AN UNHAPPY COUNTRY

Loretta Miles Tollefson

PALO FLECHADO PRESS

Other Books by Loretta Miles Tollefson

Old New Mexico Fiction
Not Just Any Man
Not My Father's House
No Secret Too Small
There Will Be Consequences
The Texian Prisoners
The Pain and The Sorrow
Old One Eye Pete (short stories)
Valley of the Eagles (micro fiction)

Other Fiction
The Ticket
The Streets of Seattle

Poetry
But Still My Child

Dedicated in loving memory to
Juanita Alice Dawkins Marquette

Epigraph

"We have declared war with the American and it is now time that we all take our arms in our hands … that we may try if possible to regain the liberty of our unhappy country."
Anonymous nuevo mexicano, circa January 1847

"Military glory—that attractive rainbow, that rises in showers of blood, that serpent's eye, that charms to destroy."
Abraham Lincoln, Jan. 12, 1848 Speech to U.S. Congress

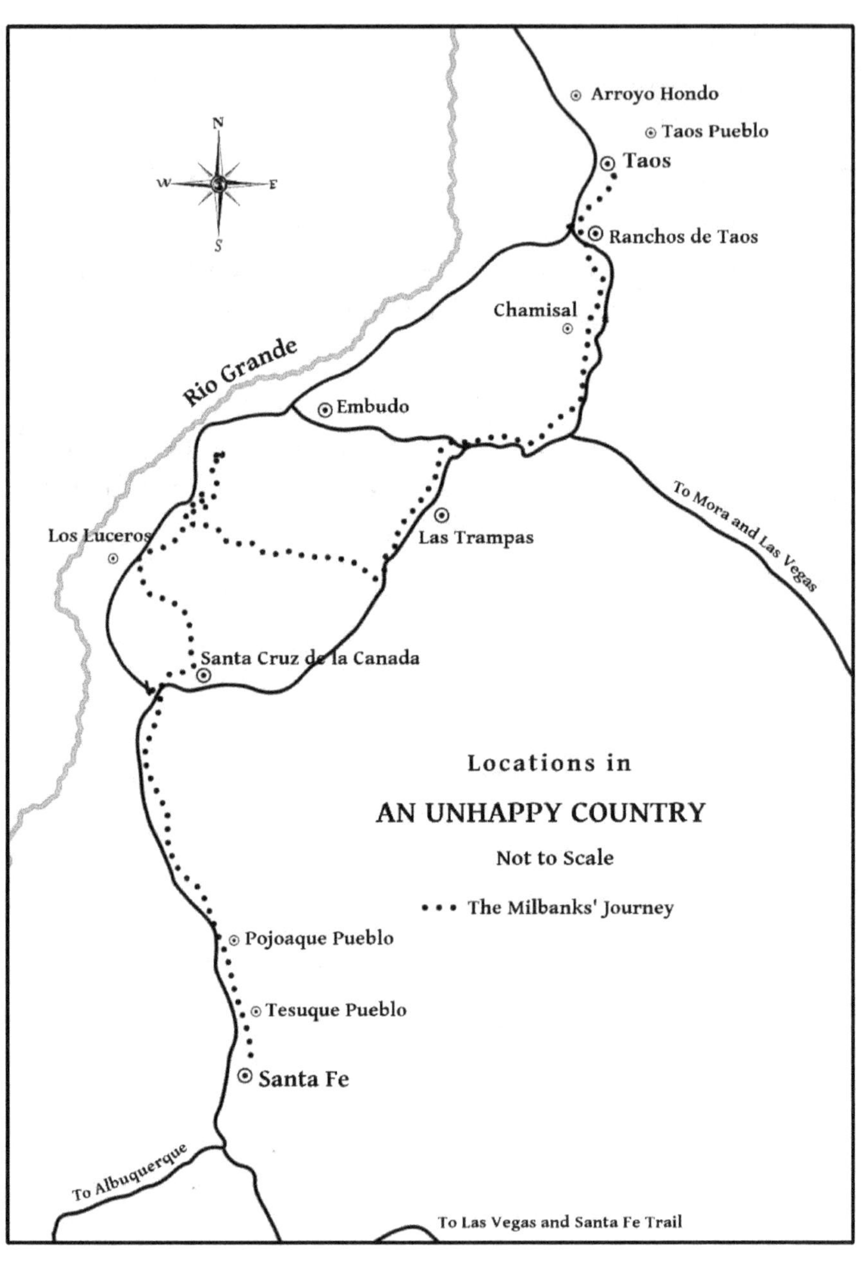

N
W
E
S
⊙ Arroyo Hondo
⊙ Taos Pueblo
⊙ Taos
⊙ Ranchos de Taos
Chamisal
⊙
Rio Grande
⊙ Embudo
To Mora and Las Vegas
Los Luceros
⊙
⊙ Las Trampas
Santa Cruz de la Canada
⊙
Locations in
AN UNHAPPY COUNTRY
Not to Scale
• • • The Milbanks' Journey
⊙ Pojoaque Pueblo
⊙ Tesuque Pueblo
⊙ Santa Fe
To Albuquerque
To Las Vegas and Santa Fe Trail

AN UNHAPPY COUNTRY

Loretta Miles Tollefson

CHAPTER 1: Wednesday, August 19, 1846

The Santa Fe plaza was dusty, crowded, and silent, the only sound the slap of the newly raised American flag responding to the morning breeze. The people below glanced up at it occasionally, then turned back to watch the long flat-roofed adobe building on the north side of the square.

Finally, the palacio's massive double doors swung open and uniformed men filed onto the covered portal. "There he is," Jessie's father said. "General Stephen Watts Kearny himself."

"And Donaciano Vigil, the traitor," Raúl muttered. "In the garments of los americanos." He tugged at the short waist of his green Mexican-style jacket, smoothed the heavy yellow embroidery on its lapels, then resettled his broad-brimmed flat-crowned black hat.

Jessie put a hand on each man's arm and stretched onto her toes to see better. The row of men on the porch gazed impassively at the crowd. Vigil was tall and so stood behind the general, only his head and shoulders visible, but what she could see of his coat was clearly American.

The flag snapped overhead. Jessie sank back, frowning a little. She was an American citizen. She should be happy that New Mexico was now part of the United States. And taken without a fight.

Beyond Raúl, her friend Juanita leaned sideways to peer around Manuelita, whose bulky middle-aged frame blocked her view. "There are others in americano garments, as well," she said. "The acting governor, por ejemplo."

Raúl tugged on the lower edge of his jacket. "Traitors, all of them."

"However, they are here and not running away as Governor Armijo has done."

Raúl moved impatiently. The silver buttons on the outer seam of his trousers flashed in the sunlight. The linen that flared from the gap below his knees was startlingly white. "His Excellency retreats strategically," he said. "He will return."

Jessie pulled her blue-and-white rebozo, the voluminous traditional Mexican shawl, closer to her shoulders. "I certainly hope not. How many people would have died if he hadn't fled?"

Her father patted her arm, his narrow face still focused on the palacio. "Hush now. General Kearny is about to speak."

She peered forward again, focusing on the hawk-nosed man on the edge of the portal, the one with the gold epaulettes on his shoulders. He spoke clearly, loud enough to reach the far corners of the square, but in English. Donaciano Vigil had stepped forward to translate. His voice was hesitant at first, then strengthened, stubbornly neutral in tone.

"We have come amongst you to take possession of New Mexico," General Kearny said. "Which we do in the name of the government of the United States."

As Vigil repeated this in Spanish, a sigh that was half groan swept through the plaza. Jessie shivered. Her father put an arm around her shoulders. "Remember, you are an American," he said into her ear.

"Juanita isn't," she murmured. "Or Raúl. We've taken their country from them."

"Peaceably."

She nodded, but as the men on the portal continued, her mind drifted, remembering the fear that had crept into the city alongside news of the oncoming army. The bitter looks. The rumors that Governor Armijo would round up all the foreigners in New Mexico. In retaliation? As tools for barter? It wasn't clear. Her father had scoffed at the idea, but some of his fellow merchants had barricaded themselves in a shop on the plaza and stockpiled weapons and supplies, sure that the governor would take them into custody.

Jessie glanced at Manuelita's stolid back. The cook had snorted when she'd heard about it. "El tímido Armijo?" she'd asked derisively.

And she'd been right. As Kearny and his men marched closer, Manuel Armijo hadn't raised a hand against either the resident foreigners or the oncoming troops. Instead, he fled south, leaving hastily raised fortifications and most of his cannon east of the city in Apache Pass.

And now an American flag flew over the plaza of New Mexico's capital. Jessie shook her head. As she refocused on the building that had housed Armijo's administration the week before, General Kearny announced, "You no longer owe allegiance to the Mexican government."

The Spanish translation was barely out of Donaciano Vigil's mouth before the hissing began, spreading across the plaza like steam from still-glowing coals. Raúl pushed his hat off his forehead and glared at the portal. "That is not for him to decide!" he growled.

The general went on as if no one had made a sound. "It is my intention to continue in office those by whom you have been governed, except the governor."

Juanita turned to Raúl. "You see? Nothing much will change."

As her cousin sniffed derisively, General Kearny went on. "I am your governor," he said. "Henceforth look to me for protection."

Raúl scowled. His spine straightened even further when the next speaker stepped forward. This was a cousin of Donaciano Vigil's and the man who'd been Lieutenant Governor under Manuel Armijo. An aristocratic-looking gentleman in gleaming American broadcloth, he turned to General Kearny and began speaking, Spanish phrases flowing elegantly.

Vigil reversed his translation, switching to English as the lieutenant governor acknowledged America's acquisition of Nuevo Méjico. The nuevo mexicanos would be cooperative, he added, saying, "It is for us to obey and respect the established authorities, no matter what may be our private opinion."

As this was translated into English, Jessie glanced at Raúl. His eyes were black with fury. Juanita placed a calming hand on his forearm, but he only scowled and jerked his chin toward the lieutenant governor. "You see?" he hissed. "Listen to him!"

Jessie leaned forward. The man's voice had dropped, as if he were speaking more for General Kearny's benefit than the people in the square, but Donaciano Vigil took up the slack. His words, still with that neutral tone, carried across the plaza. "Do not find it strange if there has been no manifestation of joy and enthusiasm in seeing this city occupied by your military forces," he said. "To us the power of the Mexican republic is dead. No matter what her condition, she was our mother."

"You see?" Raúl hissed again. "Even he, the bastard handing over the reins of power, admits we should be sad." His chin lifted. "¡Viva Nuevo Méjico!" he muttered.

Juanita shook her head anxiously and a thickset stranger standing behind them leaned forward to put a quieting palm on Raúl's shoulder. The younger man frowned impatiently, but subsided. His face was still glum when the speeches finally ended and New Mexico's former officials had all sworn allegiance to the United States of America.

When that was over, General Kearny stepped to the edge of the portal and announced that a ten p.m. curfew was now in effect. He waved a hand toward the hilltop just visible behind the palacio roof. Jessie looked up. A row of cannon stared back at her, aimed directly at the plaza. They would be fired each night at ten o'clock, the general said. After that, everyone was required to be indoors.

She glanced at Raúl. His jaw was tight and his fists clenched, eyes dark with fury.

Kearny raised his arms, dismissing the crowd, and Juanita laid a restraining hand on Raúl's sleeve. "¿Mi primo? Cousin? Will you be so kind as to bring tu amor Guadalupe to me tomorrow evening and stay yourself for a little refreshment?" She turned to Jessie. "And you? Will you join us?"

Jessie nodded, but her father frowned. "Your uncle and aunt are kind and hospitable people, but will they be in the mood to entertain?" he asked. "I expect they'll wish for quiet, to mourn this week's events."

Juanita's chin lifted. "We Senas are descendants of los conquistadores españoles who came to this land with General Diego de Vargas. We do not bow our heads before what others might call defeat." Then she shrugged, her face rueful. "Besides, one must learn to dance to the tune that is played."

Jessie's father's dark brown eyes crinkled in amusement. "I bow to the Sena experience and resilience." He turned to Raúl. "If you will promise to see my girl safely to the Sena compound and back tomorrow evening, I will gladly agree."

Raúl smiled, his irritation seemingly forgotten. "I will be happy to escort her, Don Hubert."

"I don't need an escort, Papa," Jessie said. "Our house is less than a quarter mile from the Senas and I've been walking that route for almost two years now. I'll be perfectly safe." She glanced mischievously at Juanita's cousin. "Besides, Raúl will want to devote his energies to escorting Guadalupe to the Sena casa and back."

Juanita grinned. "Yes, the little Guadalupe, who lives closer, on the street on the other side of el palacio!"

Jessie's father shook his head. "The streets and plaza will be full of soldiers."

Jessie's lips tightened. She glanced at Raúl. His hands were no longer clenched. The invitation and responsibility of escorting her had done their work. As he said, "I will be happy to escort your daughter, señor," Jessie and Juanita exchanged bemused glances and Jessie nodded, accepting her role as female in need of protection, if only to keep the male out of trouble.

The girls gave each other the customary sideways hug, murmured affectionate farewells, and turned with their men toward their respective homes.

Manuelita had disappeared while the others were talking. Jessie and her father moved through the remnants of the crowd, cutting diagonally toward the street to their house and shop. They were almost across the square when Jessie spied the cook in front of the half-ruined Spanish military chapel on the south side.

Manuelita stood with her hands on her hips, facing a small bronze-skinned man who slouched against the chapel's weather-beaten door. Above his head, the marble bas-relief of the Virgin rescuing sinners contrasted sharply with his rough, uncombed black braids, but his thin face was alert, his eyes bright. A small smile played across his face and widened when the cook put a hand on his arm and lifted the other beseechingly, though her face was set in its usual frown.

Jessie's head turned as she and her father went past. "I think that's the first time I've ever seen Manuelita with a man she wasn't buying provisions from."

Her father glanced over. "She is a quiet one," he agreed. "A woman who keeps herself to herself."

Jessie lifted a brow. "And you prefer that to a more open-hearted approach to life?"

He grinned. "There are advantages to a less outgoing demeanor."

She opened her mouth to argue the point, but was interrupted by a dark-skinned man in a brown coat who had stopped in their path and removed his battered broad-brimmed hat. "Mr. Milbank!" he said, beaming.

"Well, if it isn't Dick Green!" Jessie's father held out his hand and the other man took it with a look of real pleasure on his square face. "Jessie, you remember Dick Green from Bent's Fort? Charlotte's husband?"

The newcomer's eyes twinkled as he turned to her. "No matter where I go, I'm always known as Charlotte's husband."

She laughed up at him. "As it should be!" She took his hand. "But yes, I do remember you, Mr. Green. It's a pleasure to see you again."

He squinted at her. "I wasn't rightly sure it was you."

She adjusted the rebozo over her head self-consciously. "It's been two years."

Her father smiled. "And she's adopted a few Mexican customs. The headgear. The sideways hug."

The other man looked confused and she stepped impulsively toward him to demonstrate. He broke away, his dark face reddening, and looked at her father, who laughed.

Dick Green shook his head. "You two are the kindest—"

Jessie's father waved his hand. "It's not your fault the Bents think they own you, Dick. We Milbanks don't hold with slavery, and we're not going to treat you as a person in bondage." He glanced around the plaza, almost empty now. "Are you here on business? Do you have time to come back with us for a meal?"

"I'm afraid I'm called to other duties at the moment, Don Hubert," the other man said regretfully. "But I do appreciate the invitation."

"Please feel free to accept it whenever it's convenient," Jessie said.

Her father nodded. "We'd be happy to see you any time. There's no need to stand on ceremony."

They shook hands again and Dick Green gave Jessie a small bow, then they separated. Manuelita and her friend had also parted. She was almost out of the plaza now, moving swiftly for such a large woman. The Milbank house and shop stood on the first corner past the square, facing the road south to Albuquerque. The building's adobe-walled courtyard bordered the street that ran west. By the time Jessie and her father arrived, the cook had disappeared into it.

Jessie moved toward the big gate, but her father shook his head. "Come into the store with me," he said, and she turned left with him to the mercantile door.

The room was dark and smelled of leather, cloth, and corn flour, with an undertone of tobacco. Jessie sniffed appreciatively and opened the nearest set of window shutters, then maneuvered between the various stacks of goods and around the potbelly stove to the counter on the back wall.

Her father had been shopkeeping in Santa Fe five years now, yet the counter was still a mere hand-adzed board set on two empty barrels. Jessie smiled as she ran her hands along the edge of the pitted wood slab. "You should get this replaced with something more permanent," she said.

"I expect it wouldn't make any difference in sales." He leaned against the end of the board and studied her, a small crease in his forehead. Here it came. He was going to start worrying again.

She began unwrapping her rebozo. "I am surprised Mr. Green didn't recognize me. I haven't changed that much since we went through Bent's Fort."

He chuckled. "That was two years ago and you were still wearing Eastern clothes." He nodded at the rebozo. "In that headgear, I expect you could pass for a Mexican girl. In fact, your eyes and hair are darker than Juanita's."

"And she's so tall and slim," Jessie said a little enviously. She folded the long length of blue-and-white cloth and laid it on the counter. Then she smiled. "She is very pretty, isn't she? That pale skin and those hazel eyes."

He nodded absently, then frowned, focusing on her face. "You need to be careful from here on out."

She suppressed a sigh as he brushed an imaginary piece of dust from the counter. "Most of Kearny's men haven't seen any females to speak of since they left Missouri," he said. "From the little I've seen of them, I expect they're a fairly raw and ill-mannered lot." He looked up. "They'll be especially impertinent to Mexican girls."

"And I look more Mexican than American."

"In the rebozo and that short Mexican skirt, yes, you do. Especially since almost every rebozo in town has that same blue and white stripe."

"There are two petticoats under the skirt, it's a mere six inches shorter than before, and I'm still wearing an American corset and bodice."

"When you're wrapped up in the rebozo, they can't see what's underneath. Not that I want them looking closely enough to do so." He rubbed at a spot on the counter. "I don't suppose you could see your way to going back to more Eastern fashions."

Her chin went up. "My clothing choices reflect Mother's philosophy of simplicity of dress. I will not change it."

He tilted his head sideways, as if he'd been expecting this answer. His fingers moved across the wood, tracing a crack in the counter. "I should never have brought you here. Violence against Americans has always been a threat, even before this summer. And now the danger has switched sides. Anyone who looks Mexican is at risk." His mouth twisted. "I should have sent you to your aunt."

"If I had to leave Missouri, I certainly didn't want to go to Pennsylvania. Philadelphia is far too prim and proper for the likes of me."

He smiled faintly and looked away, toward the glassless windows with their carved wooden bars. "I should have insisted." In the street beyond, a harsh Yankee voice shouted a curse. He shook his head. "No matter what path I choose, I put my women in danger."

"Oh, Papa!" She moved down the counter and reached for his hands. "I am to blame for Mama's death, not you."

"You are not to blame. Besides, you were a child at the time."

Now it was Jessie's turn to look away. "I did nothing to stop them."

"If you had, I expect you would have died too." His face twisted, clearly recalling the frantic search two years before when he returned to Missouri and discovered his wife and daughter missing.

Then he shook himself, dropped her hands, and gave her a stern look. "This war between the United States and Mexico is not over. Not in the rest of the country and certainly not here. The men who arrived with Kearny are itching for a fight they didn't get. And Raúl isn't the only nuevo mexicano who wishes Armijo had stood up to them. It's difficult to tell what will happen next. There's danger from both directions. You will be careful. Do you understand?"

She opened her mouth to argue, but the memory of what they had both endured in Missouri stopped her tongue. "Yes, Papa," she said.

CHAPTER 2: Thursday, August 20, 1846

It was dark in the walled Sena courtyard, but the door to the sala was open, and the light streaming from it picked up the new silver ornaments on Raúl's hatband.

"How much more silver trim can that strip of leather contain?" Juanita asked, laughing.

Guadalupe pulled away from Raúl's protective arm to study his head. "A few spots remain."

He released her and took off the hat. "I believe I have attained the proper balance between elegancia and bravado," he said, twirling it. He turned to Jessie. "¿Qué opinas?"

Jessie grinned, but before she could give her opinion, the bells in the adobe church towers across the road began pealing. It was nine o'clock.

Juanita glanced in their direction and sighed. "A week ago, that sound would have told me we should go inside, but only to assist in settling my little cousins to sleep."

Raúl grimaced. "Now, it is the signal that one mere hour remains in which to move freely about our own city." He reached for Guadalupe's hand. "Come, mi amor." He turned to Jessie. "If you are ready, señorita."

She nodded. "Give me a minute to thank our host and hostess."

They all trooped indoors. The goodbyes took more than a minute. By the time the young people left the compound, the church bells had long been silent.

There was no moon, and Jessie paused, letting her eyes adjust to the starlight. The town seemed ominously still. Not even the dogs were out. She shivered, pulled her rebozo closer to her throat, and hurried up the street ahead of the others.

She'd reached the end of the street, where it met the southeast corner of the palacio and was about to turn into the plaza when she realized Raúl and Guadalupe were no longer directly behind her. Jessie turned, squinting into the darkness, then grinned.

There was a small alley halfway up the street, where the walls of the Sena compound didn't quite touch those of the nearer property. Raúl and Guadalupe were tucked just inside its entrance. His hat was off, his curly head bent toward hers as she stretched to meet his lips. Starlight touched the white stripes of the rebozo which had fallen to her shoulders.

Jessie chuckled and retraced her steps. "Can't you wait until you get her home?" she asked Raúl. She gave Guadalupe a mock frown. "What would your mother say?"

The younger girl giggled. "Doña Tules would only laugh. She, too, was once young." She put her hand on Raúl's chest. "It has been so long."

Raúl smiled and reached to smooth a loose curl from Guadalupe's forehead. "I have not had her to myself at all today or yesterday," he told Jessie. Then he glanced up at the sky and put his hat back on his head. "However, I must get you both home before the maldito curfew begins."

Guadalupe shivered and pulled her rebozo over her head. "The sound of the guns last night startled me greatly."

Raúl tucked an arm around her shoulders and kept it there as they moved up the street. At the corner, he offered Jessie his other elbow and they moved into the plaza and angled across it toward the Milbank's street.

The young cottonwoods that edged the square were ghostly in the half dark, the silence broken occasionally by muffled sounds from the adobe-brick homes and drinking establishments beyond them. Voices, a somber guitar. Curfew might be about to fall, but people still went on living.

"It seems a little silly to take you out of your way like this," Jessie said to her friends. "I have made this trip so many times without accompaniment."

"It is my pleasure," Raúl told her as they neared the flagpole. Then there was a bark of laughter off to their left. A small group of soldiers moved toward them from the hotel on the plaza's southeast corner. Raúl tucked his elbows closer to his torso and hurried the girls forward, but the newcomers surrounded them, blocking the way. A snag-toothed man with a shaggy head bent to peer into the girls' faces. "Ooh la la," he said. "You're a couple right pretty ones."

Guadalupe shrank against Raúl, but Jessie broke free of his restraining arm. "How dare you?" she snapped. "Where are your manners?"

The soldiers laughed derisively, but they moved off. "She speaks English!" one of them said. "That's even better!"

Jessie half turned, glaring, but Raúl murmured, "Por favor, señorita. I cannot fight them all."

Jessie gave him a startled look, then glanced toward the soldiers. They had reached the palacio and paused near the outlet to Guadalupe's street. The shaggy one's head was turned, watching. "How dare they!" she hissed, but she returned her hand to Raúl's arm.

They moved on, his torso stiff with tension, but the soldiers turned and surged back toward them. Jessie's breath caught, but Raúl, warning the girls not to react, muttered, "Mantente firme," and the oncoming men circled around them and back toward the hotel.

Jessie's chest released and Guadalupe murmured a prayer of thanks, and they continued on, Raúl aiming toward the half-ruined chapel, the carved marble slab above the door glowing in the starlight. They were almost to it when Guadalupe gave a little exclamation of surprise. "What is that?" she asked.

A man lay huddled against the chapel wall. The ground beneath him was darker than the surrounding soil.

"It is someone overcome by strong drink," Raúl said in disgust. "A fellow mexicano, by the look of him. Someone determined to make los americanos think the worst of us."

Guadalupe leaned forward, biting her upper lip. "That is not the smell of alcohol. It is blood."

Raúl pulled her back. "I will deliver you both home, then return to assist him."

But the girl had slipped away from him. She leaned over the man on the ground. "There is a knife!"

Raúl and Jessie moved toward her. A long knife with a brown horn handle like the ones Jessie's father sold in his store protruded from the center of the man's back. His disheveled black braids splayed out from his narrow head.

Raúl reached to turn the man onto his side. When his face appeared, Jessie's breath hissed between her teeth. "It's Manuelita's friend!"

Raúl crouched down and reached for the man's neck, then rose. "He's dead, I—"

The cannon on the hill above the town blasted just then, cutting off his voice. Guadalupe gave a little shriek and Raúl turned to her. "I must escort you home."

"It's far too late for that," a British voice drawled from the darkness. A tall young man in the blue coat and wide white belt of an American dragoon materialized beside them, his face pale under his soft black cap. He gave Raúl a sharp look. "You are under arrest." He glanced down at the body at their feet, and his hand went to the big pistol at his waist. "For murder as well as for breaking curfew."

"He didn't kill him," Jessie said. "We just found the poor man."

The dragoon's lips pursed as he turned toward her. "Your voice is not Mexican."

And his wasn't American, but Jessie didn't think this was the time to point that out. She pushed the rebozo from her head. "I'm from Missouri. My father has a shop just down the road there." She nodded toward the street beyond, then saw her father coming toward them, holding up a lantern, his face pinched with concern. "There he is now."

"What has happened?" he asked as he approached.

Raúl pointed toward the man on the ground. Jessie's father lowered the lantern and sucked in his breath when the light hit the blank face.

"Do you know him?" the dragoon asked officiously.

"No." Her father straightened. "I don't know him." He gave Jessie an anxious look, then refocused on the dragoon. "I am Hubert Milbank, a merchant here in Santa Fe. I came out to find my daughter and her friends." He glanced toward Raúl. "I expected them well before now."

"Please accept my apologies, Don Hubert," Raúl said.

"Yo tengo la culpa," Guadalupe said.

Jessie shook her head. "You are not to blame. You saw someone in apparent distress and stopped to find out if you could help."

Jessie's father looked from the girls to the dragoon, who now had a hand on the pistol tucked into his belt. "May I have permission to see them safely home?"

"The girls, but not the boy."

Raúl's face darkened at being called a boy, but Don Hubert shot him a warning look. "He has done nothing but stop to help a stranger."

"He has blood on his hands."

Raúl looked down. A dark splotch stained his left palm and fingers. "It is from the wound," he said. "From when I turned him."

"That is not for me to decide." The dragoon stepped forward and grasped Raúl's elbow.

The younger man flinched, but then steadied. They were about the same height and Raúl was a good twenty pounds heavier, but he left the dragoon's hand where it was. He looked at Guadalupe, then Jessie's father. "You will see her home, señor?" When the older man nodded, Raúl turned to Guadalupe. "Por favor informe a mi familia."

She nodded. "Mañana early."

The dragoon made a dismissive sound. "Mañana," he said. "I've already come to understand that word and what it means here." Then he seemed to think better of his tone. He looked at Jessie and her father. "Good evening, sir. Miss." His eyes skimmed over the dark-skinned Guadalupe. "I'll send someone to remove the body." He tugged Raúl's arm and they moved across the square toward the palacio.

Jessie's father touched her elbow and gathered up Guadalupe. They trailed the dragoon and Raúl toward the palacio, then veered left to the street along its west flank, the one called la calle de la muralla. As they entered it, Doña Tules looked out her gate, then hurried toward them, the big gold crucifix hanging from her neck dull in the gathering night.

"Guadalupita!" she exclaimed. "What has happened?" Laughter flashed in her eyes. "Did that Cabeza de Baca boy desert you already?"

The girl's eyes filled with tears and Doña Tules' face changed instantly. She pulled Guadalupe into her arms. "Pobrecita," she murmured. "Perdóname, my child." She looked up at Jessie's father. "Thank you for bringing her home, Don Hubert."

"It was my pleasure."

"But please, come inside, or someone will decide we're breaking ese maldito curfew."

She ushered them into the house, where they stayed just long enough to explain what had happened and see that Guadalupita was calmed by her adoptive mother's presence. By the time Jessie and her father returned to the plaza, the dead man was gone, the only evidence of his existence a dark patch on the ground.

"What will we tell Manuelita?" Jessie murmured as they passed.

"I have no idea." Her father shook his head. "So much for the peaceful American invasion."

She glanced up at him. "You think he was killed by a soldier?"

"That knife was not made here in New Mexico and the horn handle did not appear to be worn with use." He was silent as they approached the store. "Though I expect it could have come in with any of the wagon trains that arrived this summer or last. And sold by any one of us." He lifted the door latch. "We may never know."

CHAPTER 3: Friday, August 21, 1846

Manuelita was more quiet than usual the day after her friend was killed. When Jessie entered the kitchen that afternoon to help with the evening meal, she barely nodded.

Juanita arrived a little later. "Guadalupe came this morning to tell me what happened last night," she said as she entered. She turned toward the big adobe fireplace in the corner, where the cook was crouched over a spider-legged cast iron skillet. "Manuelita, I feel so sad about la muerte de tu amigo. I cannot imagine how difficult it must be for you."

Manuelita nodded at the girl, then turned back to the meat sizzling in the pan.

"Sometimes the best thing is to keep busy," Jessie said from the table. She looked at the apple she'd been peeling. She'd dreamed of her mother again last night, only this time the face on the body in the clearing was thin and male. She shuddered and concentrated on moving her knife across the surface of the fruit, removing its mottled red-and-gold skin.

"Sí, this is so," Juanita said. "I feel quite restless myself, because I have heard no further news of mi primo." She sat, reached for an apple, picked up a nearby knife, and began peeling. She glanced at Manuelita. "Are you going to make a pie? An American one?"

Manuelita nodded without turning and poked at the meat with a long-handled fork. The girls exchanged glances.

Jessie placed her peeled apple in the black, mica-flecked pottery bowl in the center of the table and reached for another one. "You haven't heard anything from Raúl?"

Juanita shook her head. "His father and my uncle went together to el palacio this morning, but no one would speak to them."

The door into the store opened and Jessie's father came in. He smiled when he saw Juanita. "I just received news that your cousin has been released into his father's custody," he said. He glanced at Manuelita's back. "So at least there's some good news today."

"That is most excellent news," Juanita said. "Gracias, señor."

"However, he has received a strong warning."

Jessie scowled. "Warning about what? Not to stop to help a stranger?"

"To be more discreet, I expect." He moved toward the fireplace and stopped a few feet from it. "Manuelita, I have arranged with the priest for the burial of your friend."

The cook nodded without turning. He and the girls exchanged glances. "Padre Ortiz will conduct the service tomorrow," he continued. "Is there anyone we should notify? Family members and so forth?"

Manuelita shook her head as she lifted a particularly large piece of meat and carefully repositioned it.

"The padre also asked for the man's name."

She glanced up. "Vidal."

"You don't know his full name? Or where he came from?"

"Not friend."

"Oh." His graying brown eyebrows twisted in confusion. "All right." He shifted slightly. "Do you know of anyone who might have more information?"

The cook shook her head and poked at the meat in the pan.

"What will happen if they can't find out who he is?" Jessie asked.

"He will be buried, but the priest's records will show only his one name," Juanita said. "It is the custom."

"And his family and friends will never know whether he's dead or has simply disappeared."

Jessie's father lifted his hands in a helpless gesture. "I have done all I can, given the information at my disposal."

"Surely someone knows something."

His hands dropped and he gave her a stern look. "You will not get involved."

Her chin lifted, but the pain in his eyes stopped her. She looked away. The image from her dream rose unbidden, and she swallowed against it. She looked at her father. "Shouldn't we at least try to see that he receives justice?"

"Jessica Matilda Milbank—"

She studied the apple in her hands. "Though, truly, I wouldn't know where to begin." She glanced at Manuelita, but the housekeeper had now moved to the soup pot. Her carved cottonwood spoon moved the broth and vegetables in a firm circle.

Jessie's father made a huffing sound, turned, and went back into the shop, shutting the door behind him.

Juanita placed a peeled apple in the bowl and reached for another one. As her knife bit into its skin, she said quietly, "Guadalupe said el dragón americano seemed to appear out of nowhere."

Jessie's knife stopped. She looked up. "The American dragoon? Now that I think about it, it was almost as if he was waiting for someone to come along." She frowned. "And why was he in the shadows?" She looked at Juanita. "Did Guadalupe tell you about the soldiers who accosted us earlier?"

Juanita nodded. "Sí. She wondered why el dragón did not come to help you. He was clearly in una posición de autoridad."

"Authority to arrest Raúl, at any rate." Jessie frowned. "It almost seemed as if he was waiting for us to come along. Or someone else. Anyone he could accuse of putting a knife—" She glanced toward Manuelita. "It doesn't make any sense."

"That is cierto," Juanita agreed. She tilted her head toward the door to the shop. "Perhaps Don Hubert is right. We should mind our own business, not be—how do you say it?—nosy."

Jessie nodded and looked away, remembering her mother. If only someone had been nosy then, perhaps her killers would have been found and brought to justice. She wiped at her eyes and went back to peeling the apples.

CHAPTER 4: Sunday, August 23, 1846

The tall thin Mexican girl and the short curvy American one had agreed to meet that Sunday under the cottonwoods at the northeast corner of the plaza. When Jessie arrived, Juanita was already there, watching the four middle-aged men smoking cigars on the benches in front of the flat-roofed hotel on the opposite corner.

Dressed in traditional Mexican clothing, they kept up a running commentary on the parishioners who streamed past them toward the big adobe church at the end of the street. The bells in its curved towers rang gaily, urging everyone inside, but the men on the benches didn't budge.

"Those gentlemen certainly seem to be enjoying themselves," Jessie said with amusement.

Juanita nodded. "I suspect they are waiting for the parade of americano officers. El general Kearny is expected to attend services this morning. Everyone has come out to see, both in church and out."

Jessie looked up the street. There did seem to be more worshipers this morning. "We should hurry."

Juanita chuckled. "There is no need to hurry. Because la parroquia contains no benches or other seats, there will be room for all who wish to attend."

"I hope chairs have been provided for General Kearny and his officers. I doubt they've ever experienced a New Mexico mass before."

"We are a very hospitable people," Juanita said drily. "I am sure the best seats in the city have been made available for them."

When they entered the church a few minutes later, Jessie saw that her friend was right. At the far end of the nave, a row of carved wooden chairs faced the altar. They all held brightly colored cushions, and the largest, throne-like one was upholstered in deep crimson.

Other arrangements had also been made. The niches in the long walls, the ones containing life-size figures of Saint Francis and Saint Dominic, were filled with lit candles. More light glowed ahead and to the left, from the chapel of La Conquistadora, the little statue of the Virgin Mary so precious to nuevo mexicanos of Spanish ancestry because of its connection to the reconquest of 1692.

The chairs for the officers had been positioned in line with the chapel entrance. Perhaps a silent reminder to los americanos that God gave this country to the Spanish long before the United States was formed? Jessie's lips quirked in amusement, then dropped. She wondered what the Indians in the various pueblos thought about this latest incursion into their homeland.

But there was no time to ponder that now. She followed Juanita to the women's side and settled in. The usual quiet chatter surrounded them as people caught up with the local news while keeping one eye on the big double doors at the back.

Finally, both doors swung grandly open, and the general and his entourage appeared. They stopped just inside, blinking as their eyes adjusted, and apparently confused by the lack of seating. Then there was a stir at the altar and Padre Juan Felipe Ortiz moved down the long aisle, looking fatter than usual in his best clerical garb. His fair skin and red hair gleamed in the candlelight as he bowed politely to the newcomers, escorted them to their seats, then disappeared through a small door near the altar.

When he returned a few minutes later, the priest was preceded by two altar boys swinging thin chains of their incense balls with concentrated vigor. An officer in the front row sneezed as they passed, and Jessie grinned. The offending man must be Protestant. The Catholic love of incense did take some getting used to.

The service seemed longer than usual. There was more music, with both guitar and violin, slow and fast tunes. The padre didn't normally give a sermon, but today he chose to deliver a short homily filled with fine phrases about respecting one another. His eyes seemed to linger on the uniforms in the front row as the interpreter put this point into English. But Jessie could have imagined that. Her legs were getting tired. Finally, it was over. The general and his officers filed out and everyone else followed.

One of the many things Jessie loved about New Mexico was the fact that no one went home right after church. Instead, men, women, and children wandered the plaza chatting, buying snacks or other items from the vendors, listening to the music of itinerant fiddlers and singers, and generally enjoying themselves.

As she and Juanita stopped to admire the black-on-red pottery a Tesuque Pueblo woman was selling, the dragoon who'd accosted Jessie and her friends three nights before came up and stood beside her.

She kept her gaze on the pottery, but Juanita peered around her, looking at his clear complexion, dark hair, blue eyes, and dimpled chin with frank curiosity. Jessie suppressed a surge of irritation. After all, Juanita didn't know who he was.

Besides, he might have answers to the questions surrounding Vidal's death. Jessie turned toward him, noting the whiteness of his teeth, the carefully combed hair. This was clearly a man to whom appearance was important.

He gave her a small bow, one hand on his heart, the other on his gleaming sword hilt. "If you will permit me," he said. "I would like to extend my sincerest apologies for my abrupt manner the other evening. I had not yet become accustomed to the duties to which I was assigned, and I fear I overextended myself."

Jessie felt Juanita move slightly, bringing herself into the conversation. The dragoon bowed again, a little deeper this time. "Ah, another lovely americana."

Juanita frowned. "Soy española."

His eyes widened. "You speak only Spanish? I beg your pardon, señorita. I find Santa Fe to be full of surprises. I fear I have offended you."

When she stared at him without blinking, his fair cheeks flushed red. He turned to Jessie. "I beg of you, please convey my apologies. I'm afraid my Spanish is extremely limited."

Jessie turned to Juanita. The other girl's eyes twinkled with mischief. "I said I was Spanish," she said in English. "The opportunity, it was too delicioso to resist."

The dragoon huffed an exaggerated sigh of relief. "Ah, you do understand. I beg your pardon and ask you to please forgive me."

She waved a hand, brushing away his concern. "De nada."

He smiled at her blindingly, then turned to Jessie. "But I have not introduced myself properly. My name is Henry Carr Fitzgerald. I am a private with Captain Burgwin's First Dragoons."

"And I am Jessie Milbank."

His eyes widened. "Are you by chance a relation of Lieutenant Abner Milbank of the Missouri Infantry Volunteers?"

"Not that I'm aware of." She gestured toward Juanita. "This is my dear friend, Juanita María de la Luz Sena."

He bowed again, his face brightening. "Of the Sena family of Sena plaza?"

The girls exchanged amused glances. Somehow, things were always a little smoother when people realized Juanita was connected to the well-to-do Sena compound.

"Sí," she said. A man came toward them, his gaze on the vendor's pottery. The three young people moved to one side.

Private Fitzgerald turned to Jessie. "And am I forgiven?"

She arched an eyebrow at him.

"For leaving you so abruptly the other evening and for arresting the young man who attended you. I'm afraid I never did learn his name."

"He is Raúl Jesús Cabeza de Baca and a cousin to Señorita Sena," Jessie said, gesturing again toward her friend.

"The señor was escorting me and his sweetheart, Guadalupe Barceló, to our homes."

"I understand he has now been released to the custody of his family," the dragoon said. "The man he was attempting to aid had died some time before you happened upon him." He gave Jessie a commiserating look. "That is not a sight to which any young lady should be exposed. I do hope you and your friend have both recovered sufficiently from the ordeal."

Jessie felt something inside her snap. Maybe it was just his British accent, but the man was entirely too glib. "The ordeal of seeing a dead body, or the ordeal of having one's friend or sweetheart arrested?" she asked.

He gave her a startled look. Juanita chuckled. "Please excuse mi amiga. She has not been in Nuevo Méjico long enough to learn our more delicate ways of phrasing such a question."

"We Missourians are more prone to plain speaking," Jessie said drily.

The dragoon chuckled uncomfortably. "Both modes of speech have their advantage." He looked around the plaza. "May I accompany you in a perambulation under the lovely cottonwoods that line your public square?" He waved a hand at the gold-tinted leaves. "Their autumn foliage reflects the glint in your hair, Señorita Sena."

Juanita chuckled and took his right arm. When he proffered the other to Jessie, she accepted it gravely. They proceeded around the plaza, moving slowly counterclockwise.

"This is a lovely custom," he said. "This promenade after church services." A cluster of Mexican men in short traditional jackets spilled raucously out of a nearby saloon, and he looked at them with distaste. "Although I'm not sure I approve of all of the Sabbath day activities which are pursued here."

Juanita smiled. "Alcohol was a gift to us from de Dios. You will find that we have very few absolute religious restrictions. Our priests accept us as we are. As we do them."

"In my own homeland, we also have relatively lenient expectations of our Anglican priests." Fitzgerald glanced at Jessie. "I suppose I assumed that your American upbringing would demand a more stringent response."

Jessie shrugged. "Not all Americans are fervent Protestants, and I value the New Mexican perspective. In fact, even though I am not Catholic, I attend church here in Santa Fe more often than I ever did back home."

They had reached the northwest corner of the plaza. Juanita nodded toward the small brass cannon that graced it. "I see that the Texan artillery has been returned to its rightful place."

The dragoon gave her a surprised look.

"This is the six-pound cannon which was captured five years ago from los invasores tejanos," she explained. "You see, their national star is engraved on the top of the barrel."

He stepped closer to the gun, then grinned at her. "That's the breech there at the back, not the barrel." He stood staring at the weapon as she shrugged.

"Governor Armijo had the cannon carried to Apache Pass to be used against el militar americano," she said. "It seems someone has retrieved it and returned it here to its corner."

Private Fitzgerald nodded absently, then seemed to shake himself. He turned to the girls. "Would you like to see the larger artillery pieces on the hill northeast of town?"

Jessie couldn't suppress a shudder. "We are quite aware of them," she said. "They've been reminding us of their presence every evening at ten o'clock sharp."

"Ah yes," he said. "The thunderous roll is quite impressive, is it not?" He turned right, toward the palacio, and they moved along its brown adobe front. They passed the big gates to the compound's interior, stepped into the shade of the portal roof, and were almost to the palacio doors when he glanced at the plaza and paused. "Here is someone you may wish to meet," he said to Jessie.

A slender fair-haired man in the blue coat and insignia of an army lieutenant moved toward them. A tall Indian man in a finely tanned leather shirt and leggings walked beside him, a white wool blanket arranged over one broad shoulder. His long black braids gleamed in the sunlight.

But the dragoon was focused on the lieutenant. He snapped a rigid salute.

"Private Fitzgerald," the other man responded as he and his companion reached the shadow of the porch. The Indian gave the dragoon a neutral look, but his eyes sparked with curiosity at the sight of the girls in their American bodices and Mexican rebozos and skirts.

"Please excuse the interruption, lieutenant," the dragoon said. He nodded toward Jessie. "I believe I may have found a long-lost relative of yours."

The other man gave her a polite bow, his soft brown eyes looking into her darker ones. "Lieutenant Abner Milbank at your service, señorita." He turned to Juanita. "And yours as well, miss."

Fitzgerald chuckled. "I see you have misunderstood the situation as I did." He raised a questioning brow at Jessie, and she smiled slightly and nodded. He shifted his arm, moving her slightly forward. "Miss Jessie Milbank, permit me to present Lieutenant Abner Milbank."

The lieutenant's cheeks reddened. "I beg your pardon, miss."

She smiled at him companionably. "It's a mistake I've encouraged since I arrived in Santa Fe two years ago," she said. "My appearance and choice of dress make me less immediately recognizable as a foreigner."

The Indian man gave her an interested look as the lieutenant nodded uncertainly. Jessie looked around the plaza, at the various American men moving across it, some on business, some heading to yet another drinking establishment. Her smile faded. "I hope I don't have to go back to wearing that stuffy old bonnet."

The Indian man's eyes twinkled. She smiled back at him and held out her hand. "Buenos días, señor. My name is Jessie Milbank."

The two American men looked startled, but his smile broadened as he took her hand. "Buenos días, señorita." Then he switched to English. "My name is Tomás Romero. I come from Taos Pueblo to meet with el general americano."

Someone with authority, then. She dropped the dragoon's arm to give the man a small curtsy. "Please forgive me, señor. I didn't realize."

He smiled and glanced at her male companions, who looked puzzled. "You are not the first," he said.

She moved to one side, opening the way for him to enter the government offices. "But you are here on important business. We mustn't keep you."

He and the lieutenant bowed slightly and moved on into the building. Fitzgerald and the girls proceeded down the covered porch and around the plaza. "So he is a chief?" the dragoon private asked.

"I'm not sure what he's called," Jessie said. "A sort of alcalde, I think, but only for the pueblo." She looked at Juanita, who shrugged and nodded.

"And what is an alcalde?"

"It's a sort of mayor and justice of the peace rolled into one." Jessie glanced at Juanita. "At least, that's my understanding."

Juanita nodded. "El alcalde is the man to whom people appeal to resolve differences between them. He also represents his community when it wishes to petition el gobernador or other officials for action or assistance of some kind."

"He is elected?"

"Sí, that is the formal process." Her eyes flashed with amusement. "However, I suspect the election is often una cuestión de confirmación rather than a choice between candidates."

Fitzgerald grinned. "A question of confirmation. That is the case in my homeland, as well."

Jessie looked up at him. "England?"

He chuckled. "Are you implying that I don't sound as if I was born and bred in the United States?"

Both girls smiled at this, and he laughed, then sobered. "I am British, but not English." He grinned at their confusion, then added, "My family is Anglo-Irish. My grandmother's English ancestor arrived in Ireland in the 1600s, and we have remained affiliated with it ever since. That makes me Anglo-Irish."

"Ah, I see," Juanita said. "It is the same with me. La familia de mi madre arrived in New Spain from Galicia." She turned toward him. "Galicia, which was settled by people from Ireland many generations ago. We might be cousins!"

He laughed and set about informing her a little more about Irish history as they circled the plaza once more. They were almost back to the Texan cannon when Lieutenant Milbank emerged from the palacio, alone this time. He brightened when he saw them and came to greet them.

"I hope we may further our acquaintance, Miss Milbank," he said when the formalities were concluded. "It would be interesting to establish whether or not we are truly relatives." He paused and looked away, his fair skin suddenly red in the sun.

She eyed him, unsure if he was embarrassed or insincere. "You must come and meet my father," she said. "I'm afraid I don't know much about his side of the family." She nodded toward the other end of the plaza. "Our home and store are on the corner of the road to Albuquerque."

The lieutenant brightened and turned back to her. "I will be happy to make his acquaintance. I look forward to it. Perhaps you and he have been invited to the ball General Kearny is hosting this Tuesday evening?"

Juanita brightened. "A dance?"

He nodded. "Perhaps an invitation has been delivered to the Sena casa as well?"

Her face fell. "Una invitación?"

He frowned in confusion.

"Here in New Mexico, we do not wait for a formal invitation to a dance," Jessie explained. "When someone holds a baile, the entire community is welcome."

"Everyone?"

She nodded, her eyes twinkling. "Sometimes even the prisoners in the jail are released for the occasion."

Juanita smoothed her rebozo over her arms. "My little cousins will be most disappointed. Even the youngest among us enjoy dancing."

The lieutenant glanced at Private Fitzgerald as if for support, then tilted his head apologetically at the girls. "I'm afraid the American custom is much like the British. Written invitations are issued and only those who receive one may attend."

Fitzgerald nodded. "If everyone who wanted to were allowed to participate, the room would become quite crowded and uncomfortable."

The girls looked at each other. "Already it is changing," Juanita said sadly.

CHAPTER 5: Wednesday, September 9, 1846

Jessie sat up with a start, her heart pounding. The dream had been so vivid. The dead man in the square, knife protruding from his back, but clad in her mother's blue-and-green dress. She shuddered, propelled herself to the window, and fumbled at the shutters.

When they were finally open, Jessie stood soaking in the morning coolness for a long time before she felt capable of starting the day. Even then, when she entered the store an hour later, she found herself unable to face her father. Instead, she crossed to the nearest window and craned to see the blue sky.

"There's something about New Mexico in September," she said. "So crisp, so clear, so nice and cool at the beginning of the day."

"Early September, that is." Her father looked up from the eggs he was settling into a basket. "I expect the mornings will be getting a little too cool for comfort in another few weeks."

"In the meantime, I'm enjoying them." Jessie moved to the counter, lifted the big brown store ledger onto it, and began turning its pages, pausing to study the entries and totals. "We seem to have a number of accounts which have suddenly become credits instead of debits."

Her father finished his task and moved to a stack of bulbous green-and-yellow-striped squash that was threatening to collapse. "Not everyone is prospering from this sudden influx of soldiers. Prices have risen. I'm being forced to pass at least part of the increase on to our customers, and some of them simply don't have the funds to pay at the moment." He shook his head. "Unless we can find a way to get more troops into the store and relieve them of their coins, the arrival of the army is going to reduce our overall profit, not increase it."

The street door opened and the army lieutenant Jessie had met two-and-a-half weeks before entered the room. His eyes brightened when he saw her, but his cheeks reddened as he said, "Miss Milbank. How do you do?"

"Lieutenant." She turned to her father. "Papa, this is the gentleman I mentioned to you. The one who shares our surname."

"Ah, Lieutenant Milbank." Her father came forward, his hand out. "I was delighted to hear that we might finally be related to someone in Santa Fe."

The other man reddened even more. "I hope we will find that to be the case. Unfortunately, I am here on other business at the moment." He glanced at Jessie, as if expecting her to turn away, and her lips twitched. Did he truly think she would not be involved or interested in her father's business dealings?

She looked down at the ledger and ran her finger down a column. The lieutenant watched her for a moment, then turned to her father. "I and my men are stationed at a grazing camp south of town near Galisteo," he said. "The villagers there cannot keep us in supplies, so I came into Santa Fe to meet with the army sutler. Even though he and his wagons arrived recently, his stock is already running low. He asked if I knew of any merchants who might be able to assist him, and I mentioned your name." His eyes flicked toward Jessie, then refocused on her father. "I hope you'll forgive me for doing so without meeting you first. The sutler asked me to bring you a message saying he'd be happy to consult with you, at your convenience."

"There's nothing to forgive," Jessie's father said. "In fact, it was quite kind of you, both the recommendation and the delivery of the message." Jessie, hearing the suppressed amusement in his voice, looked up, but his face was bland as he turned toward her. "My dear, could you bring us some coffee?" He smiled at the lieutenant. "That is, if you have time to stay for a bit and discuss our possible mutual connections."

The lieutenant beamed at him. "I would like that very much indeed."

He seemed even more pleased, and a little relieved, when Jessie returned with the tray of coffee and a small plate of bizcochitos, the anise-flavored cookies Jessie's father loved so much.

The two men plunged into a discussion of ancestors and Jessie contented herself with watching them. Her father's narrow face and tired brown eyes softened a little as his mind turned to grandfathers and great aunts. The lieutenant relaxed as well, losing his hesitancy as he dove into the details of a family tree which left Jessie thoroughly confused. By the time they'd established that they might be fourth cousins twice removed, both men seemed quite comfortable with each other.

Lieutenant Milbank left with a standing invitation to supper, and Jessie's father returned to his tasks with a jauntier step. Jessie went back to the ledger, checking totals. She was deep in a complex set of rubbed out and rewritten figures when her father said, "Now that is the kind of man I would like you to marry."

Jessie looked up. "Who says I have to marry anyone?"

"Your mother and I didn't always see eye to eye, but I wouldn't have missed that experience for all the world."

She dropped her eyes. "I'm sorry she isn't here anymore, Papa."

"It wasn't your fault."

"I didn't try to save her."

"As I understand it, the house was burning, she was lying in the yard with a half-dozen bullets in her chest, and the men who had done it were busy looting. I can only thank God you had the sense to hide in that outhouse."

She looked at her hands, suddenly flattened against the battered counter top, knuckles white. "I still dream about it." She looked up at him. "Not as often, now, but—"

He put down the box of saleratus he'd been holding, crossed to the counter, and wrapped her in his arms. "Oh, Jessie girl," he murmured into her hair.

CHAPTER 6: Sunday, September 13, 1846

"It turns out that he and my father may actually be related," Jessie told Juanita as they emerged from the church the following Sunday morning.

"That is so fascinating," Juanita said. "They arrived in Nuevo Méjico separately only to find they are family." Then she laughed. "It is only fitting. After all, everyone here is related to everyone else."

"Yes," Jessie said. "I have spent the last two years envying you your cousins and now it turns out that I have one. And here in Santa Fe, of all places."

"I can't imagine life without dozens of primos."

Jessie chuckled. "I'm not sure I can imagine a life with quite that many." Behind her, someone coughed politely. She turned to find Henry Fitzgerald, his white leather belt and polished pistol grip gleaming in the sun. He looked so pleased with himself and so happy to see them that she couldn't help but smile back at him.

Juanita chuckled. "Ah, Señor Fitzgerald," she said. "You have come to join us for another promenade?"

He bowed politely, she laughed, and he offered his arm. As they moved up the street toward the plaza, chatting aimlessly, Jessie found her attention wandering. Had Lieutenant Milbank already returned to his grazing camp?

She mentally shook herself at her foolishness and refocused on her friend and the dragoon.

"I have not had the pleasure of seeing you these past two weeks because I and my fellow dragoons have been touring with General Kearny," he told the girls. "We marched south to Albuquerque, and then down the Rio Grande as far as the village of Tomé. "He pressed Juanita's hand to his side. "I am glad to be back."

"Tomé has a lovely church," Jessie said. "We passed through it last year when my father made a merchandising trip to Belén."

"They mounted a rather grand fireworks display for us," the dragoon said.

Juanita tilted her head. "This was last week? I suspect los fuegos artificiales may have been in honor of the birth of la Virgen María as much as it was for el general."

Jessie didn't hear Fitzgerald's response. Lieutenant Milbank was coming toward them, his face bright with pleasure. She felt an unaccustomed shyness, then forced herself to meet his eyes. Milbank women did not lower their gaze for anyone.

"I hope I find you well," he said as he reached them. He nodded to the dragoon and bowed to Juanita. "And you as well, señorita."

Fitzgerald's lips pursed as he snapped a salute, but the lieutenant smiled. "That is unnecessary, private," he said. "We are all friends here." He turned to Jessie. "May I join you?"

When she nodded wordlessly, he took her arm and they proceeded into the plaza. Here they found a vendor with late season grapes and the lieutenant bought them each a bunch.

The juicy sweet fruit lightened the mood and the four young people chatted amiably as they circumnavigated the square.

When they reached the northwest corner and the Texan six pounder, Fitzgerald's mood shifted. "The journey here from Missouri was very tame and we saw no action during our recent tour," he said. "Everyone has been most polite and even obsequious." He glanced at the cannon. "I had hoped for at least a little fighting."

The lieutenant raised an eyebrow. "Are you unhappy that the conquest of New Mexico has been achieved peaceably?"

"There are some here who merit punishment," the dragoon said stiffly. He nodded at the little cannon. "That artillery piece reminds me of that fact every time I see it. My older brother, Archibald, was a member of the Texan-Santa Fe Expedition and there never was a braver and more good-hearted man. Now he is no longer with us." He looked at the lieutenant, his chin up. "I would avenge him."

Juanita frowned. "Your brother was of los tejanos who were taken captive five years ago?"

Fitzgerald nodded, his eyes on the star on the cannon's breech. "Yes, he was a tejano, as you call them. And he died as a result." There was a long pause as the others studied him. Then his head lifted. "I recently learned that Antonio Lopez de Santa Anna is once again President of Mexico and has ordered Manuel Armijo back to New Mexico with five thousand men. I hope it is true and not a rumor. To meet the man who was the cause of my brother's death on the field of battle would be a grand opportunity." The dragoon's white teeth glinted in the sun. "Revenge, and glory besides."

"Or death," the lieutenant said. "Destruction. Bullets and agony and blood."

"And la disrupción," Juanita said. "Others have also heard these rumors. Some are leaving town for fear of what might happen when el gobernador returns."

"There is no need to be afraid," Fitzgerald said. "We American troops are here to protect you. Should there be a battle, which I sincerely hope will take place, there is no question of the outcome."

"Your American troops didn't protect the man who died on the plaza three and a half weeks ago," Jessie said.

"Sí, this is most true." Juanita turned to Fitzgerald. "Has anything more been learned about el hombre or how he died?"

Lieutenant Milbank frowned. "What man is this?"

"Some Indian who was stabbed on the plaza two nights after we entered Santa Fe," Fitzgerald said. "I happened to be on patrol in the vicinity at the time and was able to assure that Miss Milbank and her friend arrived safely home after curfew had sounded."

Jessie's jaw tightened. No mention of Raúl? But now was not the time. She turned to the lieutenant. "The man who died was named Vidal," she said. "He was an acquaintance of our housekeeper, but she doesn't know his last name or where his family lives. We hoped someone from the army would take the time to discover more about him so his people could be informed, but nothing seems to have been done."

He gave her a troubled look. "I'm afraid that's not much to go on. But I'll see what I can find out before I return to my men."

"He was only an Indian," Fitzgerald said.

The lieutenant gave him a sharp look and turned away, then took Jessie's arm and guided her east along the front of the palacio. "I hope you will not feel it too forward of me to comment on the uniqueness of your dress," he said. "I find it a fascinating mixture of the Mexican and the American styles, with none of the furbelows that so weigh down the bod—" He reddened, then hurried on. "Skirts I have seen in Saint Louis. Or the amount of jewelry I have seen here in Santa Fe. At the dance the governor hosted, I was somewhat startled by the quantity of silver and gold used by the ladies to adorn themselves."

Jessie smiled, amused at the way he had avoided the use of the word "bodice." Or had he meant something else? "My mother disliked fussy display and preferred what she called 'simple dress.' She taught me to appreciate that, as well. Mexican skirts are much more comfortable than American ones, and easier to wear." Jessie touched the corner of her blue-and-white striped rebozo. "And this is something I gladly added when I discovered bonnets were not normally worn here. I've always hated the restrictive things. My mother disliked them too, but felt they were necessary in order to preserve some measure of respectability. I think she would have appreciated this option."

"She sounds like a remarkable woman."

Jessie's throat closed. She looked away. After a long moment she said, "She was. It's been three years, but there are still times that I miss her dreadfully."

Behind them, Juanita moved forward to take Jessie's free hand. "It pains her to speak of it," she explained to the men. "It was not an ordinary death, but un asesinato."

"An assassination?" Fitzgerald asked.

Jessie shook her head. "She was murdered." She looked away.

There was a hiss of distress from the dragoon, and the lieutenant pressed Jessie's hand, his face stricken. "Please accept my deepest condolences," he said.

She gave him a small smile and made a small helpless gesture. "I should have accepted it by now."

"There is no timetable to grief," Private Fitzgerald said, a little bitterly. "It creeps up when one least expects it." He bent toward her. "And the men who did this deed?"

She shook her head. "They were never found."

"Then you can understand my own need for justice."

She met his eyes. "Justice, yes. Revenge, no." She looked up at the lieutenant. "Perhaps someday I will tell you more. But today—"

He pressed her hand again, and they proceeded silently along the edge of the town square, the cottonwood leaves golden in the September sun, the brown adobe walls beyond them warm in the light.

CHAPTER 7: Friday, September 25, 1846

"¡Dios mío!" Juanita said as she entered the Milbank shop a couple weeks later. "The plaza is so crowded with men that I began to wonder if I would ever reach you!"

Jessie turned from the stack of calico she'd been arranging on a shelf near the door to the kitchen, and her father looked up from the accounts ledger. "So Kearny is leaving for California at last," he said. "I will be glad to see the back of him and the men going with him. This city has been entirely too full for too long." He glanced toward the street door. "They'll be marching right past us. We might as well go out and watch. I doubt there'll be very many customers this morning." He looked around the room and smiled. "There are certainly none now."

"It might be well to look out a window, Don Hubert," Juanita said. "The plaza is truly quite crowded."

"An excellent plan." He moved toward the one nearest the street corner. "I only opened one shutter this morning, because all the horses and men going back and forth were raising so much dust." He folded the other window covering back and lashed it into position against the wall. "This should give us a nice vantage point."

The girls moved to stand beside him. They couldn't see into the plaza itself, but uniformed soldiers filled the street leading to it. Two men emerged from the crowd, heading toward the shop. Their faces lit up when they saw the girls watching.

"Lieutenant," Juanita said through the window. "You see we have found a good place from which to watch the parade." She dimpled at Fitzgerald. "Buenos días, señor."

Jessie turned to her father. "Papa, I don't believe you have formally met Private Fitzgerald. He is a dragoon with Captain Burgwin's company."

Jessie's father nodded politely, clearly remembering him but not wanting to refer to the experience. "You are not among the men going to California?"

Fitzgerald shook his head. "Unfortunately, no. My company is being left behind."

"He will be among those helping to enforce the new law code General Kearny promulgated on Tuesday," Lieutenant Milbank said.

"Ah, yes." Jessie's father said. "I will be interested to hear your thoughts on the potential effectiveness of the code, as well as your knowledge of the civil officials he's appointed."

"I can only speak to what I know of the men who came with us from Missouri," the lieutenant said. "I myself will be interested in what you know of the men who were already here. Governor Charles Bent and the new Judge Carlos Beaubien, for example."

Don Hubert tilted his head sideways toward Juanita. "I suspect this young lady knows more about Judge Beaubien than I do. He is a good friend of the Sena clan."

Juanita dimpled at him. "It is true. Señor Beaubien and my uncles have been involved together in many transactions." Then her face brightened. "And I learned this morning that his son Narciso is even now returning to us."

She turned to Fitzgerald. "He has been in Saint Louis these last three years, attending una universidad. He is very knowledgeable."

Jessie suppressed a chuckle. From what Juanita had told her, the new college graduate was also very good looking. And rich. Or, at least potentially rich. He was co-owner with the Taos Sheriff of a million-acre land grant. Fitzgerald did not look at all eager to hear about his accomplishments.

A trumpet sounded from the direction of the plaza. They all turned toward it.

The street had emptied now. General Kearny rode into sight, swinging around the corner on a splendid bay stallion. Behind him were the riders responsible for the Stars and Stripes and the unit colors. The flags snapped proudly in the late September breeze. Somewhere behind them a drum rolled and a sergeant barked an order. The troops moved past with proud shoulders, their feet marking time.

The lieutenant turned to Jessie. "It is quite a sight, isn't it?"

She nodded. Even though she didn't approve of war, of conflict for the sake of empire, she had to admit the marching men looked very fine. These were the same soldiers who'd haunted the plaza the last two months, ducking in and out of drinking houses, accosting her and her friends, and generally making life uncomfortable. They looked completely different this morning. As if they had some place to go and a purpose in life. They looked almost admirable. Or maybe it was just the uniforms.

The parade ended at last, the troops disappearing down the road to Albuquerque, and the lieutenant and dragoon joined the others inside the store. They gathered around the little cast iron stove in the center of the room and Jessie's father shared his knowledge of the New Mexican residents who'd been appointed to the new government. Then the lieutenant added information about some of the newcomers, including the private who'd been furloughed indefinitely so he could serve as Prosecuting Attorney for the area around Taos.

Fitzgerald didn't participate in the conversation. He sat off to one side, soft black dragoon cap in his hands, his lips pursed, and left foot tapping irritably. Even the coffee and bizcochitos Manuelita brought in didn't calm him.

"I understand Colonel Price will be arriving in town shortly," Jessie's father said.

Lieutenant Milbank nodded. "In about a week."

Fitzgerald scowled. "He's bringing a battalion of Mormons with him. They will go on to California, but once again I will be left behind."

"There's work to be done here, as well," the lieutenant said. He glanced at Juanita and looked away. "I'm not at all sure everyone in New Mexico is quite as delighted with our presence as our leadership assumes."

"I expect that's why work on the fort continues to move forward," Jessie's father said.

The lieutenant nodded. "That and the desire to complete the walls before winter sets in. It's actually coming together quite nicely. The fortifications are well engineered."

The dragoon stared at the floor. He truly did seem dejected. Jessie didn't sympathize with his need to fight someone, but she did feel a little sorry for him. Impulsively, she leaned forward. "Are we allowed to visit the fort?"

He lifted his head. "Would you like to?" He turned to Juanita. "And you as well, señorita? Would you like to do so today?"

She glanced at Jessie, then nodded. The corners of her hazel eyes crinkled in wry amusement. "It seems appropriate to spend the afternoon examining the fortifications el general has left behind to keep us in our place."

Jessie looked at Lieutenant Milbank questioningly, but he shook his head. "I'm afraid I must return to my men." He smiled a little sheepishly. "In fact, I should have been on my way an hour ago."

And yet he lingered while the girls gathered their outdoor things. And took the time to accompany them as far as the barracks behind the palacio, or what was now being called Government House.

Jessie hadn't been to this part of town since the takeover and was bemused to discover that the former Mexican troop quarters now housed Americans. Its former residents had been accompanied by their wives and families, giving this section of town the air of a small village. Now, the low adobe buildings had an air of general neglect, as if no one was responsible for airing blankets, picking up debris, and making sure food was secure from rodents and dogs. Fitzgerald hurried the girls past and up the road to the hill on the northeast edge of town.

The path up the slope was churned to dust and the summit buzzed with activity. A wide moat had been carved into the hillside that faced the town and lined with two thick, double-bricked walls an arm length apart. Farther along, men dug steadily, extending the trench. Others carried buckets of excess material to the center of the hill and dumped them beside a pit where more workers mixed a slurry of soil, straw, and water together, then poured it into a line of wooden forms. Long rows of sturdy adobe bricks, slabs perhaps eighteen by twenty-four inches, lay farther on, drying in the sun.

Private Fitzgerald and the girls moved around this area to one of the cannon that overlooked the town. Jessie stared past its big barrel to the flat-roofed houses and the palacio below. Government House, she corrected herself, then forced herself to trace the plaza cottonwoods instead. They were golden in the September sunlight, a brilliant contrast to the brown buildings.

A little boy crossed the square, a shaggy yellow dog at his heels. Jessie smiled and looked east toward the parish church, its brown bell towers steadfast against the clear blue sky. She turned slowly to the right, taking in the view. The three chapels were also visible from here, each within a cluster of houses. On the land between, men and women moved through long narrow fields, harvesting chile and corn, checking pumpkins, shooing stray chickens and goats. The sight filled Jessie with an odd sense of comfort.

"I have always loved this view," Juanita said wistfully. She looked down at the big brass cannon, bent to gaze along its trajectory, then jerked upright. "This monstruosidád aims directly at my uncle's casa and the church beyond!" She stepped back. "La parroquia itself." She opened her mouth, then closed it and turned to look blindly at the adobe-making activities. "The church," she muttered, then stalked off, as if only movement would allow her feelings the expression they needed.

Jessie, searching for something to distract Private Fitzgerald, pointed at the fortifications along the edge of the hill. "Why are there two walls, one inside the other?"

"It will be a single wall when construction is completed," he said. "The space between will be filled with stones and mortar." He waved a hand at the hilltop. "The resulting structure will enclose an area sufficient to accommodate up to one thousand men. The pit there where the adobe is being mixed will be reinforced and turned into a magazine for powder and shells."

"Cannon shells?"

He nodded. "Of course, they will only be used in case of actual insurrection. The sound you hear at curfew each night is the product of powder only."

She made a little face. "I doubt I will ever get used to that sound or the restrictions it places on us."

"The curfew has been instituted to assure your safety from our troops as much as ours from insurrection," he said, reciting as if from memory. "None of us are allowed out of quarters after curfew unless we know the counter sign, and only authorized personnel and the men on guard duty are provided that information."

"So if I'm found on the streets after ten p.m., it will be by somebody who is supposed to be there, and unlikely to insult me?"

He squinted at her. "I sincerely hope you don't attempt to test that theory."

"I assure you I have no desire to do so."

"Jessie!" Juanita hurried toward them, her rebozo half off her head and her face lit with pleasure. "Raúl is here!" She turned and pointed toward the center of the hill. "There, making los adobes." She hurried off, waving her hand, and calling "¡Primo!"

Jessie looked at Fitzgerald. "I thought the work here was being done by soldiers."

His lips pursed in disapproval. "The majority of the men assigned to the task departed earlier today with General Kearny. Local men have been hired as replacements."

They moved to join Juanita, who hovered at the edge of the adobe-making area. Raúl stood near the forms, grinning at her. When he saw Fitzgerald, his smile faded.

The dragoon touched Jessie's elbow. "I must take a moment to speak to the captain of the works," he said. "I'll leave you here to talk with your friend." His eyes skimmed over the men mixing adobe and across the top of the hill. "Until I return, then."

As Fitzgerald moved away, Raúl said something to a man nearby, then headed toward the girls.

"Primo," Juanita said as he reached them.

"Buenos días. Have you come to see the sights?" He looked down at his arms and hands, which were splashed with wet and drying mud. "I'm afraid I am unable to greet you properly."

She waved off his apology as she asked, "What are you doing here?"

He grinned sardonically. "I and mis compañeros assist our conquerors in the task of la supresión." He looked around, as if checking to see who might hear him, then smiled at Jessie. "Excluding present company, of course."

"Private Fitzgerald tells me you replaced the troops who were making the bricks," she said.

He nodded. "Sí, and it is well for los americanos that we are willing to do it, or the whole thing would have toppled. Los soldados, they are not adoberos and they do not know how to build with them, either." He turned to his cousin. "The money I earn will enable Guadalupe and me to purchase a little land and construct una casa for ourselves."

Juanita's eyes widened. "You have permission to marry?"

He grinned. "No, but a little dinero will speak loudly when we seek it."

She chuckled and shook her head, then nodded toward the fort perimeter. "There seems to be a great amount of wall still unfinished. By the time it is finished, you will be able to purchase much land."

"That is my hope." There was a shout behind him. The man he'd spoken to earlier was gesturing for him to get back to work. Raúl waved a hand to indicate he was coming, then leaned toward Juanita as if to give her a hug. She stepped back involuntarily and he stopped, looked down at his hands, chuckled, and shrugged apologetically. "Adiós por ahora," he said.

"Goodbye for now," the girls echoed as he loped back to his task.

Juanita turned to study the hilltop. "So many picnics," she said. "So many late afternoon walks up here to watch the sun set." She sighed. "The changes, they multiply."

Then she saw Fitzgerald moving toward them and her shoulders straightened. "And we will adapt as we must."

The three young people made their way back down the hill and into town. They had just turned into the street to the Sena compound when Dick Green emerged from its gate.

Fitzgerald stiffened at the sight of him, but Juanita didn't appear to notice. She moved toward the dark-skinned man. "Buenos días, Señor Green! You have been to see mi tio?"

The slave removed his hat and smiled broadly. "Sí, señorita, I have brought your uncle news you also may be glad to hear." He glanced at the dragoon, then back at her. "But then, perhaps not."

She tilted her head at him, and he grinned and relented. "I'm told Señor Saint Vrain's caravan has reached Bent's Fort on the Arkansas river. I reckon we'll be seeing them in another six weeks or so."

"Already? I am so glad!"

Private Fitzgerald gave Jessie a puzzled look and she shrugged. Juanita caught the look and smiled self-consciously. Dick Green chuckled, bowed to them all, replaced his hat, and moved toward the plaza.

"Is this Saint Vrain a friend of yours?" the dragoon asked.

"He is a mountain man and part owner, with our new governor and his brothers, of Bent's Fort, there north of the Arkansas River," Juanita said.

"I know Bent's Fort. We spent several days there on the march here. After the endless plains, it was quite a sight for sore eyes."

Juanita nodded and smiled. "I am told it is most impressive."

There was a suppressed excitement about her that couldn't be ignored. Jessie's eyes narrowed. "Is there someone on that caravan you are particularly anxious to see?" she asked. "A certain college graduate named Narciso Beaubien, perhaps?"

Juanita smiled demurely. "Perhaps. I am also told he comes with Señor Saint Vrain's train." She turned to Private Fitzgerald. "We were good friends before he entered la universidad."

"Ah, I see." The dragoon studied the empty street, with its brown walls and thick dust. A burro overloaded with firewood trundled toward them from the direction of the mountains, a small boy guiding it with a stick. "Forgive my presumption, but I cannot bring myself to believe that even the most educated Mexican could give you the life you deserve." His eyes flicked to Jessie, then back to the burro. "You both deserve Americans." He smiled flirtatiously at Juanita. "Or at least an Irish Englishman."

Juanita laughed and took his arm. "Come in and meet my aunt and uncle and los primos."

"Primos?" he asked as they walked away.

"The cousins," she said gaily. "All of them!"

CHAPTER 8: Friday afternoon, September 25, 1846

Later that day, Jessie was crossing the plaza alone when she again encountered Dick Green. "Your news seemed to please Juanita," she observed with a grin.

"I certainly hope so." His brows contracted. He studied her, glanced around as if to make sure no one overheard, then lowered his voice. "I beg your pardon for saying so, but I can't say I much care for that young dragoon who was escorting you all."

She tilted her head. "Why is that?"

"It's more a feeling than anything else. He's very slick and courteous and all that, but—" Green shrugged. "I reckon it's none of my business, and I'm certain sure both you gals are old enough to know your own minds, so it may be that I'm just making up stories in my head." His eyes twinkled. "Or it's that smooth British drawl of his. Makes him sound like a river boat gambler."

She laughed and put her hand on his arm. "My father and I have not seen much of you since you've been in town. I believe Manuelita is baking bizcochitos this afternoon."

He chuckled. "Is that an invitation?"

"It certainly is."

He grinned. "I reckon what I was heading to can wait a mite longer. That woman's baking is worth a detour or two."

They set off toward the store, Jessie's hand on his arm, but found it closed. Jessie's father had gone to a meeting with the army sutler. Jessie led Green into the courtyard instead, where they found Manuelita extracting cookies from the beehive-shaped outdoor adobe oven.

They followed her into the kitchen. She set the platter of bizcochitos on the table, and Green seated himself while Jessie poured them both some coffee. He lifted a buttery, cinnamon-dusted sphere to his mouth, took a bite, and turned to the waiting cook. "Mmmm, mmm," he said, nodding to her. "You sure do know how to bake a good biscuit, Cookie. I wish you would come visit the fort and teach my Charlotte how to make these."

A smile touched Manuelita's usually taciturn lips as she turned away to tackle the dirty dishes. Jessie grinned. Green was the only person she knew who could get away with calling the woman Cookie. She reached for a bizcochito. "Ah, but that wife of yours makes quite a pie," she said.

"She does that." Green took another cookie from the platter. "If we ever get our freedom, we could start us up a bakery and make a right comfortable living."

"You know, there isn't any slavery in Mexico." Jessie looked down at the table, pinched at a crumb, and gave him a swift glance. "If you ever want to go south—"

The dishes on the worktable went silent, then clattered loudly.

Green smiled slightly and shook his head. "It would have to be a good way south, beyond Mexico. By the time this war is over, I reckon all that country will be U.S. territory. I surely wouldn't want to be caught by American soldiers who thought I'd deserted to the enemy." He dusted bizcochito crumbs from his fingers and leaned back from the table. "Besides, I wouldn't leave Charlotte. And anyone who's met her would remember the occasion. You can't hide that pair of bright eyes and those hips. We'd be picked up by nightfall the first day."

"If you should ever change your mind—"

He smiled again and raised a quieting hand. "I know you mean it kindly." He swallowed the last bit of his coffee and stood up. "I'd best be getting along. I need to locate a space for Saint Vrain's caravan to settle into when it gets here. The town's still a mite more crowded than usual, so I reckon finding a good spot is going to take somewhat longer than it has in the past." He looked at her gravely. "The Bents and Saint Vrain have come to rely on me. I don't think I could rightly live with myself if I disabused that trust."

He was barely out the door before Manuelita turned on Jessie. "Not your bizness, he slave or free!"

Jessie blinked at her. It was one of the longest sentences she'd ever heard from the woman. "It was just an idea," she said mildly. "If he and Charlotte needed assistance, I would be more than happy to provide it. I thought he ought to know that."

Manuelita scowled and turned back to the worktable.

Jessie frowned. "You were a slave yourself, as a child, weren't you? An Apache girl captured by the Navajo?"

"Four winters. Then Utes come."

"And they sold you." It was hard to believe anyone could steal or sell an innocent being as if they were a blanket or pot. Jessie shook her head. "To a Spanish family, wasn't it?

Doesn't that make you genízaro? What exactly is an genízaro, anyway? I've never understood what it means."

The cook's back was still turned. "No tribe Indian."

Like Dick Green was a no tribe African. But Jessie didn't say it. Instead she said, "I thought it meant you were from what they call the wild tribes and decided to become a Catholic."

The cook began stacking bowls a little more sharply than strictly necessary. "Baptize eight winters. No choice."

She finished her task. A log fell in the fire. Manuelita began wiping down the worktable.

"I can't imagine," Jessie said.

The cook didn't respond. Jessie gazed at her broad back. "But you're not a slave now." She brushed at the cookie crumbs on the table, gathering them up. "I still don't understand why you think I shouldn't offer to help Dick and Charlotte. They are slaves. The Bent family owns them. Someone else could come along tomorrow and buy one of them, take them off to a distant land, and leave the other behind. I can't imagine why anyone would choose to remain in such a condition."

Manuelita shook her head. Jessie waited. Surely she would explain why she was so upset. Perhaps the offer to Dick Green wasn't the real issue. "I'm sorry I haven't been able to learn anything more about your friend."

The cook didn't turn.

"Is there anything more you may have remembered? Something that could help us find Vidal's family or understand why he was killed? Or who killed him?"

Manuelita grunted in exasperation. "From north in mountains." She moved across the room to return the bowls to their shelf.

"North? Was he from Taos? Or somewhere more in the mountains like Las Trampas? East of there, around Mora?"

The cook shrugged. Jessie watched her a little longer, then gave up. She should check the shop. If her father still hadn't returned, she ought to go ahead and open it. But first she would check the animals. Perhaps Manuelita would be in a better mood if there were eggs from the chickens.

Jessie tossed her rebozo over her shoulders and slipped out into the courtyard. She stood for a moment, soaking in the sunshine, then skirted the oven and maneuvered around the covered wagon to the chicken coop on the far wall. The hens pecked at her feet and she shooed them away. "Silly birds," she said. "I came to get food, not give it." But when she poked around in the nest boxes, she found nothing.

She moved back into the courtyard and stood with one hand on the wagon, just below the bench seat. She should open the shop. Instead, she turned toward the far corner and went through the covered passage that led to the corral behind the house.

The two mules saw her immediately and came to peer over the fence of cedar posts jammed end first into the ground. When Jessie stroked their brown muzzles, they reached for her rebozo, and she laughed and batted them away. "I don't have any treats," she told them apologetically. "I wasn't planning to visit you."

"They'll stop greeting you so happily if you continue that habit," her father said from behind her. She turned and he smiled at her from atop Saturn, his big black gelding. "I thought you would be in the shop by now."

"I met Dick Green in the plaza and invited him back for coffee and Manuelita's bizcochitos. After he left, I just couldn't settle."

He swung from the horse. "Help me get the gear off Saturn, and we'll go in together."

CHAPTER 9: Tuesday, October 6, 1846

"These are really beautiful melons." Jessie plucked a large pale-yellow fruit from the top of the little pyramid and admired its smooth skin. She held it to her nose. "They smell delicious."

Her father looked up from the counter. "They are good-looking, aren't they? Someone from Santo Domingo brought them in. I expect that's the last of them for this year. I've never seen them later than early October."

She placed it carefully back into position. "I'm surprised you're getting them even now. I noticed yesterday that the eastern mountain peaks are completely white. The snow must be thick up there."

He chuckled and nodded toward the windows to the street. "You'll notice I only opened one set of shutters this morning. It felt a little too cold and wet for both of them."

She studied them. "One of these days, we need to order window glass." Then Lieutenant Milbank's head appeared and she waved impulsively. He smiled, touched his hat, and a minute later, came through the door.

"Good morning," he said cheerily. He turned to her father. "How are you, sir?"

"We are well. And yourself?"

He smiled wryly. "A bit chilly." He turned to Jessie. "But I am not feeling as under the weather as some of my compatriots. I thought you might want to know that Private Fitzgerald has come down with what appears to be typhoid."

"Is he very ill?"

"The doctor holds good hope of his recovery, but it may be some time yet. With typhoid, it's always difficult to be certain." He turned to her father. "The cold weather is exacerbated by the fact that the troops have still not received their winter uniforms. Colonel Price has finally arrived, but the wagons detailed to accompany him were left behind. Unfortunately, they contained the cold weather uniforms as well as extra blankets." He smiled ruefully. "The men in Washington City responsible for our equipage don't seem to understand that Santa Fe is not in the same temperate zone as Veracruz."

"Yes, we Americans often misunderstand the range of temperatures possible here," Jessie's father said. Then he grinned. "On the other hand, that misapprehension can be quite good for shopkeepers such as myself."

The lieutenant chuckled and glanced around the room. "I wonder if you would happen to have a few blankets at a reasonable price."

"That all depends on what you consider reasonable." The two men contemplated each other, eyes twinkling.

Then the lieutenant sobered. "I had hoped to take at least one to Private Fitzgerald." He turned to Jessie. "In honor of your friendship with him."

"That is kind of you," she said. "Is there anyone providing him with nursing care?"

"The military doctor and his assistants are doing the best they can, but there are many who are suffering with it or other ailments."

She turned to her father. "I can take him some of that soup Manuelita made yesterday—" But her father was already shaking his head and the lieutenant looking at her in horror.

Jessie pulled herself up, ready to do battle, then forced her face into calmer lines. "I'm sure the doctor and his assistants are stretched beyond their limits," she said patiently. She turned to the lieutenant. "Yesterday I overheard a customer saying that some of the lower ranks are sleeping on mere boards, because there isn't enough straw to fill all the mattresses. Would a sheepskin help Private Fitzgerald rest more comfortably? We have extra pillows, as well."

The lieutenant stared at her, then looked away, his face suddenly red. Her father heaved an exasperated sigh. "If you want to send some items with the lieutenant, feel free to do so," he said. "However, typhoid is highly contagious. You will not go anywhere near that barracks. Do you understand?"

He didn't use this tone with her very often. When he did, she knew there was no point in arguing. Jessie blew out an impatient breath and made a small gesture of acceptance. But then she glanced at the lieutenant, saw the relief on his face, and felt a surge of irritation. The dragoon was a fellow human being. One way or another, she was going to find a way to assist him. She gave the lieutenant an icy look. "If you would be so kind as to wait a few minutes, I will gather what I can and bring them to you." She turned and swept out of the room without waiting for a reply.

By the time she'd gathered what she wanted, she'd cooled off a bit and started to think of solutions to her dilemma. Private Fitzgerald needed nursing, but her father was going to be obdurate about this. She doubted the dragoon actually had typhoid. If the disease was truly in the city, half the population would be sick by now. Perhaps someone in the Sena compound could be persuaded to take food and bread to the barracks.

After the lieutenant left, she put on her heavy brown winter cloak, threw her rebozo over her head, and headed to Juanita's house.

As she entered the plaza, she saw Guadalupe Barceló just ahead. The younger girl stood in front of the old chapel, bareheaded and shoulders hunched, and surrounded by American soldiers. One of them had snatched her blue-and-white rebozo and was waving it like a flag, while another reached for her curly black hair. As she flinched away from him, Guadalupe saw Jessie and gave her a pleading look.

The American girl was already moving forward, her eyes snapping. "What are you doing?"

"Ah, another one," the nearest soldier said. He reached for her rebozo, but she slapped him away. "Leave me alone!"

"That one ain't no Mex," a pockmarked man said, peering at her.

The one holding Guadalupe's rebozo dropped it into the dirt and put his hands on his hips. "I didn't know any of our wagons had women in 'em. You a Mormon?"

"Camp followers!" said the man who'd been trying to pat Guadalupe's curls. He moved toward Jessie.

She stepped back, chin high, shoulders back. "I am an American merchant's daughter." She jerked her head toward the street behind her. "Shall I scream for my father or would you like to call him yourself?"

"Oh, no ma'am." He raised his hands, palms forward. "My apologies, ma'am." He backed away and the others followed, heads down and eyes shifting from side to side. They headed off in the direction of a drinking establishment on the other side of the plaza.

Jessie turned to Guadalupe, who had picked up her rebozo and was shaking it vigorously. "Are you all right?"

The other girl nodded, blinking away tears as she rearranged the shawl. "Thank you," she whispered.

"Why are you out here by yourself?" Jessie demanded. Then she stopped. She was also alone. But then, she was four years older than Guadalupe. And, as filthy-minded as most of the soldiers were, they often had a respect for American females which gave her some protection. All she had to do was open her mouth, say her name. She hated that fact, but it was true. She turned back to her friend.

Guadalupe chewed on her upper lip. "I came out to search for Raúl."

"Isn't he at the fort making adobe bricks?"

Guadalupe glanced toward the retreating men who'd accosted her. "The new soldados americanos make them now."

"So he's no longer working?"

Guadalupe nodded. "Sí. So now he has no means to earn." She looked around the square as if willing him to appear. "He came to me two days ago and requested half of that which we had set aside for a small casa and land. He said he had una oportunidad de inversión, so of course I gave it to him." She looked away. "However, late this morning, a man who arrived to speak with mi madre told us he saw Raúl gambling in one of the saloons."

"So his investment opportunity is a game of cards?"

Guadalupe nodded, her eyes flicking across the square. "I have been trying for the last two hours to find him. I know many of our people gamble. Mi madre keeps the roof over our head with her skill as un comerciante de monte—" She broke off. "How do you say it?"

"A monte dealer?"

Guadalupe nodded and went on. "Only a person acting in that capacity can truly make a living at cards. For the rest, it is truly a gamble." Her chin went up, her mouth firm. "When I find mi amor, I will tell him that I will live most happily with him in a shack, but I will not live with un jugador, no matter how large the plot of land or casa he may be able to provide."

A group of soldiers went by, their heads turning to study the two girls. Guadalupe shrank toward Jessie, who glared at them. "What are you looking at?" she snapped. The men's eyes shifted and their steps quickened as they moved away.

Jessie turned back to Guadalupe. "You are too young and too pretty to be out here on your own." She peered into the girl's tearstained face. "Let me take you home and then I will try to find Raúl and give him your message."

Guadalupe shivered and nodded. She wrapped her rebozo closer to her face and clung to Jessie's arm as they crossed the square.

CHAPTER 10: Tuesday afternoon, October 6, 1846

By the time Jessie reached the fourth saloon, it was late afternoon and she was shivering with cold. It seemed unlikely that she would find Raúl here. It was the largest gambling room in town and the one where Gertrudis Barceló usually set up shop. Surely Raúl wouldn't want Guadalupe's adoptive mother to know what he was doing.

Jessie paused outside the open door and took a deep breath. She could hear laughter, though it was curiously distant.

Her experience in the other three places hadn't been all that unpleasant. The Mexican men and women in them had shielded her from the americanos' more lewd comments. But she was uncomfortable with gambling. Her mother would have been horrified at the thought of her daughter in such an establishment. And her father. If someone told him where she'd been, the resulting conversation would not be pleasant.

But she couldn't think about that now. Guadalupe needed her help. She'd promised to find Raúl and give him his sweetheart's message, and she was determined to do so. Jessie straightened her shoulders and went through the door.

But this wasn't a gambling salon, it was a bar. A long counter, much like the one in her father's mercantile, filled the back wall. Behind it were shelves of bottles and drinking utensils. To her left, flames crackled in a corner fireplace. Small tables were scattered around the room. The men sitting at them eyed her curiously. No one spoke. Then the man behind the counter caught her eye and jerked his chin toward a half-open door on her right. Behind it, someone laughed triumphantly.

Jessie nodded gratefully to the bartender and moved toward the inner room. She paused on the threshold, letting her eyes adjust to the haze of cigarillo smoke. The only light was from the candles in a wooden chandelier suspended from the ceiling. And a small corner fireplace. Jessie headed toward it and stood with her back to the flames while she studied the crowd.

Donaciano Vigil leaned against the adobe wall near the door, his dark head bent toward a man she didn't recognize. They were both dressed in fine wool American suits. A young man in Mexican clothing edged toward them and said something that caused Vigil's head to go up, but then the taller man smiled dismissively and the younger one shrugged and turned away.

Jessie's eyes moved on, to a rectangular table centered on the back wall. Doña Tules sat behind it on a cushioned chair. Her henna-tipped black curls, usually so carefully done up, were loose on her shoulders, the ends brushing three thick gold chains around her neck. Her gold crucifix flashed in the light from the candle sconce behind her, which softened the lines in her face, but her dark brown eyes were sharp and intent on her work. The monte cards slipped steadily through her long fingers.

A short sleek man with smooth salt-and-pepper hair and dressed in a short red Mexican jacket and split trousers sat opposite the dealer, his back to the crowd. His eyes never left the cards as he smoked a cigarillo and occasionally spoke a few words in a low voice.

Then he suddenly threw up his hands and pushed back his chair, turning sideways as he rose. "Ah, señora," he said, laughing. "Once again I am indebted to you. You have relieved me of the anxiety of great wealth."

Doña Tules smiled back at him. "Ah, Don Agustín," she said. "I have done more than that. I have given you the opportunity to experience the delight of winning and the drama of losing." She tilted her head coquettishly. "And also the anticipatory pleasure of knowing that tomorrow the scales may swing in your favor."

The people around him laughed as the man gave her an elaborate bow and turned away. He nodded cheerfully at them and headed toward the door, then veered off to clap a young man in a short green Mexican jacket on the back. The person he greeted was taller than he was, but still the touch seemed bestowed like a blessing.

Jessie's breath caught. The younger man was Raúl. She surged forward and was at his elbow the instant the older man moved off.

Raúl looked down at her in surprise. "Buenos días, Señorita Jessie," he said. "I wouldn't have expected to find you in this place."

She put her hand on his elbow. "I'm here because you are."

"Because of me?"

"Guadalupe asked me to come. She wanted me to give you a message."

He glanced toward the monte table. The chair Don Agustín had vacated was still empty. "This is not a good time."

Doña Tules' hands were moving again, the cards flipping smoothly, but her eyes were on Raúl. She gave Jessie a sharp look and flicked her eyes toward the young man, then the door. Jessie nodded at her and squeezed his arm. "Please. It will only take a few moments." She smiled at him. "Un momento."

Raúl sighed, shook his head, and moved toward the door. He paused in the outer room, looking at the tables, but she tugged him toward the street.

The air which had been so cold before felt sweet after the tobacco-shrouded gambling saloon. Raúl didn't appear to notice. "¿Cuál es el mensaje?" he asked.

Jessie gave him a questioning look.

"You said you brought a message from mi amor Guadalupe. What is it?"

She paused, not quite sure how to begin. All the time she had been looking for him, she hadn't thought out what she was going to say. She closed her eyes, trying to remember the Barceló girl's exact words.

Raúl moved impatiently. "There are cards waiting for me."

"That's what the message is about."

He frowned. "I am quite aware that Guadalupe disapproves of los juegos de azar."

"Then why are you playing them?"

"If I am to provide us with a home, I have no alternative."

"You told her you had an investment opportunity. Is this what you meant? Games of chance? Card games?"

He looked away. "There are few alternatives now open to me." Then he brightened. He pulled out a small leather bag and jingled it at her. "I already have enough to purchase a large parcela de tierra. With a little more, there will be sufficient for more than a small casa. I can build for her una hacienda."

"Guadalupe told me she would rather live in a shack. That is the message she asked me to give you."

"She deserves more than a shack. I will earn enough to provide it for her."

"Money won at gambling is not earned. It is acquired."

"This is una conversación I will have with Guadalupe and Guadalupe alone. I beg your pardon, señorita, but it is truly none of your concern."

She looked up at him, her mouth half open, ready to give him more arguments, but his jaw was tight and his eyes angry.

He shrugged and looked away. "It is another means of taking from los americanos. Every dealer in the city has been blessed with a sudden influx of dinero because los soldados americanos do not know when to stop losing." He grinned. "They are all a great deal like Agustín Durán, el hombre I was talking with before you came up. He has la adicción. Almost all these new soldiers are also possessed with it. This is a most excellent time to be un repartidor de cartasa in Santa Fe."

"But you are not a card dealer."

"But the money I earn—" He glanced at her face and began again. "El dinero que gano, it is in americano coin, acquired by the dealers from soldados who seek entertainment." He grinned. "And then passed on to me by las cartas. It is a kind of revenge against the conqueror."

Jessie shook her head. Raúl shrugged. "I must take advantage of la oportunidad while it is available to me. They say Santa Anna has been replaced en la ciudad de México and the new president now prepares to prosecute the war with great vigor. We must fleece los americanos before they run away home."

Jessie bit her tongue. Rumor in the shop that morning had said just the opposite. That Santa Anna was still in power and negotiating with the American officials. That the war could very well be over already. But nothing was certain. Besides, if Raúl thought the conflict was going to end soon, he would probably become even more intent on his personal method of revenge.

He jingled the little bag again, the coins clinking. "General Armijo will arrive with a victorious army, these americanos arrogantes and that bastardo Henry Fitzgerald will leave once and for all, and we can return to una vida normal," he said. "And then I will buy the land and construct la hacienda my Guadalupita deserves."

There was a shout of laughter from the building behind them. He glanced at it, tucked his money away, and turned toward the door. "One more round and I will take Guadalupe my winnings." His lips twisted. "And be home before ese maldito curfew." His chin lifted. "But los soldados de mexico march north." He gave her a sharp glance. "Los americanos may not always be here, amiga," he said. "It would be well to remember that."

Then he was gone. Jessie stared into the gathering dusk, pondering the irony that Raúl was pleased with news that would also make Henry Fitzgerald happy. That more bloodshed was possible. She closed her eyes, fighting the sudden memory of her mother's shattered corpse, then turned toward home. As she moved across the plaza, it began raining, thin icy drops that seemed to go right through her rebozo. She pulled the hood of her cloak clumsily up over the head covering, but it didn't help much.

CHAPTER 11: Saturday, November 7, 1846

Nothing came of the rumors that Manuel Armijo was heading to Santa Fe. The city was quiet. It became even quieter when Colonel Doniphan took many of the American troops with him to parlay with the Navajo before heading south to Chihuahua and the main American army.

Lieutenant Milbank seemed relieved they were gone, glad to see the last of Doniphan's men. He approved of Colonel Sterling Price, the man who'd arrived with reinforcements the month before and was now in charge at Santa Fe.

"He has a more refined sense of military discipline," the lieutenant told Jessie when he saw her on the plaza in early November. "He's ordered all the officers to drill on the square twice a day, beginning this Saturday. Then we're to transfer that knowledge to our men." His lips quirked. "I'm not at all sure how effective that knowledge transfer will be, but hopefully the drilling itself will have the intended effect and the men won't be tested in a fight with anyone local."

"I certainly hope not," Jessie murmured.

"At any rate, I'm sure the training itself will be quite a spectacle," he said. "It will give us all a chance to wear our dress uniforms."

She wasn't sure she really wanted to watch the officers train, but when Juanita appeared at the store the following

Saturday morning, she couldn't help but smile at her friend's enthusiasm.

"The officers are forming in the plaza," Juanita said breathlessly. "And the weather is clearing. The morning clouds are turning back toward the mountains."

Jessie looked down at the fourounce packets of sugar she was trying to form into a reasonably sized display. The weather had been exceptionally gloomy the last few days. It would be nice to see sunshine. And she'd never seen an American officer in dress uniform.

"I expect you aren't going to be able to make that stack look more substantial than it actually is," her father said from the other side of the room. "There's hardly any sugar left in the city." He made a shooing motion at her. "Go and enjoy the scenery."

"I merely want to see what a training drill is like."

He grinned. "Go on now."

There was a sudden boom from the direction of the plaza and the girls jumped. Jessie's father grimaced. "I suppose the cannon fire is necessary to call them to formation."

"I believe it is el cañón tejano," Juanita said. "There were men doing something with it when I went by." She turned to Jessie. "Some of the officers are even wearing gold lace."

Jessie tapped the last sugar packet into place, crossed to the row of pegs by the door, and took down her rebozo. "It seems odd that the colonel would have ordered the officers to be trained and not the men," she said as she lifted it over her head.

"Many of the officers are volunteers," her father said. "They've never served before. That's part of the reason the men under them have so little discipline." He went to the stove and added a log. "Though some of them do seem to know what they're doing. Our lieutenant, for example."

Juanita raised her eyebrows at Jessie. "Our lieutenant?"

Jessie gave the lower edge of her rebozo a little shake, working out a fold. "I suppose since he and my father are related, that makes him ours." She glanced at her father, who was grinning at her. "Papa's, at any rate." She headed for the door and Juanita followed, eyes twinkling.

They found a place near the old military chapel from which to watch. The officers stood in a neat rectangle in the plaza's center, sunlight glinting on the gold lace at their sleeves and throats and contrasting sharply with the dull copper of the leaves on the cottonwoods. Juanita looked at Jessie. "Do only certain ones wear the lace?"

Jessie shook her head. "I have no idea." Someone touched her elbow and she turned. "Raúl! How are you?"

Guadalupe was on his arm. Jessie and Juanita greeted her affectionately, then they all turned to watch the officers.

"They do look rather fine, don't they?" Jessie asked. She slid a glance at Raúl. "Although I don't think I've ever seen an officer quite as well turned out as General Armijo used to be."

Raúl's eyes were fixed on the parading men. "I see your lieutenant is among them."

Juanita frowned, her eyes searching. "Where? Oh there, in the center."

"Sí, there in the center, not out fighting los indios bárbaros which I am told now raid from Albuquerque south to Sabinal."

Guadalupe looked up at him and made a small cautioning motion, but Raúl went on, eyes still on the officers. "Instead, they remain here, spreading measles and typhoid and other enfermedades."

"There are those who believe living conditions here have created those diseases, including the measles," a voice behind them said.

Jessie turned. Fitzgerald smiled at her wanly, bowed to Juanita, then bent to kiss Guadalupe's hand. "Señoritas y señor." He turned to Raúl. "You see. I have been turning my convalescence to good use by schooling myself in your language."

Raúl gave him a skeptical look. "Three words."

The dragoon shrugged and turned back to the girls.

"How are you feeling?" Jessie asked.

"I am standing again. That is an accomplishment in itself." He turned to Juanita. "I am as well as I am due to the kind services of the servant you sent me."

"Mi tía was delighted to do so."

"Please accept my thanks for thinking of me and also convey them to your aunt." He flashed a triumphant look at Raúl, as if to point out that he knew what "tía" meant. "I hope to call upon her soon and express my appreciation in person," he added. "I was quite disappointed when I was informed that I was too unwell to accompany Doniphan's campaign. However, I comforted myself with the knowledge that I could see more of you, in consequence." He smiled at Jessie. "Both of you."

So gallant, even if he was bloodthirsty. Jessie smiled in amusement and turned away. Juanita maneuvered around her to stand next to the dragoon.

"You should ask your aunt to continue to send him nourishing food," Raúl told Juanita. "There is word that a large force of los soldados de mexico marching north from Chihuahua even now. The plan is to separate Señor Doniphan and the troops he left behind here and so destroy both parties once and for all." He looked at Fitzgerald. "Perhaps you will finally be provided la oportunidad you seek. One that will send you back to where you belong."

"¡Primo!" Juanita said. "Where are your manners?"

Fitzgerald smiled at her and shook his head. "He's merely repeating one of the many rumors so rampant during a time of war. There is no cause for concern."

Raúl looked away. "¡Arrogante!" he muttered.

Guadalupe jiggled his elbow. "I see mi madre there just near the corner," she said. "Will you take me to her?"

He ignored her and gave Fitzgerald a stony look. "It would be well for you to consider the wisdom of lacking concern for what you deem mere rumors. When el militar mexicano appears, I assure you its leaders will find many supporters throughout Nuevo Méjico."

The dragoon shrugged. "My information says otherwise. You may hate us because you're a rico, but the poor of this country appreciate what we have done for them."

"¿Rico?" Raúl spat. "Me? What little land mi familia holds is insufficient to feed us. And it is all we have. Even that will not be in our hands for long, if you americanos have your way!"

"The land will always be there," Juanita murmured.

"They are demanding papers now," he told her. "All of la tierra must be registered and proved to be owned by those who hold it. El gobernador Bent is behind this. He is a rico with much property, but still he desires more. That Donaciano Vigil you admire so much is responsible for the books where it is all to be recorded." He shook his head. "No good will come of these demands for proof of what we all know!"

Raúl's raised voice had caught the attention of others nearby. A man in a Mexican-style jacket turned and raised his hand in a cautionary signal. Raúl saw him, nodded, and took a breath. He leaned toward Fitzgerald, his voice lower now, but no less intense. "Again, I say to you. Consider carefully the wisdom and the possible repercusiones of a lack of concern." Then he straightened and turned to Guadalupe. "What did you say of your mother, mi amor? Let us go to her."

CHAPTER 12: Sunday, November 22, 1846

After that first training session, Jessie didn't return to the plaza to watch the officers. She went about her business, helping Manuelita prepare for the oncoming winter and assisting her father in the mercantile. When she had a few spare minutes, she threw on her cloak and hurried across the plaza and past the east end of the palacio to visit Juanita, careful to keep out of the way of wandering American soldiers.

There were more of them in town by mid-November, all of them excited because Colonel Price had ordered Lieutenant Colonel Mitchell south to Chihuahua. Soldiers poured into town from the grazing camps, eager to join him. When Jessie and Juanita came out of church that Sunday morning, they seemed to be everywhere.

The girls stopped outside the big doors and studied the street to the plaza. The dirt thoroughfare was crowded with soldiers, many apparently the worse for drink. Past the hotel at the corner, the square seemed to teem with them.

Jessie shook her head. "Has every member of the United States Army in New Mexico come to town today?" she asked.

Juanita chuckled. "It is very possible. With the exception of Señor Fitzgerald. Raúl informed me with great pleasure that la compañía de dragones americanos is now stationed in Albuquerque."

"Are you disappointed?"

Juanita shrugged. "He is very galante and has a most pleasant acento británico."

Jessie laughed. "That's true. He is very gallant. I doubt he'll be content in Albuquerque. I'm sure he, too, is hoping to go south with the Colonel. It's the only topic of conversation among our military customers these days." She shook her head. "They're all burning to fight what they call 'the greasers'."

Juanita raised an eyebrow. "Your lieutenant, as well? He holds this view?"

"No, Lieutenant Milbank is the only military American in town who seems to have any sense. He says he'll go, but only if he's ordered to do so. He's worried Mitchell will take so many men with him that there won't be enough left behind to protect us from the Navajo." She glanced at her friend. "Or an uprising."

The lieutenant had also reported that he'd been unable to find out anything about the dead man, Vidal. Before Jessie could say so, there was a sudden "Hurrah!" at the end of the street. A surge of uniformed men erupted from the hotel as others tried to enter it. The girls looked at each other.

"Perhaps we should promenade along el río today and admire los árboles," Juanita said.

"All the trees have lost their color."

"Cottonwoods are beautiful any time of year."

Jessie smiled. It was true. Like the trees on the plaza, those by the Santa Fe River were still young, planted as saplings only two or three years ago. They didn't have the majestic branches and thick gray trunks of mature cottonwoods, but they were still beautiful. Besides, the American troops didn't seem to care much for the path along the river. It would be more peaceful there. Jessie nodded and the girls turned left simultaneously.

The stream was gray under the thickly overcast sky, but it ran freely, and there was little wind. In fact, the weather was oddly warm for November. Jessie took a deep breath and walked backward for a moment, studying the Sangre de Cristo mountains which loomed east of the scattered houses and fields. The peaks were swathed in clouds, the foothills gloomy with shadows. And yet it felt strangely warm. She shook her head.

Juanita nudged her arm. "Look at that!"

Jessie turned. To the west, a row of low hills blocked the view of el Río Grande del Norte, or what newcomer Americans called the Rio Grande River, and framed the snow-capped peaks of the Jemez mountains beyond. Clouds rose above them all in banks of black, gray, and white. The cumulus clouds had broken apart in the center and sunlight poured triumphantly through the resulting split, blazing the white mountain tops with glory.

Jessie's breath caught.

"My country," Juanita said simply.

"It's incredible," Jessie said. "I don't think I will ever get used to it."

Juanita smiled. The two girls moved forward with new energy, as if they could walk across the entire valley, over the hills and the river itself, to reach the glittering peaks.

"Have you heard reports of la producción teatral that los soldados americanos presented to each other the week before last?" Juanita asked. "I understand Padre Ortiz received una invitación."

Jessie nodded. "Yes, Lieutenant Milbank told us about it. The men responsible must have gone to some effort. They even had playbills printed." She wrinkled her nose. "I'm not sure we missed much, though. They presented a melodrama called *Pizarro* and a comic musical drama titled *Bombastes Furioso,* which sounded very silly indeed."

Juanita frowned. "The play was *Pizarro?* About el conquistador of the Incas? What a strange topic!"

They reached the chapel of the Virgin of Guadalupe and moved south, their heads turned to admire the ever-changing light on the Jemez peaks. Then the clouds directly overhead began to break, and the branches on the old cottonwoods beside the road brightened. Jessie turned to her friend. "Thank you for suggesting this."

Juanita smiled. "This walk is the one I have always loved best." The houses in the vicinity were farther apart now. She gestured at the empty road. "Especialmente when I have it all to myself."

Hoof beats thrummed on the hard-packed dirt ahead. Juanita grinned. "For un momento, at least."

Then the horse came into sight, a solidly built roan with a white star on her forehead and carrying a man in dragoon uniform. He lifted his hand and Jessie chuckled. "I see he found his way north, after all."

Private Fitzgerald reined in and pulled off his soft dragoon cap. "Buenos días, señoritas," he said. "I am delighted to see you once again. It has been far too long since I have had that pleasure."

The girls curtsied demurely as Juanita said, "Buenos días, Señor Fitzgerald. I hope you are well."

"I am, most certainly." He reached to pat the mare's neck. "As you can see, I have recovered completely from my illness. However, I am now stationed in Albuquerque with the rest of Captain Burgwin's company, so I have not had the pleasure of calling upon you." Then he brightened. "However, I have recently been tasked with carrying dispatches between Albuquerque and Santa Fe. In consequence, it seems I will be in town at least occasionally."

"So you've been assigned to carry dispatches on a regular basis?" Jessie asked.

The dragoon nodded. "I have. And I find the assignment allows for a certain amount of flexibility, of which I intend to take full advantage." He looked at Juanita. "In fact, I may well be in Santa Fe all this week or, at the very least, return well before the next theatrical production on Wednesday."

Juanita raised her eyebrows. "Another?"

"Ah, I see you have heard about our officers' little troupe."

"And *Bombastes Furioso*," Jessie said drily.

Fitzgerald grinned. "That particular portion of the program was apparently not a rousing success. This Wednesday it will be replaced by a farce called *Perfection*, which also contains music." He chuckled. "Sentimental songs, that is. I can't vouch for how well they will be performed."

Jessie laughed. "*Perfection*? How perfect!"

"Indeed, I hope so." He bent toward Juanita. "Would you do me the honor of accompanying me to its performance?"

She considered him, then glanced toward Jessie. "I am not sure I would feel quite comfortable going alone."

"I would protect you from any disturbances."

Juanita shook her head. "I am quite certain mi tía will not agree to me going out at night under la protección of un hombre who is not of mi familia."

Jessie, watching his face, saw the dragoon suppress a sigh but his expression was polite enough when he turned to her. "May I have the honor of escorting you both to the event in question?"

She glanced at Juanita, who gave her a slight nod, then turned back to him. "I would be delighted to accept your invitation."

He looked at Juanita, who dimpled and nodded.

Private Fitzgerald returned his cap to his head. "Until Wednesday then." He paused. "Shall I collect you at the shop or at the Sena casa?"

The girls looked at each other. "The house, I think," Jessie said. She turned to Juanita. "If that's all right. It's so much closer to the palacio."

Juanita nodded agreement, then the dragoon bowed to them both, tapped the mare with his stirrups, and headed toward town.

Jessie turned to Juanita. "Would your aunt truly have objected to you attending the play with him by yourself?"

The other girl shrugged. "She might be concerned, but she would leave la decisión to my discreción."

Jessie lifted a brow.

Juanita tilted her head. "Although I find Señor Fitzgerald very agreeable, I am unsure of his intentions. He has made no effort to make himself known to mi tío. Also, Narciso has not yet returned. I will make no decisions until I have seen him." She took Jessie's arm. "Gracias for agreeing to come with me. I would very much like to see una producción teatral americana." Her brow furrowed. "And this thing called *Pizarro*."

They turned back toward town and had reached the river again when they saw a young couple sitting on a log under the trees. The girl's head was nestled into the man's green-clad shoulder, his flat-brimmed hat bent toward her. As Jessie and Juanita drew closer, he tilted it to look up at them and Jessie saw that it was Raúl.

"Well! Well!" Juanita said, stopping in the middle of the path. "The two of you appear very cozy."

Guadalupe blushed as she straightened, but Raúl kept his arm firmly around her waist. "Nosotros estamos comprometidos," he said with great dignity. Then he grinned. "We can do as we like."

Juanita clapped her hands. "You are betrothed? Then it is official? You are to be married? ¡Qué maravilloso!"

"Congratulations!" Jessie said. Guadalupe seemed very young to her, but early engagements were the custom here. The two of them certainly seemed happy with the arrangement. Raúl almost glowed with contentment. He gave her a small triumphant smile and she wondered how much he'd collected during his gambling spree.

"Now we can spend evenings together with no one to criticize us," he said.

Jessie gave him a puzzled look. She had thought Mexican society was more relaxed about such things. Almost shamefully so. "You couldn't do that before now?"

Raúl smiled at her confusion. "There are many in Nuevo Méjico who do not place such restrictions on young people, however Doña Tules is most protectora. Always before now, we must have someone in the room with us."

Guadalupe nodded, smiling self-consciously. "It is true. But in three days from today, mi madre attends the theater of los americanos." She glanced at Raúl bashfully. "We will be alone in the house for the very first time."

Juanita turned to Jessie. "Perhaps we should plan to pay them a visit instead of going to la producción teatral ourselves."

Raúl's eyes widened in alarm, but Jessie chuckled and shook her head. "I, for one, plan to attend the play."

Guadalupe laughed in sheer relief. "I look forward to hearing the details."

CHAPTER 13: Wednesday, November 25, 1846

When Jessie arrived at the Sena house late Wednesday afternoon, she found Juanita's aunt trying to convince her to wear something besides her everyday skirt, bodice, and rebozo. After two hours of coaxing, negotiation, and digging through cedar chests, both girls were attired in necklines cut considerably lower than usual. Fine lace mantillas held back by elaborately carved tortoise shell combs fell elegantly from carefully twisted hair and hid their exposed skin from direct view.

Private Fitzgerald was all compliments when he arrived, gazing at them both as if he'd never seen them before. As if he wanted to do more than simply escort them to a play. Jessie began to wish she hadn't succumbed to Juanita's interest and her own curiosity about the production.

She felt a little better once they arrived at Government House and the long room set up for the theatricals. At the far end, a row of large unmatched silver candlesticks lined the foot of the stage. Jessie grinned. Several of them had graced the church altar the previous Sunday. The chairs in the first row also looked familiar.

The rest of the room was filled with backless benches. A few near the front sported cushions. Fitzgerald settled Juanita and Jessie on one of these, with Jessie on the center aisle and himself between the two girls. They were a little early, so they entertained themselves by watching their fellow audience members arrive and commenting on their appearance and clothing.

The room was almost full when there was a sudden commotion at the door. Lieutenant Colonel Mitchell had entered. He was perhaps forty, with dark hair combed straight back from a high forehead, his good looks marred by perpetually anxious eyes. Señora Gertrudes Barceló was on his arm, dressed in a green velvet gown and her long red-highlighted curls glowing under a resplendent black lace mantilla. The gold chains and crucifix on her chest glittered triumphantly as she and the colonel proceeded to the chairs at the front of the room. As she passed the girls, she smiled at them mischievously.

"She appears most pleased with herself," Juanita murmured.

Fitzgerald chuckled. "She ought to be. I understand that the lieutenant colonel's wife is quite prone to jealousy. Although she is safely in Saint Louis, she pays close attention to what the American newspapers report about events in Santa Fe. If she learns that he escorted another woman to the theater, the repercussions could be quite serious."

Jessie frowned. "So why is he risking her wrath?"

"I assume you're aware of the pending mission to Chihuahua?"

She nodded.

"The funds for the expedition haven't arrived yet from Missouri, but Colonel Price has ordered Mitchell to march post haste. To do so, he must borrow money for the journey.

La Tules is the only person in New Mexico who possesses the necessary sum."

Jessie smiled in spite of the inappropriate diminutive for her friend's mother. As Raúl had pointed out, the city's card dealers were making a good deal of money from the American troops. So, the funds Lieutenant Colonel Mitchell hoped to borrow from Doña Tules were actually American dollars she had garnered from his men. And she would be sure to charge a substantial rate of interest for the loan. No wonder the woman looked so pleased with herself.

Juanita was frowning in confusion. "Was her attendance tonight as his guest a condition of la transacción?"

"That's my understanding." The dragoon pursed his lips as he looked around the room. "I hope he obtains what he needs and that the report doesn't get back to his wife before he returns home to explain why he was forced to do what he did."

"It's only a play," Jessie said.

"His wife believes all Mexican women are promiscuous and eager for er … connections with American men. Also, she has undoubtedly read about La Tules in the Saint Louis papers and would be horrified to learn that her husband was consorting with such a person."

Juanita and Jessie exchanged glances. Juanita's lips were tight with annoyance. "That person—" she began.

But then there was another stir at the door and Colonel Price arrived. He was a tall man with broad, self-conscious shoulders and sharp eyes under a wide forehead and receding hairline. His hair was thin, gray, and carefully combed. Everyone stood at attention as he moved toward the front of the room, then settled in. After a short pause, the makeshift stage curtains rattled aside.

A woman in an American dress lay on a couch. Juanita leaned forward, studying the figure intently, then turned to her companions. "¡Es un hombre!"

"A man?" asked Fitzgerald. He grinned and nodded. "It is a military custom to follow the old Shakespearean practice of men playing female roles."

Juanita shook her head, her lips quirking in amusement.

On the stage, the "woman" was busily resisting the blandishments of a man in an oddly shaped paper helmet and insisting that she loved the Spanish Captain Pizarro. Jessie rolled her eyes at the silliness of it all and looked instead at the cover of her program.

Then she straightened in surprise. According to this, the play had been written by the man who'd created *Lovers Vows*. She knew the title of that theatrical piece. It was in Miss Austen's book. Then she frowned. Surely it couldn't be the same author.

She turned the pages of the program, looking for more information. Private Fitzgerald leaned toward her. "Is it not to your liking?" he asked quietly. "I'm told this production has been presented on the Saint Louis stage annually since 1827. It's based on Francisco Pizarro's conquest of Peru and is said to be true to life."

Jessie raised an eyebrow. Was there such a thing as a true-to-life play? But the piece's historical accuracy wasn't why she felt so flustered. The central theme of *Lovers Vows* was infidelity. If the author of *Pizarro* was the same person, the play was likely to be what her mother used to call "racy." If Jessie had known, she wouldn't have agreed to attend.

She glanced at Juanita, who was leaning forward, her eyes darting from one actor to another, and suppressed a sigh. "It is well enough," she murmured to the dragoon. "Though I suspect Señorita Sena will need help with translation."

But Juanita didn't need help. She understood English well enough to understand what was going on. And she was also irritated, but not by the likely infidelity. When the first act ended, she sat back, lips tight with disapproval. "These americano officers have chosen this play to speak to themselves and to us of the supposed ferocity of los conquistadores," she said. She looked around the room and sniffed contemptuously. "As if americanos are not capable of such things."

By the end of the second act, she was even more annoyed, her hazel eyes snapping with indignation. "They portray los españoles as perfect horrors and the natives as ángeles perfectos," she growled. "No individual is entirely one or the other."

Fitzgerald smiled knowingly. "Do you truly believe so? Certainly, there are traits of character that rise from the blood and cannot be denied."

When she scowled at him, he turned to Jessie. "You see?" He nodded toward Juanita. "Look how her Spanish eyes flash! There is that temperament!"

"Eyes that are lighter colored than mine," Jessie said drily. "And I have no Spanish ancestors." She leaned forward to look at her friend. "It is only a play."

"It is a play with a message." Juanita sat back and stared at the stage, hands clenched together in her lap.

"Forgive me, señorita," the dragoon said contritely. "I thought you might enjoy the theatrical production but I was truly unaware of the message it could be construed to convey. If you like, I will gladly escort you home at once."

Juanita shook her head. "I would prefer to remain and learn the full lesson la producción is intended to teach los estúpidos mexicanos."

As he gave her a disappointed look, the curtains opened again and the third act began. Juanita's face was stony. Jessie, leaning forward to watch her, didn't pay much attention to the action on the stage. It seemed to go on forever. Finally, the act ended. As the curtains closed, there was a stir at the far end of the front row. A uniformed man bent toward Colonel Price, who frowned, rose, and followed the messenger out of the room.

"I hope there is no trouble," Juanita said.

Private Fitzgerald shook his head. "I'm sure it's nothing of consequence."

The fourth act began. The play's female lead was deep in her pursuit of illicit love when the same messenger moved down the center aisle, stopped just behind Jessie, and leaned past her shoulders to hand a note to Fitzgerald. The dragoon opened the missive, read it, then quickly refolded the paper and tapped it on his knee as he stared blindly at the stage, lips pursed.

The messenger remained at the end of the row, hovering anxiously. The dragoon glanced at him, frowned, then bent toward Juanita and said something into her ear. She gave him a startled look, then nodded and refocused on the play. He half smiled and turned to Jessie. "I have a message from the colonel," he murmured. He glanced around the hall, eyes anxious. "I will do my best to return to you before the entertainment concludes."

She nodded and he rose, edged past her, and followed the messenger up the aisle to the door.

Jessie moved closer to Juanita, moving the gap Fitzgerald had left to the end of the bench. Juanita glanced at her and shook her head. "Nothing about this evening is quite as I anticipated," she murmured.

"He said he'd try to return for us."

Juanita smoothed her mantilla, rearranging it over her bodice. "I certainly hope so."

Someone behind them hissed, "Ladies, please!" and the two girls turned back to the play.

As the final scene began, Jessie felt someone settle beside her on the bench. She glanced around, expecting Fitzgerald, but it was someone she'd never seen before, an American soldier who leered at her drunkenly.

She frowned and focused pointedly on the stage. He leaned toward her, muttering, and she scooted closer to Juanita. The other girl glanced at her, saw the stranger, and frowned at Jessie inquiringly.

Jessie shrugged and shook her head. The two girls leaned toward each other, doing their best to ignore him, but as the act ended and the curtains closed, the man edged closer and poked Jessie's arm with his finger. "Señorita," he hissed as the curtains closed. "¡Señorita! My love!"

She stiffened. He reeked of alcohol. Would rebuking him make him stop or would it trigger more impertinence? But she couldn't allow it to go on. As she set her jaw and turned, he suddenly tumbled sideways into the aisle, his arms flailing against the back of the man in front of him.

"What the—," the other man said, turning.

Lieutenant Milbank stood at the end of the bench, holding the drunk by his collar.

"That will be all, private!" he snapped as he flung him to the floor. "Get out before I have you up on charges!"

The drunk scuttled toward the back of the room and the door. Lieutenant Milbank turned to Jessie. "I see your escort has been detained," he said politely. "May I have the honor of taking his place until he returns?"

Jessie stared at him, speechless, as Juanita said, "Please, señor. Gracias."

The lieutenant looked at Jessie and she nodded wordlessly. He settled himself on the end of the bench. The man in front of them turned back to the stage, and the curtains opened.

The fifth act began. Jessie, still startled by the lieutenant's appearance and chagrined at her own inability to handle the drunk soldier, didn't pay much attention. But Juanita did. When the play was over, she sat back with an audible sigh of relief, then leaned forward and looked at the lieutenant. "Please reassure me that the remainder of el entretenimiento will be more truly entertaining," she said.

"I believe we are to have a minstrel show and then a comedy or farce or something similar. Not more drama, at any rate." He studied her face. "I'm sorry the production wasn't more to your liking."

"The choice of topic appears to have been designed to emphasize the aspects most negative of the character of my people," Juanita said drily. "Negative from la perspectiva de los americanos, that is."

Jessie smiled at the lieutenant's confused look. "The play doesn't present Pizarro or his companions in the best of lights," she pointed out.

"That's true enough." He looked at Juanita apologetically. "I'm not sure it was intended to affront anyone. It was the only play for which there were adequate copies on hand for all the players."

Juanita frowned skeptically and Jessie cast about for another topic of conversation, but the lieutenant came to her rescue. "The gentleman who wrote the play in question also wrote a piece that appears in a well-known English novel," he told her. "Can you guess what it is?"

"So it truly is by the same author?"

He smiled. "I take it you know the book to which I refer."

"*Mansfield Park*? Miss Austen's novel about the family with sugar plantations in the West Indies?"

His smile widened. "Yes, that's the one."

Jessie smiled back. "A man who reads novels."

Juanita laughed, her equilibrium restored. "Perhaps it is the only one he has read," she teased.

The lieutenant chuckled and was about to respond when a man appeared just beyond the candles at the edge of the stage, lifted his hands, and called, "Silence, please!" He swung his arms toward the wings, then back at the audience. "Ladies and gentlemen, may I present to you, the Virginia Minstrels!"

A group of men with tattered clothes and blackened faces pranced onto the stage and began performing a song-and-dance routine interspersed with various jokes and repartee. The mangled English they spoke was apparently meant to imitate that of plantation slaves. While this meant Juanita couldn't understand most of the words, she seemed to find the facial expressions and physical humor amusing. She laughed along with the rest of the audience while Jessie grew more and more serious.

Lieutenant Milbank leaned toward her. "You don't like this sort of thing?" he asked quietly.

Jessie shook her head. "I've never met anyone, slave or free, who speaks like that. Or dances around like that, for that matter."

"Actually, I have seen slaves caper in that way."

She glanced at him in surprise. He shrugged. "Their owners expected it. It's apparently a traditional way of expressing one's thanks." His face darkened. "It's demeaning, but still better than some of the other expressions of gratitude the male owners feel they have the right to demand."

She shivered and looked away.

Someone behind them muttered, "Quiet up there!" but the lieutenant bent toward her again.

"Forgive me," he said softly. He sat back and shook his head, his eyes on the stage. "I find myself saying things to you which I would never say to another young lady. I'm not quite sure why that is."

She slid him a half smile and looked away. Continuing the conversation was going to aggravate the people behind them. Besides, she wasn't sure how to respond. She should be annoyed with him for the allusion to the rights male owners had over female slave bodies. After all, the topic was completely inappropriate for unmarried people of the opposite sex.

And yet, she didn't feel insulted. She felt touched that he was so comfortable with her. He was right, there was an odd kind of familiarity between them. As if they'd known each other all their lives. She'd never felt anything quite like it. Did being distant cousins create an automatic connection?

Jessie was uncomfortably aware that this wasn't an explanation she particularly cared for. But she also wasn't sure how she did want to explain the thread of understanding that seemed to exist between herself and this man.

The minstrel show ended and the final theatrical piece began. It featured yet another soldier dressed as a woman and singing the higher notes remarkably well. Jessie didn't hear a word.

The curtain closed for the last time and the crowd began to disperse. As Lieutenant Milbank turned to the girls with a questioning look, Henry Fitzgerald appeared, his face anxious. He moved into the now empty row of benches in front of them and reached for Juanita's hand. "I apologize for deserting you, señorita," he said. "My duties kept me away longer than I expected." He gave Jessie a broad smile. "However, now I have returned." He turned to Lieutenant Milbank. "Thank you, sir, for seeing to them."

"It was my great pleasure." The lieutenant smiled into Jessie's eyes. "May I escort you home?"

Jessie looked at Juanita, who glanced toward the dragoon and shook her head slightly. "Perhaps we could all walk together," Jessie suggested.

Neither man seemed especially delighted with this idea, but they nodded politely enough. The four young people made their way out of the hall.

The plaza was crowded with theatergoers who weren't quite ready to end the evening. The sky was clear, the new moon and November stars gleaming. Lieutenant Milbank looked at the girls. "Shall we proceed to the Sena casa first, or to the Milbank mercantile?"

"I am a little tired," Juanita said. "I would like to return to la casa."

The dragoon glanced toward the east end of the palacio and the street to the Sena compound. "Would you care to take a stroll around the plaza before doing so?"

Juanita looked at Jessie, who shrugged and nodded, and they turned right, moving counterclockwise around the square. The cottonwoods stretched overhead, light from the thin moon highlighting their dry copper-colored leaves. Jessie looked up at them. "I do love the look of these trees at night," she said. "It's one of my favorite things about Santa Fe."

Juanita chuckled. "There are so many things in Santa Fe which are your favorite."

Jessie smiled, pleased to hear a little humor in her friend's voice. "This is very true," she replied. "And I plan to collect even more of them."

When they had circled the square and turned into the street to the Sena house, their footsteps slowed. Even Juanita didn't seem to want the evening to end. The niche where Raúl and Guadalupe had lingered on the night of Vidal's death was just ahead on the left. As they reached it, a man lurched out of the shadows and fell sideways into the road.

"Here now!" Lieutenant Milbank said, jerking to a stop.

"Another drunken soldier," Juanita said in disgust. "They are everywh—" Then she dropped Fitzgerald's arm and ran toward the silent form. "Raúl?"

She knelt in the dirt, careless of her fine skirt and the mantilla falling across her face, and reached for his shoulder.

"Primo? Oh!" She jerked back and covered her mouth with her hands. The pale moonlight gleamed obscenely on the horn-handled knife in Raúl's chest.

Jessie was at her side now, bending forward. Raúl's eyes flickered open and she gripped Juanita's shoulder. "He's alive!"

Raúl's lips twisted. His hand moved toward the knife and the patch of blood staining his white shirt.

Jessie looked up at the lieutenant. He turned to the dragoon. "A doctor," he said. "quickly!"

Fitzgerald stood frozen, eyes oddly angry as he stared at the bleeding man.

"Private!" Lieutenant Milbank snapped, and the dragoon's head jerked. He opened his mouth, closed it, then snapped a salute and turned and ran back toward the palacio.

Raúl's eyes followed him. He clutched at Juanita's hand. "Lupe," he said hoarsely. "Tell her—" There was a pause, then he croaked, "Sin aviso,'" his body twitched, his eyes rolled back, and he was gone.

Juanita shrieked. As Jessie reached for her, the gate to the Sena compound opened. Men rushed out. "What have you done?" one shouted as they ran forward.

Juanita's aunt was right behind them. A few yards from the body, she stopped abruptly, then came slowly to kneel opposite Juanita. "Dios mío," she groaned as she reached to close Raúl's eyelids. She shook her head. "Pobrecita Guadalupe."

On the hill north of the house, the cannons of Fort Marcy began to boom, marking the ten o'clock curfew. When they finally stopped, the woman rose with a grim face. She turned to the lieutenant. "Please sir, may we send for the priest?"

CHAPTER 14: Thursday, November 26, 1846

The three rebozo-wrapped girls entered different corners of the bleak rain-threatened plaza at the same time the next afternoon and convened at the base of the flagpole. Guadalupe's face was puffy and her brown skin splotchy. Jessie reached for her, then stopped herself, but Juanita felt no such compunction. She wrapped the younger girl in her arms.

"He is to be buried mañana," Juanita said.

Guadalupe nodded against her shoulder. "I know it. Padre Ortiz himself came to tell us, which was a great kindness." She looked from Jessie to Juanita. "Did mi amor say nothing before he—"

Jessie looked at Juanita, who hesitated, then said, "He spoke your name." She frowned. "And he said to tell you 'sin aviso.'"

Jessie nodded. "Yes, he said 'no warning."

Guadalupe's eyes widened slightly, but she was already shaking her head. "I do not know what that could mean." She bit her upper lip. "Mi pobre amor."

"Why would someone stab Raúl?" Jessie asked.

Guadalupe shook her head again. "He was un hombre without enemies. Everyone loved him."

Behind them, someone coughed politely. The girls turned to find Lieutenant Milbank. "I beg your pardon," he said. He looked at Jessie. "I was on my way to you, to tell you what little I have learned about the death last night."

Jessie touched the younger girl's arm. "Guadalupe, may I present Lieutenant Abner Milbank?"

Guadalupe nodded dully, not bothering to wipe the tears from her eyes.

"Lieutenant, this is Señorita Guadalupe Barceló," Jessie said.

"Ella era su prometida," Juanita added.

He looked at her blankly.

"She was his fiancée," Jessie explained.

He nodded and bent toward Guadalupe, sympathy in his blue eyes. "Please accept my deepest condolences." She nodded without looking at him and he studied her for a long moment before turning to the other girls.

Rain had begun to mist across the square. He brushed it away from his face. "Colonel Price acted quickly in this matter. He ordered an investigation, which took place this morning and determined that the young man's death was the result of an altercation over a gambling debt."

"¿Deuda de juego?" Juanita asked as Guadalupe lifted her head. "A gambling debt?"

"¡Es imposible!" they said in unison.

The lieutenant looked at Jessie. The rain was gathering force now. A drop hit her cheek. She pulled her rebozo closer and looked away. He turned to the other girls.

Guadalupe glared at him as she swiped tears from her cheeks. "It is untrue," she said. "Él estaba ganando." She shivered and closed her eyes, then said it again. "He was winning. We had almost enough." She looked up at the lieutenant. Raindrops stained her rebozo. "There was no debt."

He gave her a puzzled look, looked at Jessie, then half turned to study the buildings that surrounded the plaza. "I would like to discuss this with you further, but not in the rain. Is there somewhere nearby that we can go?"

The closest establishment was the saloon where Jessie had found Raúl gambling. As she led them toward it, the lieutenant gave her a questioning look. "It's perfectly all right," she told him. "Here in New Mexico, a woman can visit a bar or gambling salon without damaging her reputation."

He looked doubtful, but didn't argue. They entered the front room and settled at the table nearest the fire. The man behind the counter started toward them, then saw Guadalupe's face and turned away. A shout of triumph came from the inner room, and he moved to the door and shut it halfway. Jessie sent him a grateful look, and he nodded sympathetically and returned to the back of the room.

Lieutenant Milbank leaned toward Guadalupe. "Again, please let me extend my sincerest condolences for your loss."

She nodded and swiped at her tears. He handed her a handkerchief. "I know this is a difficult time for you," he said gently. "However, it would be helpful if you could explain why you believe your fiancee wasn't stabbed in consequence of a gambling debt. Private Fitzgerald was the chief witness in the investigation and he seemed certain that a debt was the cause of the deceased's demise. There was a note—"

Guadalupe's shoulders straightened. "Él no era 'the deceased.' His name was Raúl Jesús Cabeza de Baca."

"Forgive me," he murmured.

She appeared not to hear him. "Mi prometido, he knew I disliked el juego, however, he was most determined to acquire funds sufficient for land and una casa and for us to marry with dignity." Guadalupe looked at Jessie. "I know you spoke to him, and I am grateful to you for that, but he was muy decidido." She turned back to the lieutenant. "There was no debt. He was careful to choose his games wisely. He was winning." She closed her eyes and said it again. "He was winning. He brought the results of each night's play to me and only took away enough to begin again the next day."

She shook her head and her voice wobbled. "We had enough, but he wanted a little more. Sufficient for a large house instead of a modest one."

She turned her head, speaking to the crackling fire. "I have no desire for una hacienda. I told him this but still he—" She put her hands to her face. "I should have said it with more force."

The street door opened and Henry Fitzgerald came in. He nodded to the lieutenant as he approached. "Señoritas," he said. He turned to Guadalupe. "Please accept my sincerest condolences on your loss."

She nodded and wiped at her face with the lieutenant's handkerchief. The dragoon turned to him. "The colonel has allowed me to show you the evidence we found concerning the activities of the deceased."

Lieutenant Milbank glanced at Guadalupe, then back at Fitzgerald. "Do you refer to Señor Cabeza de Baca?"

The dragoon pursed his lips, then nodded and pulled out a piece of paper which he unfolded carefully and handed to the lieutenant.

The other man looked down at it. "This is in Spanish."

"Yes. The Army translator tells me it's something called un pagaré, a promissory note which commits the deceased to pay a debt of one hundred pesos. It is dated two months ago."

Jessie reached for the paper and the lieutenant gave it to her. Raúl's name was scrawled inelegantly across the bottom of the sheet, although the words above didn't state who the money was to be paid to, or what it was for.

Guadalupe's face was dry now, her eyes sharp. "He did not attend los salones de juego two months ago," she said. "He worked for los americanos, making adobes."

Private Fitzgerald frowned. "Los salones—"

"Los salones de juego," Jessie said absently. "I suppose the best translation is 'gambling parlors.'" She tilted the note, letting the firelight play across it. "Where did this come from?"

"It was found on the body," he said. "We believe it to be a debt to one Agustín Durán." He turned to the lieutenant. "Durán has been making a nuisance of himself all morning, asking what happened and where the body was found. Colonel Price doesn't believe he is responsible for the death, but Durán does seem inordinately concerned about the contents of the deceased man's pockets and whether he spoke to anyone in authority before he died."

Guadalupe took the slip of paper from Jessie and stared at it, shaking her head. "Él estaba ganando," she said.

The dragoon looked at Jessie, but Juanita translated instead. "He was winning."

Guadalupe nodded. "He would have told me if there was a debt." She frowned. "Además, esta no es su letra ni su firma."

Both men looked at Juanita this time. "Also, it is not his handwriting," she said.

Fitzgerald pursed his lips. "The note itself was likely written by the man to whom the debt was owed. And the signature appears to have been scrawled in great haste."

Guadalupe turned to the lieutenant. "Please, señor, will you speak with mi madre, Señora Gertrudes Barceló? She is in a position to be familiar with all those who contract debts en la ciudad, most especially those related to gambling. She can tell you the truth of el documento." She handed him the note.

"Also, she may recognize that handwriting," Jessie said. "Doña Tules has business dealings with many of people here, both American and New Mexican."

Lieutenant Milbank nodded, tucked the piece of paper into a pocket, and rose from his seat. He turned to Guadalupe. "I will be happy to go to her now, if you like."

She nodded and stood slowly, as if she had suddenly aged forty years, then lifted her chin and straightened her shoulders. "I would be most grateful, señor."

The lieutenant put some coins on the table and nodded to the bartender. "For your time," he said. He bowed to Jessie and Juanita, offered Guadalupe his arm, and they went out.

Private Fitzgerald turned to Juanita and Jessie. "May I escort you home?"

"I was on my way to the Milbank mercantile to purchase una cinta negra," Juanita said. "Perhaps you can accompany us both there."

"Certainly," he said. "But first I must ask. What is 'cinta negra'?"

Juanita frowned. "How do you say it? Ribbon that is black."

"Ah. You wear it for mourning?"

"On occasion."

Jessie's breath caught in her throat. She took Fitzgerald's proffered arm silently and they went out into a drizzling rain. "It's a very sad event," he said.

Juanita sighed theatrically. "It was especially upsetting coming as it did after una producción teatral. The two events were indeed a contrast." She glanced sideways at the dragoon. "I wish you could have seen more of it. The minstrels were muy divertidos. When Colonel Price came back, I worried that perhaps you had been sent to Albuquerque."

He gave her a confused look. "Albuquerque? Oh, yes." He pursed his lips, then added, "Fortunately, the colonel didn't need my services after all."

"Ah, I suspected as much." She flashed him a coquettish smile as she glanced meaningfully at Jessie. "You had other business to occupy you."

Jessie shot her a puzzled look. Did Juanita think the dragoon had something to do with Raúl's death? Surely not. But Jessie could at least help her friend fish for information. She lifted her face to the dragoon's, willing herself to smile flirtatiously. "I suspect there is another señorita here in Santa Fe vying for your affections," she teased.

His laughter had a relieved sound to it. "Why would I wish for anyone else's smiles but yours and the señorita's?" They'd reached the southwest corner of the plaza now, and the Milbank store was in sight. "Ah, the lights of home," he added. "I fear I must leave you at the door today. I'm told there will be dispatches for Albuquerque this afternoon."

He bowed them across the threshold, then hurried off, shoulders hunched against the rain.

"Well, that was quite interesting," Jessie said as the girls removed their rebozos and shook water droplets onto the top of the little wood stove.

"There is something muy peculiar about all of this," Juanita said. "I caught a glimpse of the handwriting on the missive Señor Fitzgerald received last night. It was not written por un americano."

"How can you tell?"

"Surely you have noticed the difference between la escritura española and that of los americanos. Ours is most decorativo, with plenty of flourishes, while yours is precise and business like."

Jessie wasn't sure she agreed, but certainly, Spanish signatures were much more given to flourishes. "So what does that imply?"

"I do not believe for one moment that the note Private Fitzgerald received yesterday evening was from the colonel. It was very descortés of him to leave us as he did, and most unlike him."

"Do you really think he had something to do with Raúl's death?"

"I must admit it seems unlikely. And yet the entire evening was so very strange and ended in the manner most horrible." Juanita moved closer to the stove. "The only positive aspect was that Señor Fitzgerald's absence brought your lieutenant to us."

Jessie nodded. "Yes. I was especially grateful for his presence and decisiveness when we found Raúl."

"I do wonder about the origin of el pagaré in Raúl's pocket."

"The promissory note? Maybe there actually was a debt and he was afraid to tell Guadalupe."

"I suppose it is possible, although it seems most unlikely." Juanita sighed. "They were so much in love. It will be muy difícil for her to recover from his death." She frowned. "However, I suspect she is not telling all she knows. While I believe she speaks truly about la deuda de juego, the gambling debt, I think she knows why he said 'sin aviso.'"

"I wondered about that. And about why she was so quick to say she didn't." Jessie shivered, remembering the anxiety in Raúl's face, the emptiness that followed. "First Manuelita's friend, and now Raúl." She closed her eyes. "That knife. And the blood."

"Has it brought the dreams back?"

Jessie nodded, her shoulder hunching closer to the cast iron stove.

"Mi pobre amiga." Juanita moved toward her, hugging her close. "So many deaths. So few answers."

The door to the kitchen opened and Jessie's father came in. "What is it?" he asked, but the girls only shook their heads and told him it was raining outside.

CHAPTER 15: Sunday, December 6, 1846

The intensity of Jessie's shock at Raúl's death faded somewhat over the next week and a half, but the cold, rainy weather lingered. As she and Juanita followed the rest of the congregation out of la parroquia after mass that Sunday, she shivered and tucked her rebozo more securely around her face.

"These skies truly produce una gran miseria," Juanita grumbled. "Tan gris, tan frío y tan húmedo."

"I suppose the grayness, the cold, and the damp explain why there were so few people at mass this morning." Jessie's eyes crinkled in amusement. "That or the fact that there are now fewer American officers to look at."

Juanita chuckled as they moved up the street toward the plaza. "La ciudad is a good deal less crowded now that la teniente coronel Colonel Mitchell and his troops have departed. It almost feels safe to once again walk alone in the plaza at night."

Jessie looked at her in alarm. "I hope you're not actually doing that."

Juanita shook her head. "No. In fact, I find I have little desire to go anywhere since mi primo was asesinado." She scanned the street ahead. "Have you received the honor of Private Fitzgerald's presence since then?"

"No, I assumed he went to Albuquerque with dispatches and there were no messages in return."

Juanita nodded, her eyes still on the street ahead. "La memoria of that event continues to linger in my mind. Señor Fitzgerald seemed so—how do you say it?—so startled when Raúl fell into the street, almost as if he had encountered un fantasma."

"A ghost?" Jessie frowned. "I didn't notice that. Though he did seem strangely angry." She shook her head. "But then, the lieutenant's first reaction was anger, too. He seemed to think Raúl was drunk."

"As did I," Juanita said. "Until I saw his face." She shuddered. "And el cuchillo. The knife." They had reached the hotel now. A squall of rain gusted across the plaza and they paused under the portal roof to let it ease. The bench by the door was empty and dark with moisture. In the street beyond, a man draped in a Navajo blanket led a similarly draped horse from one house gate to another, both keeping their heads down as they tried to find the least muddy path.

"Private Fitzgerald went to great lengths to ensure we knew about the promissory note," Jessie said thoughtfully. "I haven't seen Lieutenant Milbank since he went with Guadalupe to speak to her mother about it. I wonder what Doña Tules had to say about the note and about Raúl and his supposed gambling debts. Whatever Guadalupe may not have told us, she was certainly sure he hadn't been losing."

Juanita nodded and looked around the empty square and the dripping cottonwoods that lined it. "I have no desire to return home just yet, and I have not seen pobrecita Guadalupe in several days. Perhaps we should pay her a visit."

Jessie nodded. "Given the fact that almost every building on the plaza has a covered portal, we shouldn't even get very wet."

Together, they dashed to the next porch and began circling the plaza. Juanita glanced toward the street to the Milbank mercantile. "Will your father approve of you seeking conversation with Doña Tules? After all, she is a monte dealer. And possibly worse, according to los soldados americanos."

"The people who think so badly of her are fools who don't appreciate a capable woman." Jessie grinned. "That's a direct quote. In fact, he told me once that she reminded him a little of my mother." Jessie chuckled. "I'm not sure how my mother would have felt about that. She didn't approve of gambling."

"Will he approve of you asking questions concerning the death of Raúl?"

Jessie sighed. "No, probably not. But my mother would have. She would have wanted to help. And even though Raúl was gambling, she wouldn't have held it against him. She would have been indignant that he was murdered and yet no one seems to be trying to identify the culprit."

They found Doña Tules at home, snug in a quilted red silk wrapper and delighted to have company. She waved the girls to cushioned seats by the fire, called for hot chocolate, and settled herself onto a small divan opposite, a low table between them.

"Gracias for coming to visit me on such a cold and miserable day," she said. "I have had no one to converse with all the morning." She waved beringed fingers toward a door on the other side of the long room. "Rather than beginning to recover from the shock of the event, my sweet Guadalupe is sinking deeper into la depresión. She has not left her room these last three days."

"We are so sad about what happened to Raúl," Juanita said.

"I understand that you were there at the time. That you found him and were with him at the last."

The girls nodded.

"Guadalupe was so upset when she heard the news that she was unable to speak with coherence. Then she seemed to recover a little, but she's worse now than before." Doña Tules' dark brown eyes studied the girls. "She became most agitated after that nice Lieutenant Milbank spoke to me about un pagaré." She paused. When neither girl responded, she reached into a wrapper pocket and pulled out the makings for a cigarillo. "Will you join me?"

Jessie and Juanita both shook their heads and reached for their cups of hot chocolate. Doña Tules smoothed a rectangle of prepared corn husk on the table and tapped a little tobacco into the center. "It is truly incomprehensible to me."

She glanced up at the girls as she began pinching the husk and tobacco into shape. "As you undoubtedly know, I am intimately familiar with the various gambling operations here in Santa Fe. When Raúl Cabeza de Baca became el amor of my daughter, I took it upon myself to monitor his activities in that regard. It seems absolutamente imposible that he could have incurred any debt without my knowledge, but especialmente one related to gambling." She sealed the cigarillo, lit it, leaned back, took a long drag, then exhaled the smoke with a little frown. "It is truly incomprensible," she said again.

"The military authorities seem to believe he was addicted to gambling," Jessie said. "That he couldn't help himself."

The monte dealer shook her head. "I am quite familiar with the signs of la adicción. Raúl did not exhibit any of them." She lifted her head and stared at the ceiling, then took another drag on her cigarillo and shook her head again. "No. Es imposible. I do not believe it."

Juanita frowned. "But there is the note."

"There is something muy extraño about that note," Doña Tules said. "Indeed, there are various strange things. The most strange thing is that the paper does not identify the person to whom money is owed. I have never seen un pagaré which did not specify both parties to la transacción. Also, the handwriting was not familiar to me."

She smiled faintly and the lines around her mouth softened. "I have seen more than a few promissory notes in my day and am familiar with the signature of most of los hombres in the city. Also a good many of the women." She shook her head. "I am not acquainted with that writing."

The girls exchanged glances. "So it may not have been Agustín Durán to whom Raúl owed money?" Jessie asked.

"I doubt very much that Raúl Cabeza de Baca owed anything to anybody, but if he did, it was certainly not to Don Ramón. Agustín Durán borrows, he does not lend." Doña Tules leaned forward to tap cigarillo ash into an empty saucer and reached with her other hand for her hot chocolate. Then she settled back against the divan. "But now let us speak of something más agradable." She looked at Juanita, mischief in her eyes. "How did you like la producción teatral? Did you enjoy la representación americana portrayal of our Spanish forebears?"

Juanita's spine stiffened. "Esa producción teatral was the most terrible, derogatory representación del carácter nacional español to which I have ever been subjected."

Doña Tules burst into laughter. "¡Dios mío!" she said. "You certainly know how to express yourself." Then she sobered. "I agree with you with all my heart, though you may wish to learn to couch your opinion in terms of less intensity." She waved her cigarillo in the air. "Unfortunately, I suspect this will not be the last time you find yourself subjected to such representaciones of both the Spanish and the Indian character."

Juanita glowered at her.

"They are here to stay, los americanos," the older woman said wearily. She glanced at Jessie. "There are some, those who have spent time among us, who are muy corteses. However, I find, in general, that many are not capable of seeing beyond their long-held preconcepciones." Then she grinned. "Though their fixed ideas and lack of understanding can be rather amusing." She leaned forward again to tap ash from her cigarillo. "You saw me with el teniente coronel Mitchell that evening?"

The girls nodded.

Doña Tules sat back, smiling wickedly. "Almost any hombre en la ciudad would have been delighted to escort me to that event, and I had already decided to make the loan to Mitchell. However, el coronel had convinced himself that persuading me to agree would require unreasonable measures. For him, escorting me to his silly entertainment was such a medida muy irrazonable. I couldn't resist the opportunity to force him to do so."

She shook her head. "He disapproves of me, you know. Disapproves of gambling in general, and me, in particular, as una mujer de negocios—" She glanced at Jessie. "A business woman. Also, he believes all Mexican women are depredadoras peligrosas whose highest ambition is to be bedded by an American big and blond."

Juanita and Jessie looked at each other and tried not to giggle. Women as dangerous predators?

"I'm sure you have been accosted by them yourselves," Doña Tules continued. "My sweet Guadalupe has suffered that indignity." She nodded to Jessie. "She told me what happened that day on la plaza. You have my deepest gratitude for coming to her rescue as you did."

Jessie's face darkened. "I was happy to help. Those soldiers—"

The older woman nodded. "As I said, unfortunately, we have no other option but to accustom ourselves to their behavior." She took another drag from her cigarillo, then exhaled and shook her head. "Don Donaciano informed me last night that los americanos have captured la ciudad de Monterrey. The war is effectively at an end."

As she spoke, a door on the other side of the room opened and Guadalupe came out. She crossed to the fire, nodded to Juanita and Jessie, then snuggled in beside her mother and reached for Doña Tules' mug of hot chocolate.

Doña Tules squeezed the girl's arm, stubbed out her cigarillo, and stood up. "And now that I have shared that bit of news, which is bueno or malo, depending upon one's perspective, I must prepare myself for my evening tasks. Sunday is a busy day at the monte tables." She nodded to Jessie and Juanita. "It has been a pleasure to visit with you, señoritas. I hope you can bring some cheerfulness to the face of my sweet Guadalupe." She bent, kissed the girl's head, and breezed out of the room.

The sound of the fire was suddenly very loud. Jessie looked around, taking in the long, narrow room. A glossy American-made table against the far wall was piled with ledgers and other business paraphernalia. A handsome brass clock hung above it, its hands permanently set at twelve and six, where they had been when she and Juanita arrived.

She was trying to decide how to politely ask if the clock was broken when Juanita leaned toward Guadalupe. "Tu amor is at peace now," she said gently. "It will do no good to continue to mourn him in this way."

"Sí, I know it." The younger girl's face twisted. "Padre Ortiz has been quite clear on the matter." The chocolate in the mug sloshed dangerously as she thumped it down beside her mother's cold cigarillo. "He doesn't understand that a woman can be troubled by many things, even beyond the death of a man such as Raúl."

Jessie frowned. "Are you—" She paused, not quite sure how to ask.

Juanita had no such hesitation, although her eyes were wide with concern. "Have your courses stopped?"

Guadalupe's lips twitched. She shook her head. "No. I wish I did have such a blessing from him. But no. It is un dilema moral. I must decide—" Then she stopped and looked away, her eyes on the clock as she chewed her upper lip.

"Decisions can be difficult," Jessie said sympathetically.

Juanita studied the fire. "Sometimes it can be helpful to obtain the advice of others," she observed.

Guadalupe glanced at her. "O muy peligroso."

The other girls stared at her.

"Dangerous?" Jessie said.

Guadalupe smiled slightly. "Perhaps," she amended. Then she shrugged. "Perhaps not." She reached for the chocolate again and took a sip, her eyes on her mother's business ledgers.

Josie and Juanita exchanged a look. "I suppose I should head home," Jessie said. "The store tends to be busy on Sunday afternoons. My father will need my assistance."

"And mi tía will wonder what has become of me," Juanita said. "My smallest cousins become very restless at this time of day. It helps her if I am there to assist in their entertainment."

They both looked at Guadalupe, who nodded absently.

Jessie leaned forward impulsively. "Perhaps you should ask Doña Tules for advice. She is a woman of great wisdom."

Guadalupe gave her a startled look, then turned her head and gazed into the fire. When the other girls rose, she trailed them to the door and murmured a half-hearted goodbye.

"¡Dios mío!" Juanita said as they headed toward the plaza. "I have never seen her like this." She looked at Jessie. "Must you truly return immediately to the mercantile? I feel in need of a walk to work off these sentimientos negativos." She tilted her head toward the sky. "Look, the sun has come out. Let us take the path by el río."

"My father doesn't actually need my help this afternoon," Jessie admitted. "The store is much less busy now that so many soldiers have gone south. And I could certainly do with a walk." They moved silently through the plaza and past the buildings beyond, feeling the weight of Guadalupe's sadness and confusion. "I wish I knew what I could do for her," Jessie said.

"Sí," Juanita replied. "I as well." She made a hopeless gesture with her hand. "It is muy difícil."

They followed the river perhaps half a mile, listening to the dry cottonwood leaves rattling in the light early-December breeze. Then Juanita suddenly stopped and put her hand on Jessie's arm, her eyes on the road ahead.

Jessie squinted against the sun. A slender young man walked slowly toward them, his gaze on the stream. He was dressed in American clothes but there was something undefinably Spanish about him. Perhaps it was the straight set of his shoulders or his fashionable black silk top hat, worn as if it were a traditional Spanish head cover.

Then he looked up, saw the girls, and stopped in his tracks. After a long moment, he rushed toward them, his hands stretched out to Juanita and his face bright with pleasure. "¡Mi amiga! Is it really you?"

She laughed, a truly joyful laugh, the first Jessie had heard since Raúl's death. "Cisco!" she said. "You are home!"

"Now I am." They stood looking into each other's face, smiling with delight.

Jessie turned away, but Juanita reached for her. "Jessie, please stay. I want you to know one another." She took a breath, then beamed at her. "Miss Jessica Matilda Milbank, may I present Señor José Narciso Beaubien?"

Jessie smiled at the slim young man, amused at Juanita's enthusiasm but still aware that she was standing outside a closed circle. "I'm delighted to make your acquaintance."

He tilted his head at her. "And I yours. I believe we are bringing goods with us for Señor Hubert Milbank." He smiled and shook his head. "That is, I believe Señor Saint Vrain has goods in his train purchased on Señor Milbank's behalf. Am I correct in assuming the gentleman in question is su padre?"

Jessie nodded, smiling a little at the formality of his language. Her father shipped goods with most of the wagon trains coming into town. He said it spread the risk of attack or loss on the journey.

Narciso Beaubien turned to Juanita. "And how is tu familia? Tu madre y padre? Tu tia y tu tio? Are you living in Santa Fe with them permanently?" He tucked her hand into the crook of his elbow and held it there protectively. They began walking up the road, their torsos slanted toward each other, heads together. Then Juanita stopped and turned to Jessie. "Please, come with us."

Jessie shook her head. "If the wagons have arrived, my father will need me in the store." She dropped a curtsy to them both. "Buenos días."

They gave her brilliant smiles, and Jessie turned back toward town and home. There were still no answers to the why or how Raúl had died. Or Vidal, for that matter. And now Juanita would be taken up by the appearance of this Beaubien boy. Not that he was truly a boy. He was older than she was, at any rate. But the city suddenly seemed very drab. Small and dirty, especially under the gray December clouds.

Jessie tugged her rebozo closer to her shoulders and didn't respond to the greetings of the men now smoking on the hotel porch when she passed.

CHAPTER 16: Sunday, December 20, 1846

In the next two weeks, Jessie became accustomed to Narciso Beaubien's presence and even began to like the young man, though she did see less of Juanita. Her friend's preoccupation with him gave Jessie more time to spend with Guadalupe, whose hollowed-out grief over Raúl's death had abated enough that she was able to leave the Barceló casa. On the Sunday before Christmas, the two girls attended mass together and met Juanita and Narciso there.

They emerged from the church to find a light snow falling from a brilliant blue sky.

"How I have missed this," Narciso said. He put out a hand, palm up, letting the flakes melt on his fingertips. "Snow, sun, the sweep and gracious solidity of brown walls." He looked at Juanita. "Good friends of long standing." He turned to the other girls. "Shall we promenade?"

They smiled and nodded, and he gestured for them to walk ahead of him and Juanita. "Please, lead the way," he said. "We will follow wherever you deem fit to lead us."

They weren't the only citizens out enjoying the sun and the bit of snow that dusted the ground. They passed the hotel and nodded to the gentlemen on the benches beside the door.

"I have been home two weeks," Narciso said. "That is, I have not yet been home to Taos, but I have been here in la ciudad. And I still am not yet weary of the old scenes. Men smoking on los portales, the cottonwoods, the Sabbath Day promenade." Jessie glanced back at him and he smiled at her. "New friends as well."

They circled the plaza. As they neared the west end of the palacio, Narciso studied it thoughtfully. "I understand we're calling it Government House now."

"It will always be el palacio to me," Juanita said.

He patted her hand. "In my heart as well. But, unfortunately, we must move with the times."

"That is what mi madre says, also," Guadalupe said. She looked at Jessie. "Mi amor Raúl thought otherwise." Then movement at the other end of the building caught her eye. "Look, it's Agustín Durán, the man to whom ml was supposedly in debt."

The sleek little man Jessie had last seen talking to Raúl in the gambling salon was ambling along the other end of the palacio portal smoking a cigarillo. He had almost reached the big doors to the interior when the farther one swung open and Donaciano Vigil came out.

Vigil paused, looking one way, then the other, then spied Don Agustín. He stepped forward, blocking the shorter man's path. "What is the news?" he asked menacingly.

Durán's head lifted. "I know nothing."

Vigil scowled. "That is untrue." He looked around the plaza as if marking those within hearing distance, then swung back to Durán. "You know!" he said, his voice just below a shout. "You know all there is to know about la conspiración against the present government and the meeting of los insurrectos yesterday night. In fact, you were present on that occasion!"

As Durán stepped back, shaking his head in denial, Guadalupe clutched Jessie's arm. "She did it!"

Jessie gave her a puzzled look, but the other girl was focused on the men on the portal.

"All has been revealed," Donaciano Vigil said, his voice carrying across the square. He gestured toward the old military chapel. "You planned to meet there this very night to finalize your wicked plans, to conspire with others in a rebellion on Thursday, on the eve of Christ's birth." He stepped closer to Durán. "You planned to celebrate the nativity of el niño Cristo by killing every americano in the city!"

Durán took a step back, still shaking his head.

"It will do you no good to run," the other man growled. "You and your friends will be arrestados y castigados for this."

Guadalupe's fingers bit into Jessie's arm. "Arrested?" she muttered. "Castigados? How punished? Dios mío, what have I done?" As Vigil stomped back into the building, she broke away from Jessie and darted toward home.

As Jessie and Juanita exchanged concerned glances, Narciso stared at the palace and Agustín Durán, who was now hurrying back the way he'd come. "Rebellion," the young man murmured. He looked at the girls. "I heard last week that two americano companies stationed here have been ordered south to Chihuahua. They will not leave until after Christmas. I wonder if the news prompted the idea that we could take back our government."

Jessie frowned. "On Christmas Eve? I would have thought they would wait until January, after the troops left."

"Perhaps there were other considerations." He stared at the palacio doors, then shook himself. "I go tomorrow to the gold fields in the mountains south of the city, on business for mi padre. Those mountains harbor more than precious metals. I believe I will investigate this matter a little more thoroughly and try to ascertain the thoughts of the people there."

Juanita clutched at his arm. "Please be careful."

He smiled and patted her hand. "I survived three years in Missouri among men who considered me a no-account greaser, even though I am half French. Here, I am among mis compañeros. There is no danger."

CHAPTER 17: Monday, December 21, 1846

"It truly is a lovely day," Jessie said as she joined Juanita, Private Fitzgerald, and Lieutenant Milbank outside the mercantile the next day. She smiled at Fitzgerald. Although she didn't care for many of his attitudes, he didn't absorb Juanita's attention the way Narcisco Beaubien did. She turned toward the lieutenant. "It's so clear and warm for December that I'm having trouble realizing Christmas is only four days away."

"Enjoy it," Juanita said as they moved toward the plaza. "Mi tía says we will receive a storm within the next two days, that it always happens this way. The cold comes on the heels of the warm."

"The weather here is so changeable," Fitzgerald grumbled as they passed the old military chapel. "I was really dreading the ride from Albuquerque yesterday, given how miserable it was getting there on Saturday."

Lieutenant Milbank smiled at Jessie. "I'm glad you and Juanita were able to join us today and take advantage of the fine weather."

She smiled back at him. "So am I."

"I am eager to see this americano sawmill east of town," Juanita said. "And the building it is housed in. Is it truly made of boards not cut by hand?"

Fitzgerald nodded. "The waterwheel constructed to power the mill blades was then utilized to saw the boards for the structure that covers it. It's the first wooden building ever erected in New Mexico."

The girls exchanged amused glances. "Not all the buildings here are made of adobe," Jessie told him. "In fact, in the northern mountains, you will sometimes see log houses like those in Missouri."

Juanita nodded. "Also, some people in el norte use stone." She smiled. "Although it is true that las casas construidas de piedras can be difficult to distinguish from those of los adobes, because their walls are also often plastered both outside and in."

The dragoon frowned. "I know 'casas.' But 'construidas de piedras'?" He smiled at her flirtatiously. "Have pity on a poor English speaker, I beg you."

She laughed. "Perdóname," she said. "It means, 'constructed of stones.' However, as I said, they are often plastered inside and out, so it can be very difficile to tell them apart."

He grinned. "Gracias for la explicación. You see, I know a tiny bit." Then he shook his head. "The use of mud to cover the walls of the buildings here is beyond my comprehension. But then, I don't understand why anyone would allow their floors to remain mere soil. It seems sheer laziness to me."

The girls raised their eyebrows at him. "Soil?" Jessie asked.

"Packed dirt," Lieutenant Milbank said. "I also have noticed the practice. Almost every building I've had the good fortune of entering here has floors of packed dirt." He looked at Jessie. "Your father's mercantile, for example."

Jessies's eyes twinkled as she looked at Juanita. "Shall we tell them? Or will they be shocked?"

Juanita put a hand to her mouth, suppressing a laugh. "They will undoubtedly be filled with horror."

The men looked at the girls and Jessie was about to explain the effort involved in creating a concrete-hard floor using the blood of slaughtered animals, when Fitzgerald said, "Ah, they are taking steps after all."

She gave him a puzzled look, and he nodded toward the hotel on the southeast corner of the plaza. Three men in Mexican jackets and flat-brimmed hats sat on the bench beside the door. Tobacco smoke drifted around their heads.

Jessie frowned. "They're smoking as usual."

"They won't be doing so much longer." He nodded again, this time to the left. A squad of soldiers marched smartly down the plaza toward the hotel.

Jessie and her friends were almost there themselves. Lieutenant Milbank's fingers tightened on her arm. "We might want to slow down a bit."

She nodded and they stopped. The men in uniform reached the building and spread out, wrapping around the corner and blocking both ends of the portal. The sergeant stepped forward and said something to the smokers. They stared at him for a long moment, then looked at each other, tossed their cigarillos aside, and slowly stood. The tallest put his hands on his hips and stepped forward, chin jutting belligerently, but the others simply spread their hands to indicate they carried no weapons.

The sergeant barked an order. The soldiers moved onto the porch. When their square reformed in front of the hotel, the three Mexicans were in its center. They began moving back across the plaza toward the palacio.

Juanita turned to Lieutenant Milbank. "What is happening?"

He frowned slightly, his eyes on the moving men. "They're being taken into custody."

Jessie followed his gaze. "Are these the arrests Don Donaciano spoke of yesterday?"

"Yesterday?"

"We saw Donaciano Vigil speaking with Agustín Durán on the palacio portal. He accused Don Agustín of conspiring against the government and said he and his fellow conspirators would be arrested and punished."

Fitzgerald nodded. "A friend of mine saw it and told me what happened." He frowned. "That was yesterday morning and yet the orders to take them into custody weren't enacted until just now. I notice that Durán was not among those on the hotel porch." He looked at the lieutenant. "Apparently Vigil spoke to Don Agustín quite loudly, almost shouting. The entire plaza heard what he had to say. I wonder who else he was warning so they could have time to leave town."

The lieutenant's eyes twinkled. "Vigil is, after all, a politician," he said mildly.

"The bastard," Fitzgerald muttered. He looked at Juanita and Jessie apologetically. "Ladies, I hope you will forgive the coarseness of my language. I fear my emotions are stronger at this moment than my self-control."

The girls barely glanced at him. The square of soldiers and prisoners had halted in front of Government House while the sergeant spoke with a slender man on a big chestnut gelding and wearing a black silk top hat.

The rider turned from the sergeant to the prisoners, spoke briefly, then lifted his hat politely and reined the horse back a few steps. The squad moved left and through the palacio courtyard gates, while he watched. Then he turned and saw Jessie and Juanita.

"I thought it was him!" Juanita murmured as the chestnut trotted across to them. Narciso Beaubien reined in, doffing his hat.

"I thought you had already left for los campamentos mineros!" Juanita said.

"Did you truly believe I would go without speaking to you?" he asked. "When I didn't find you at la casa, I thought perhaps you had gone to visit Señorita Milbank." He smiled at Jessie. "I'm pleased to see that I was correct in my assumption." His eyes narrowed as he took in the men with them, then focused on the one with the most rank. "Lieutenant Milbank, I believe?"

The lieutenant smiled and nodded. "Yes, and you must be the illustrious Señor Narciso Beaubien of whom Miss Sena has spoken so highly. I am delighted to meet you."

"And I you." He turned toward Fitzgerald and gave Juanita a questioning look.

"Cisco, permíteme to present to you Private Henry Fitzgerald of the First United States Dragoons," she said, then, to the dragoon, "Señor, this is Narciso Beaubien, Judge Carlos Beaubien's son, who has recently returned from la universidad near Saint Louis."

As the two men nodded to each other, Jessie suppressed a grin. Neither looked particularly happy. Fitzgerald glanced toward the palacio gate, then returned to Narciso. "I see you spoke to the men arrested just now. Do you know them well?"

The younger man's lips smiled but his eyes were cold. "They are old friends of my father's. The sergeant claims they have been detained under suspicion for plotting insurrection. Indeed, your men seem to be rounding up half the city."

"I doubt there were that many involved," Lieutenant Milbank said. "Though I do hope everyone responsible has been identified and safely taken into custody."

Fitzgerald huffed impatiently. "Safely? I hope not. We need to teach these greasers a lesson in blood if they are ever to truly submit to our superior rule."

Narciso Beaubien gave him a long look, his dark eyes hooded, then turned to the lieutenant. "If there was indeed a plot, I believe you are correct. Only a handful of people will have been involved. However, I'm sure many of my countrymen harbor concerns about the administration General Kearny appointed before he moved on to California." The horse stirred under him, and he reached to stroke its neck. "I understand that the U.S. Secretary of War and the President himself instructed the general to keep in their places the Mexican officials already in office. However, he does not seem to have obeyed that particular directive."

Jessie looked up at him, frowning. "Your own father is among the men he appointed."

He moved the hat in his hand deprecatingly. "I am delighted to see my father in a position which utilizes his talents. However, I cannot help but notice the paucity of men with Spanish surnames in the new administration. That fact has undoubtedly been observed by others, as well. Men with long experience in governance who are held in great esteem by their neighbors."

The horse stirred, as if in agreement. "Not everyone General Kearny appointed is as respected as he might believe," Narciso went on. "For example, although Governor Bent is my father's friend, not everyone here in Nuevo Méjico feels kindly toward him. Most especially in Taos." He shrugged. "I'm sure the general had his reasons for making the choices he did, but they do appear to contradict the orders he was given. And the promises he made." He gave the lieutenant a sharp look. "That is, if my sources are correct. Did he not say soon after he arrived that he would retain men of power in the offices they held?"

The lieutenant shifted uncomfortably. "I can't speak to the orders the general may have received, but yes, I understand that he did say something to that effect. However, I believe the reference was more to the local positions of alcalde and similar posts than to those in higher offices."

"He might well have striven to make himself more clear," Narciso said drily. "And to utilize the expertise of the local men. Individuals who know this country far better than even my father or Governor Bent." His smile flashed. "Though he does seem to have taken advantage of Donaciano Vigil's long experience and skills." He sobered. "I hope to God it is enough to keep us from bloodshed."

They all stared at him. He returned his hat to his head and adjusted his reins. "However, the changes General Kearny made are now in place, and I doubt there is room for modification without direct orders from Washington City. And I must be on my way." He smiled at Juanita. "So that I may complete the business of mi padre and return as quickly as possible."

As she smiled back at him, he touched his hat to the ladies, bowed to the men, and trotted south and out of the plaza.

"That is an interesting young man," the lieutenant said, watching him go. "A New Mexican educated in the United States. A very articulate one with friends among the ricos. I foresee great things for Señor Narciso Beaubien if he chooses to involve himself in the leadership of his country and countrymen."

Juanita gave him a brilliant smile.

"Ah, but still a Mexican," Henry Fitzgerald said. "No matter how civilized, there will always be a question of how well he can be trusted."

Juanita pulled her hand away from his arm as Jessie stiffened.

"I don't believe it's a matter of race, but more one of different approaches," Lieutenant Milbank said. He smiled at Juanita apologetically. "Because you all have such beautiful manners, it can be difficult to determine whether you speak from the heart or are simply being polite. It makes the issue of trust rather complicated."

Juanita stared at him, eyes wide. Then her expression hardened. Her lips flattened. "Must we all become as rude as los americanos?" She glanced at the dragoon. "And those who fight alongside you?"

Fitzgerald put his hand on his chest. "Forgive me, I beg of you. It was a general statement and I certainly did not—"

Juanita looked up at the brilliantly blue, cloudless sky. "I fear the change in weather has already arrived, and it has become a bit too cold for una excursión," she said coolly.

She turned to the lieutenant. "I bid you good day." She bobbed a general curtsy and moved regally up the plaza toward home.

The men turned to Jessie. "I agree with Juanita, it is rather cold," she said without looking at either of them. If she did, she would either rage or cry, and neither would be helpful. Instead, she said, "I find I have lost interest in experiencing more American expertise." Then she tugged her rebozo closer to her shoulders and turned blindly toward the corner and the mercantile beyond.

When she reached the store, she stood outside the door for a long moment, taking deep breaths. When she finally went inside, she found her father at the counter, smoothing lengths of calico into neat squares. He looked up. "I hear Governor Bent has suppressed a planned insurrection," he said.

"Yes, we saw some of the men being arrested."

"I hope there was no resistance."

She shook her head and turned to hang her rebozo on a peg by the door. "No, they went peaceably enough."

"Well, that's a relief." He paused, his hands on the stack of folded cloth, a mischievous look in his eyes. "I might as well take this opportunity to point out that identification of the men responsible and the discovery of their plans did not require any involvement on your part or mine."

When she didn't respond, he frowned and leaned forward to peer at her. "Are you all right? I thought you and your friends were going to inspect the new sawmill."

"It's only a sawmill. And the weather is too cold for that long a walk, anyway."

"It's only a mile east of town."

Jessie shrugged and kept her eyes averted as she crossed the door to the kitchen. Manuelita didn't turn from the fire and Jessie didn't greet her. She went on through to the courtyard and stood staring into space. The chickens clucked at her feet but she didn't respond to them either, just turned and went to her room.

She slipped through the door, sank onto her bed, wrapped a red-and-black wool Navajo blanket around her shoulders, and tried not to think about the conversation in the plaza. Fitzgerald's comments about Mexicans hadn't surprised her. He was jealous of Narciso Beaubien. Also, he wanted revenge for his brother's death. Insurrection and battle were exactly what he hoped for. He wasn't going to get it if there was no one to fight.

But the lieutenant. Abner. How could he? Perhaps he wasn't as intelligent and observant as she'd thought. Her mind veered from their final interaction to the question of dirt floors. He had apparently never truly looked at what was under his feet, never bothered to investigate a culture that could take simple materials like animal blood and soil and turn them into something beautiful. Something durable and solid as concrete.

Jessie shook her head. But that was a small thing. It was his comment about the people here that so appalled her. To say their politeness, their manners, made them untrustworthy. And the look on Juanita's face when he said it. The shock.

Jessie's breath hitched. How could he? She should have slapped him. Screamed at his idiocy. She should have turned instantly and walked away. Well, she had walked away. But not soon enough. Angrily enough. She shook her head, wiped futilely at the tears on her cheeks, curled into her pillow, and wept.

CHAPTER 18: Thursday, December 24, 1846

In the next few days, Jessie found herself returning again and again to the scene in the plaza, inventing new responses to the lieutenant and wishing he would come into the store so she could tell him what she thought.

Finally, on Christmas Eve, she gave up. He wasn't coming, and she didn't intend to spoil the season fuming over a man who clearly wasn't all she'd thought he was. When Juanita and Guadalupe arrived that afternoon, she was in the kitchen, finishing the lattice top of a pie crammed with fat raisins.

"Other than griddlecake, this is the only food I know how to make," she said in response to Juanita's raised eyebrows. Jessie maneuvered a strip of pastry into place. "My mother used to bake it when Father came home from Santa Fe. He always brought us a special treat of El Paso raisins and she would use some of them to make a Christmas Eve pie."

Manuelita, who was stirring a mixture of rice, egg, and milk in a pan over the right-hand section of the fire, sniffed loudly, and Juanita grinned. "Pie seems an odd use for raisins," she said. "Though mi madre bakes with them, also, in las empanadas."

"Turnovers are delicious, but this pie has so many memories to it." Jessie smiled at her friends. "I wanted to share it with you." Then she sobered. "My father can't bear to eat it anymore. He says it carries too many associations. Since he's going to the artillery officers' Christmas banquet tonight, this seemed like a good opportunity."

Juanita smiled and nodded. "Cisco has been invited to the same entretenimiento."

Guadalupe looked at Jessie. "¿And your teniente also?"

Jessie's lips tightened. "He never was and never will be my lieutenant." She turned abruptly to the left-hand side of the fire, where she'd already positioned the little tin reflector oven, its open side facing the flames. She touched the top gingerly, checking the temperature. It was definitely hot enough. She scooted one end slightly away from the flames, placed the pie in the oven, then carefully maneuvered it back into place.

"Now we simply have to wait," she said. She turned to Guadalupe. "I'm so glad you were able to join us tonight."

The younger girl smiled wanly. "Mi madre wished me to attend un baile with her, but I didn't have the spirits for una celebración, especially with dancing. A meal with you and then church is much more to my liking."

Jessie moved impulsively to hug her, then thought better of it. Guadalupe had a fragile look about her, as if this night held too many memories.

"I was worried Colonel Price would be so angry about la conspiración that he would cancel all the events planned for tonight," Juanita said. "Instead, he suspended ese maldito curfew so everyone can enjoy themselves and the mass can be held at midnight, as usual. I'm so glad."

"He must be confident that the plot was completely suppressed," Jessie said.

Manuelita snorted. The girls looked at her. She didn't look up. "Maldito curfew is insult," she said to her pot.

"It does keep the soldiers from the streets late at night and maintains at least a little control," Jessie pointed out.

"Us controlled." The cook sprinkled a liberal dose of cinnamon across the top of her rice-and-milk pudding and lifted the pan toward them, showing the contents off.

"That looks delicious." Jessie turned to her friends. "Let's set the table."

They were well into the meal when Guadalupe looked up, a slight frown creasing her brow. "What burns?"

"Oh, my pie!" Jessie said. She rushed to the fireplace, pulled the oven away from the hearth, and lifted the pastry dish out. The edges were a little dark, but otherwise it looked fine. "You see?" she said to Manuelita. "I actually can bake something."

The cook's lips quirked. "With help."

Jessie laughed. "That's very true!"

They had finished the meal and were sampling the pie and Manuelita's rice pudding when there was a knock on the door to the inner courtyard. They looked at each other uneasily and the cook went to open it. Narciso Beaubien followed her into the room.

"Narciso!" Jessie said as Juanita rose to greet him. "¡Feliz navidad!"

"Forgive me for interrupting la celebración," he said, removing his hat. "Juanita told me you planned to dine together and then attend services at la parroquia. I came to offer to escort you there and back."

"I thought you planned to attend the artillery banquet."

He glanced at Juanita, who smiled at him, then turned back to Jessie. "I find a mixed company more enjoyable, especialmente on Christmas Eve." Then he grinned. "Tu padre was there. He told me you were baking your mother's famous raisin pie."

"Oh, it was my pie you were interested in, not Juanita's company," she teased. "Or ensuring that we make it safely to the church and back." Then she burst out laughing at the chagrined look on his face and waved a hand toward the table. "Please join us."

They polished off the desserts and headed toward church and midnight mass, Manuelita behind a little and off to one side. Jessie eyed her, wishing the cook felt more welcome to join them. But she seemed content enough, her usual grim expression relaxed as the little group ambled along the south side of the plaza, admiring the traditional bonfires that dotted the square and lined the street up ahead, where the bell towers of la parroquia gleamed invitingly under a bright winter moon. Closer to, revelers stood around the fires playing guitars, singing songs, and cracking jokes.

"It feels almost as if the last few months never happened," Juanita said, smiling.

Then a gun boomed from the center of the square. Everyone froze in place, then carefully turned toward the sound. A small boy stood near the flagpole, holding an old musket longer than he was tall, its barrel aimed at the stars. There was a stunned look on his face, but when he saw the others looking, he broke into a delighted laugh. "I did it!" he shouted.

A cheer went up from the fires and Narciso laughed. "It makes me happy to see that weapon being used for such a harmless purpose," he said. "If the plans of los conspiradores had come to fruition, this night could have been one of great bloodshed." He glanced at Jessie, his brows knotted. "It is the nature of mobs to lose control, to confuse friend and foe. I fear what might have happened to all los americanos here."

Guadalupe turned toward him. "Los conspiradores, they have been arrested? Every one of them?"

"One of the leaders escaped south. He is undoubtedly in Chihuahua by now." Narciso grinned. "Did you hear the story of what happened?"

When the girls shook their heads, he continued. "The man is half brother to Padre Ortiz and hid in the priest's house. When the soldiers came, he dressed up as a servant girl and escaped from a balcony by being lowered with ropes into the priest's garden. He slipped away to a casa by the river, but when he was leaving it, still in women's clothes, he was almost caught. He actually talked to los soldados americanos looking for him, but then he got scared and started running and the way he handled his skirts gave him away." Narciso grinned. "Some local women saw him and told los americanos how stupid they were, and they almost caught him."

Guadalupe didn't smile in return. "¿Él escapó?"

"Yes, he escaped, in spite of his costume. Which annoyed the men after him. They had been told he carried a list of the leaders of la conspiración. If they captured it, they would know for certain whether they had caught all of them."

"¿Pero él escapó?" They were almost to the church now and passing the final bonfire. Its flames cast deep shadows on the girl's face.

"Yes, he did escape," Narciso said. He grinned. "Why so anxious? Do you have a sweetheart among los insurrectos?"

Juanita hissed something at him, then turned to the younger girl and took her arm.

"Forgive me, mi amiga," the boy said contritely. "I meant no harm."

She nodded without looking at him and they proceeded into la parroquia.

Narciso left them at the door and moved to the men's side. As the girls settled into their places, Jessie noticed that he'd found a spot near Dick Green. The Bent slave was gazing at the altar, his eyes dark with what seemed to be a cross between worry and exhaustion.

But then, he wasn't the only preoccupied congregant. Guadalupe was near the center aisle, but focused on the nearest wall, not the altar, and chewing on her upper lip as she gazed at the locally made paintings of Christ's passion. They were simple designs, hand-painted on lovingly smoothed boards. The light from the candles on the little shelves below them filled the depictions with emotion. The girl looked almost as sorrowful as they did.

She remained pensive throughout the mass, tears dampening her face as everyone else celebrated the sacred child's birth, and silent as the little group made their way back to the mercantile. She accepted Narciso Beaubien's repeated apology with a small smile and nod, but didn't speak until the three girls were in bed and Jessie had snuffed out the candle.

"Narciso spoke truly," she said into the darkness. "One of los conspiradores was mi prometido."

The bed clothes rustled as Juanita sat up and turned toward her. "Raúl?"

"Sí. But I convinced him not to continue his participación." Her voice wavered. "I told him he should inform someone. Los autoridades. Perhaps Don Donaciano. Or mi madre. Doña Tules would know what to do."

There was a long pause as the other girls absorbed this information, then Guadalupe's soft voice went on. "I knew it to be dangerous. But I said he must. He had una obligación. What bloodshed might result if he remained silent?" Her breath hitched. "He promised that he would tell someone that evening before he came to me. I do not know who." She was weeping now, silently, the tears filling her voice. "But he was prevented. With un cuchillo. A knife." Her voice was muffled, as if she had covered her face with her hands. "Dios mío, I sent mi amor to his death."

Jessie pushed herself onto her elbows. "So you think someone killed him because they found out he was going to tell?"

"Sí." The answer was barely a whisper.

"That note they found in his pocket—"

"Los americanos believe it was from Agustín Durán," Guadalupe said. Her voice was stronger now.

"That was un pagaré for a gambling debt," Juanita said.

"What if it wasn't?" Jessie asked. "What if it was actually a code? Perhaps a message about a meeting or the details of the plot? After all, it didn't include the name of the person to whom the debt was owed. Doña Tules said it wasn't Don Agustín's handwriting." She laid back and stared at the ceiling. "In fact, she didn't recognize it at all."

"Los autoridades must have had a reason to think it was his."

"Because they saw Raúl with him." Guadalupe sniffed. "Los americanos saw them together and decided they were of the same kind. Raúl would never have gambled as Don Agustín does."

"Señor Durán is not gambling at all at present." The bedclothes rustled again as Juanita returned to her pillow. "He is in prison because la administración believes he took part in la conspiración."

Jessie turned toward her. "Are prisoners allowed to have visitors?"

"I do not know what the rules of los americanos are about such things," Juanita said. "It was always possible before."

"Why would you wish to pay him una visita?" Guadalupe asked.

"If he didn't write that note, he might be willing to help us find out who did," Jessie said. "Do you remember how Private Fitzgerald spoke of Don Agustín's repeated inquiries after Raúl died? He seemed to think Durán was acting suspiciously. Other people might also think so. Conspiracy to insurrection is one thing, but a man's actual death is quite another. If the authorities think Durán had something to do with that, he might be willing to tell us what he knows in order to protect himself."

"Can your lieutenant help us to speak with him?"

Jessie stiffened. "He is not my lieutenant."

Guadalupe chuckled. Jessie smiled reluctantly. It was good to hear a sign of amusement from the younger girl, even if it was about Lieutenant Milbank.

"Would Private Fitzgerald be able to provide assistance?" Guadalupe asked.

"I have not encountered him since the day of los arrestos," Juanita said. "He undoubtedly has been sent to Albuquerque with los despachos and has not yet received any to bring back. Jessie, has he visited the mercantile?"

"No, I haven't seen him."

"Could Don Donaciano arrange for a meeting?" Guadalupe asked.

"Would Doña Tules be willing to ask him?"

"Mi madre wishes me to keep the past en el pasado, where she says it belongs." All trace of amusement had disappeared from Guadalupe's voice. "She says she is grateful la conspiración did not result in the shedding of blood, and, for the time being, is unwilling to associate herself with los hombres arrestados."

The girls lay in the darkness, contemplating this hard fact. As a woman in business, especially the gambling trade, Doña Tules was already viewed with suspicion by the Americans. If she wanted to continue making a living, she needed to at least appear to be cooperative. Visiting jailed conspirators, or arranging for family members to do so, would be unwise.

"We must wait until he is released," Guadalupe said.

"Sí," Juanita said. "If we explain to los americanos that Raúl was of los conspiradores, they will be even less concerned to find out what truly happened to him. They certainly will not believe he intended to warn them about what was planned. After all, he was simply one of many untrustworthy greasers."

Jessie raised herself on her elbow. "The private didn't say that exactly."

"He did not use the word 'greaser,' but it was clearly implícito."

"¿Quién?" Guadalupe asked. "Who?"

"Private Fitzgerald, el dragón americano," Juanita explained. "He said no matter how civilized Narciso Beaubien is, because he is Mexican, there will always be a question of how well he can be trusted."

"Cisco?" Guadalupe sat up. "Narciso Beaubien? How long was he at la escuela in Saint Louis? ¿Cuatro años? Four years? And he is still not to be trusted?"

"He attended tres años," Juanita said. "Three very long years. But that will not suffice. No matter how much he agrees with them, no matter how many of their customs he adopts, he will never be trustworthy."

"But his father is French!"

Jessie pulled her blankets up to her chin. "It doesn't matter. If people want to be close-minded, they will be."

"I do not know what I ever saw in ese dragón," Juanita said.

"His manners are muy agradables," Guadalupe said.

Jessie chuckled. "And he has a very British accent, which makes his manners seem even more agreeable. But the more he talks, the more I realize how biased and bloodthirsty he really is."

"And the more I compare him to Cisco, the less pleasant his manners appear to me," Juanita said.

Guadalupe giggled. "Si, we all know Narciso Beaubien is perfecto. He can do no wrong."

A pillow flew across the room. Guadalupe huffed as it hit her. "Gracias," she said. "I had just wished for another one."

But in the middle of the night, Jessie woke to hear muffled sobs from the other side of the room. She lay listening, feeling her friend's grief and knowing there was nothing she could do to assuage it.

CHAPTER 19: Friday, January 1, 1847

A week later, Jessie rolled over, burrowed into her pillows as she tried to blank the dream from her mind, then sat up with a jerk. It was New Year's Day. No time to think about dreams, especially bad ones. She had work to do. She bounded out of bed, threw her rebozo over her nightgown, and hurried to the kitchen.

Manuelita was already at the workbench, mixing corn masa and water for tortillas.

"What are you doing?" Jessie demanded.

Manuelita frowned. "Morning work."

"Today is your saint's day."

The cook shrugged and moved to the fire to check the temperature of the cast iron skillet. "Un día."

Jessie crossed to the workbench and stood in front of it, blocking Manuelita's return. "We discussed this last year. And the year before. Today is the day of everyone named Manuel or Manuela, or Manuelita. The day we honor the saint you were named for and celebrate you, as well."

Manuelita's lips flattened. "Spanish day. Not mine."

"It isn't mine either. In the States we celebrate the anniversary of the actual date a person was born. But you said you didn't know when that was."

The cook shifted to one side, reached around the girl, pinched off a ball of tortilla dough, and began patting it into shape. Jessie held out her hand. "Let me do that."

Manuelita's mouth was still set in a straight line, but her eyes glinted with amusement. She put the dough into Jessie's hand, who began to pat it between her palms, trying to flatten it. Chunks fell onto the floor. "Ugh!" Jessie said.

Manuela held out her hand for what was left, but Jessie shook her head. The cook stepped back and watched. More dough landed on the floor. "This is more difficult than I thought," Jessie muttered.

"That's what you said last year," her father said from the door to the shop. "Manuelita, do we have any bread?" He looked at Jessie. "Maybe you could make toast instead."

"But then this will go to waste." She turned to the cook. "Isn't there a way to roll this out, instead of patting it with my hands?"

Manuelita nodded. "I show."

"Or perhaps some corn meal mush," her father said. When the women ignored him, he shook his head and headed back into the shop. "We're going to starve today."

"You said that last year!" Jessie called after him. She turned to the cook. "Please just sit down and tell me what to do."

The cook shook her head, but she seated herself at the table. "Flour." Jessie moved toward the gaily painted supply cupboard in the corner. "And roller," the cook added as the girl opened the lower door.

They were still at it when Juanita arrived an hour later, Manuelita with a mug of coffee and Jessie gingerly removing an oblong tortilla from the skillet. The Mexican girl chuckled as she looked at the misshapen cooked ones on a plate on the table. "These are quite *bonitas*," she said sardonically. "Especially since you only do this once a year." Then she turned to Manuelita. "May I wish you a happy saint's day?"

The cook nodded an acknowledgment, and Juanita grinned at Jessie. "If we were celebrating properly, I and your other friends would have arrived at midnight to sing you a birthday song. But then you would have had to prepare for us a *banquete completo*." Her eyes danced with mischief. "In addition to los tortillas, that would include *bizcochitos* and *posole* and *empanadas*."

Jessie put the tortilla on the platter. "So I finally have a reason to be thankful the 'maldito curfew' is still in place."

Even Manuelita chuckled at this. Jessie's father reappeared in the doorway. "Are the tortillas ready?"

Jessie bobbed him a curtsy. "Sí, señor. And there are boiled eggs in the bowl on the shelf."

"And *miel*?"

Jessie laughed, retrieved the eggs and the corn-based syrup, and set them on the table. Then she turned to Manuelita. "And what would you like to eat this morning?"

The cook pursed her lips, thinking. "Grid cake."

Jessie and her father broke into laughter. "Griddlecake?" Jessie said. "Now that I can do!"

"May I join you?" he asked Manuelita.

"And I?" Juanita added.

The cook's eyes twinkled as she nodded. Jessie set to work.

"And I will prepare el chocolate caliente," Juanita said.

"Hot chocolate sounds delicious," Don Hubert said. He turned to Jessie. "I'm going to go back into the store until you're ready."

Half an hour later, as Jessie poured the last spoonful of batter onto the skillet, he was back, with Private Fitzgerald beside him.

"What a delicious aroma," the dragoon said.

Jessie looked up from her stool by the fire. "Happy New Year," she said. "Today is Manuelita's Saint's Day, so I'm doing the cooking."

"Which means we'll eat griddlecake for breakfast, dinner, and supper," her father said.

"That isn't fair," Jessie said. "I can also make soup."

Juanita chuckled. "As long as you aren't distracted by conversation. That's what happened last year."

"That soup was edible."

Her father grinned. "It didn't taste like Manuelita's."

Jessie made a face at him as she transferred the griddle cake to the platter beside her. She carried it to the table and they all dug in.

"I'm glad my task brought me to Santa Fe today," Fitzgerald said. "Not only do I have the pleasure of partaking of these delicious griddlecakes, but I also have the knowledge that I recently contributed to the peace and security of New Mexico."

Jessie raised an eyebrow at this change in the dragoon's usual bloodthirsty tone. He clearly wanted to explain himself, and she wasn't sure she wanted to let him. She glanced at Juanita, who didn't look up from her plate.

"Oh yes?" her father asked politely.

Fitzgerald sat back, stretching out his legs. "The Albuquerque alcalde reported that a relative of the late governor was hiding out in a tumbledown house on the edge of town. When we investigated, we found the culprit in a decrepit old adobe not fit for pigs to inhabit. The man had been there a good week, but was still reluctant to leave his place of refuge. Eventually, I arranged for a bit of gunpowder and a fuse to be applied to the situation, and he decided to surrender." The dragoon grinned. "I must say, that little explosion was rather enjoyable, although I was surprised at how well even crumbling adobe bricks withstood it. I suspect it was the smoke that brought him out, rather than the risk of the walls tumbling down any further."

Jessie and Juanita exchanged a glance. Private Fitzgerald bit into another piece of griddlecake, then washed it down with hot chocolate. "The prisoner wasn't terribly enthusiastic about coming to Santa Fe. He said it was too cold, that we should wait until the weather broke. I suspect he was hoping we'd put him in the town jail and forget about him. I gather that was a common enough occurrence under the old regime."

Jessie frowned. "Didn't you say the alcalde turned him in?"

"Yes. We believe there's some kind of personal animosity between the two men. Or between the alcalde and Manuel Armijo for running away the way he did."

"I, for one, am glad Armijo ran away," Jessie's father said. "I expect his doing so prevented a good deal of bloodshed."

Fitzgerald nodded reluctantly. "I begin to think I will never see battle," he said. "I was too ill to go with Doniphan, and now more artillery are following him, but not dragoons.

Exploding an old hut may be all the action I experience." Then he brightened. "The men going south next week aren't taking the Texan six pounder, though. Perhaps we'll still have occasion to use it."

Jessie's father raised an eyebrow. "That isn't a very big gun. I doubt it would do much damage on whatever it's used for."

"It's a matter of principle. The Texan Expedition didn't have an opportunity to employ it before they were captured and treated so ignominiously by Armijo and his menials." The dragoon leaned forward to help himself to another griddlecake. His teeth flashed in amusement, though his eyes were hard. "And now Texas has become part of the United States, Armijo has fled, and New Mexico is finally in the appropriate hands. It would be only fitting to use that cannon to put the final seal on the achievement, as a reminder that we have not forgotten how the Expedition was treated. And to commemorate the men like my brother who were killed on that dreadful march to Mexico City."

"Ah, yes. Jessie told me about your brother's death. Please accept my condolences."

"Thank you." Fitzgerald placed his utensils on his plate. "And please accept my wishes for a prosperous New Year." He looked at Jessie, then Juanita. "May more adventures lie in wait for us all." He pushed back from the table. "But now I must be on my way to Government House, to collect Colonel Price's dispatches to Albuquerque." He turned to Jessie. "Miss Milbank, I thank you for the delicious meal." He glanced toward Juanita, then nodded to Jessie's father. "I bid you all good day." He gave them an elegant bow and went out.

Jessie's father rose and followed the dragoon through the store, then returned to the kitchen, shaking his head. "That is a very interesting young man," he said as he sat back down at the table.

"Thirst for blood," Manuelita said.

Jessie glanced at her, unsure if the cook was expressing admiration or disgust. "He seems to feel the loss of his brother very deeply."

Juanita frowned. "Killing someone else will not return life to his brother."

"I wish more people understood that," Jessie's father said. "Revenge tends only to beget more revenge, and then the cycle goes on unceasingly." He stared bleakly into space, then drained the last bit of chocolate from his mug. "Well, that was quite a repast. I expect I'm well fueled for a session of opening bundles and crates, and stocking shelves."

He stood up. "I will leave you ladies to your task." He grinned at Jessie. "I assume you will not be joining me in the shop, but will instead be preparing our dinner." He nodded toward Manuelita. "If nothing else, this annual day of cooking is a reminder of all the work Manuelita does for us."

"Yes," Jessie said. She smiled at the cook. "And how very forbearing she is."

Manuelita's forehead knotted at the strange word.

"Paciente," Juanita told her. She pointed her chin at Jessie. "Especialmente with her."

Manuelita's lips quirked as Jessie's father laughed and went out. The cook gathered the plates within her reach and started to rise, but Jessie waved her back to her seat. "Have more coffee. Or go for a walk. Do whatever you like. I will clean up."

"And I will assist," Juanita said.

The cook frowned. "And dinner? Supper?"

Juanita chuckled. "I think we can manage a simple soup for midday. And Jessie can always make more griddlecake for supper."

Manuelita looked around the kitchen as if she wasn't sure she should trust it to them, then shrugged and went out. Juanita began gathering dirty plates while Jessie checked the level of hot water in the kettle.

They washed, rinsed, and dried in silence until Juanita said, "I wonder if Private Fitzgerald is truly driven merely by el deseo de venganza."

Jessie gave her a surprised look. "A desire for vengeance?"

"Perhaps he is more anxious for la gloria, and la muerte of his brother is merely an excuse," Juanita said.

Jessie frowned. "I see what you mean. But if he was only seeking glory, he could have gone anywhere. He could have stayed in Europe and joined the French Foreign Legion. Or volunteered with a U.S. regiment that was being sent deeper into Mexico. He didn't have to come here." She looked down at the plate in her hands, then sighed. "It can be so difficult to tell what motivates another person. Or what they'll do as a result."

"Sí, this is so." Juanita crossed the room to return the griddlecake platter to its shelf. "For example, Raúl told Guadalupe and you that he gambled to obtain funds for land and a house. But he also said it was in venganza against los americanos. I wonder if he truly would have stopped once he accumulated suficiente dinero."

Jessie nodded, remembering what he'd said about owning a hacienda instead of a small house.

Juanita was beside her again, reaching for another plate. "The death of mi primo is still difficult for me to retain in my memory," she said. "I find myself often at the gate, watching for him and Guadalupe as they arrive to spend an afternoon."

"You may do that for a long while yet," Jessie said. "Even now, I sometimes look up, expecting my mother to enter the room with a letter from someone she's helped, or to ask if I've gathered the eggs." She took a deep breath. "I miss her so much."

Juanita squeezed her arm and crossed the room to put the plate away. "Surely it is impossible that Raúl was involved in the planning for la insurrección," she said as she returned. "Yes, he was angry. He certainly was unhappy that el gobernador Armijo gave up without trying. But to conspire actively against the authorities—" She reached for a mug and stared into it, letting water drip onto the floor. "Ojos vemos, corazón no sabemos," she murmured.

"Eyes we see, heart we know not?" Jessie asked.

Juanita nodded. "It is something mi tía says quite often." She sighed. "It truly is a difficult thing to know another person's heart."

When Jessie didn't answer, Juanita bent her head over the mug, dabbing it with the cloth. "I have told mi tio and my parents that I wish to proceed with caution in regard to Narciso Beaubien." She lifted her head. "He has expressed a desire to request permiso oficial for us to court."

Jessie dropped her dishcloth in the dirty water and reached to hug her friend. "He has requested permission? I'm so happy for you!"

Juanita smiled faintly and moved out of reach, still clutching the mug. "He has spoken to mi tio, but not mi padre y mi madre. And I will not be rushed. I will look into his heart as closely as possible before I commit myself."

Then she gave herself a little shake and went to put the mug in its place. "He has had no opportunity as yet to speak with his own padre y madre. They must agree before he goes to my parents, and I do not know how they will respond to the idea. It has been a long while since I last saw su madre. She has always been kind to me, but the attributes of a potential spouse for a beloved only son are not the same as that of una amiga de la familia."

"But surely she will approve. And a courtship doesn't mean you would marry immediately."

"Here in Nuevo Méjico, it could mean that. There is simply the matter of an agreement and la confirmación by Padre Ortiz that we are not closely related."

Jessie turned back to the dishes. "You are still young. There's plenty of time."

"Guadalupe is only fourteen."

"I assumed that acquiring land and then building a house would take a good while. That years would go by before they actually married."

"In the Sena family, and with the Beaubiens, it is not uncommon for un matrimonio to take place as soon as the girl is able to bear a child. Narciso's sister, Luz, was not quite thirteen when she wed Lucien Maxwell." Juanita smiled. "Although I suspect acquiring land and building una casa might have delayed the marriage of Guadalupe and Raúl longer than he would have liked."

"Yes, I suspect you are right." Yet, even as she smiled at the memory of Raúl's impatience, Jessie's heart constricted. So much ambition. So many plans. Snuffed out by a knife in the chest. Her morning dream touched the edges of her mind, and she pushed it away firmly. "Someone must know something about that night in November," she said. "I still think it would be useful to speak to Don Agustín."

"Agustín Durán? Is he not still in el calabozo?"

"I haven't heard that he was released. I'm sure there would have been talk among our customers if that had happened."

"Cisco thinks he knows nothing."

Jessie raised an eyebrow. "So you two do talk about something other than your love for one another?"

Juanita laughed and flicked the dish towel at Jessie's shoulder. "¡Muy divertido! How do you say it? Most funny!"

CHAPTER 20: Tuesday, January 5, 1847

Jessie continued to mull over ways to learn more about Raúl's death, but she had no one to discuss ideas with. She'd seen Juanita three times in the last four days, always farther along the street or on the other side of the plaza and arm in arm with Narciso Beaubien. Each time, Jessie turned away and proceeded with whatever task she had in hand, but the disappointment lingered.

Perhaps it was the icy gray January weather, but everyone seemed preoccupied. Even Fitzgerald didn't acknowledge her when she saw him emerge from the old military chapel with Tomás Romero, the leader from Taos Pueblo, by his side.

Jessie was returning from an errand to the sutler's office when she spied them. There was something about the turn of Fitzgerald's head, the quiet dignity of Tomás Romero, that stopped her in her tracks. They looked so sure of themselves, so oblivious to anything else.

Something twisted inside her. The entire city was full of people focused on their own concerns. It was as if Raúl had never lived, much less died with a knife in his chest.

She turned and studied the flagpole in the center of the square. The stars and stripes whipped straight out in the icy wind, colors sharp against the clouds. Tears stung her cheeks. Someone ought to do something. It wasn't right.

But she knew her father wouldn't intercede, what he would say if she spoke to him: That the death of young Cabeza de Baca was unfortunate, but finding out who killed him was not the Milbank family's responsibility. Her mother would have thought differently. But her father? Jessie's shoulders dropped. There was no point in even bringing it up.

The rain started up again and was pelting hard by the time she reached the store. Jessie handed the sutler's information to her father, hung her rebozo and cloak by the door, and went to stir up the flames in the little stove. As she reached for another piece of firewood, she found herself saying, "I wonder if Agustín Durán is still in jail."

Her father looked up from the counter, where he was entering the sutler's order into the register. "Dick Green was here while you were gone. He said Don Agustín has refused to provide any information about his fellow conspirators or to take the oath of allegiance to the United States. I expect it will be some time before he's released from jail."

"I wonder why they haven't put him on trial."

"They charged one of the other men with treason, but the defense argued that New Mexico is occupied territory, and therefore the people here aren't U.S. citizens and can't legally commit treason against it." He made a note in the book, closed it, and looked up at her. "The strategy seems to have worked. He was acquitted of all charges."

She closed the stove door. "So that's why Don Agustín is still in jail? Because they can't figure out what to accuse him of?"

Her father shrugged and picked up the account book. "I expect Colonel Price hopes Durán's urge to gamble will eventually become so strong that he'll identify his fellow conspirators in exchange for release."

"All I want to know is whether the promissory note found on Raúl really was for a debt owed to Don Agustín." This wasn't the truth, of course. She wanted to know a good deal more than that. "Doña Tules didn't think it was," she continued. "But only the parties involved would know for sure."

The ledger thudded back onto the counter. "That's the military's business. Not yours."

Jessie straightened, her chin up. "They don't appear to be very interested in finding out who killed him."

"You don't know that. They may be pursuing numerous lines of inquiry."

"If they were, someone would have come to ask me what I know. What I saw that night."

He gave her a sharp look. "Something other than what you told me?"

"No, but—"

His lips tightened. "You have enough to do here. If Colonel Price needs more information from you, he will send someone. Raúl's death is unfortunate, but finding his killer is not our responsibility." He put his hands on the counter and leaned toward her. "Trying to do so could be dangerous. Leave it alone."

She glared at him. He looked away. "You are so much like your mother." He grabbed the ledger, thumped it onto the shelf under the counter, and left the room.

Jessie's shoulders slumped. She wasn't sure that it really was dangerous to ask questions, to try to identify Raúl's killer. But she clearly wasn't going to get her father's help, or even his blessing, to pursue the matter. She moved around the room, neatening displays, returning items to their stacks, and doing a little dusting, as she tried to reestablish her equilibrium.

Twenty minutes later, he returned. "The rain has stopped, at least." When she didn't respond, he went to the counter, took out paper and ink, and began writing. When he finished, he looked up at her. "I need to respond to the army sutler about a few items," he said, his voice carefully neutral. "If you could take this to him, I'd appreciate it."

An hour later, Jessie was returning from this errand and passing the palacio doors when Donaciano Vigil came out, flanked by Dick Green and Ceran Saint Vrain.

"Señorita," Vigil said, doffing his hat. "How are you this fine day?"

Jessie glanced at the gray clouds overhead. The day was anything but fine. Her eyes glinted with amusement. "I am well, Don Donaciano," she said, dipping a curtsy. "And you?"

He waved a hand at the sky. "The rain has ceased, I have amigos beside me, and a pretty girl to talk to. What more could a man desire?"

"Fewer enemies," Ceran Saint Vrain said drily. He uncovered his own head, his broad forehead pale above his hat line, and addressed Jessie. "How do you find Santa Fe now that we Americans have taken over, Miss Milbank?"

"I would prefer fewer soldiers," she said.

Dick Green chuckled. "That's our Miss Jessie. She sure will tell you what she thinks and no mincing about it."

She smiled at him. "We haven't seen you at the store lately."

"Guv Bent's been keeping me right busy." He glanced at Don Donaciano. "Along with a few other small things."

"Like trying to make sure Vigil here stays in one piece," Saint Vrain said. "That's keeping us both occupied."

Don Donaciano smiled at Jessie. "Mis amigos, they worry too much," he said. "They are all convinced I live in danger of repercussions as a consequence of the December arrests." He gestured toward the men beside him. "As a result, I now have an escort wherever I go."

"You've been threatened?"

"No one has been threatened. As I said, mis amigos worry too much. There is no reason to be concerned, señorita." He glanced toward the plaza. "And now, if you will excuse us, I will torture my friends with more government business." He grinned at Green and then Saint Vrain. "That will teach them to hover about me like so many flies."

Impulsively, Jessie put out a hand. "Please sir, before you go, could you advise me about a government matter?"

"I suppose that would depend on the matter in question."

"How would I go about getting permission to visit a prisoner?"

He grinned. "You have a sweetheart in el calabozo? One of the troops perhaps? That British dragoon?" He shook his head mockingly. "Lieutenant Milbank will be disappointed."

Her jaw tightened. "I don't have a sweetheart," she said evenly. "However, I do have an interest in visiting Señor Durán. I understand that he is still incarcerated."

He raised an eyebrow. "And what is your interest in visiting that old reprobate? Are you among those to whom he owes a gambling debt?"

She shook her head, wondering how to answer, hearing her father's disapproving voice in her head, then plunged in. "No, but he is believed to have lent money to Raúl Cabeza de Baca, the young man who was killed in November. Raúl was a cousin of my friend, Juanita María de la Luz Sena. I thought perhaps learning about the debt might provide a clue to the circumstances of his death."

"Ah, yes. I was very sorry to hear about what happened to the cousin of your friend. However, I am a simple funcionario público. I cannot provide you access to the prisoners in the military jail. Entry there requires permission from Colonel Price. I suggest you ask your father to go to him." His lips twitched. "The colonel has very americano ideas regarding the proper role of women and the activities appropriate to them. Señor Milbank is more likely to be able to obtain the permission you seek."

Saint Vrain nodded in agreement, then frowned slightly. "I'm not sure even Don Hubert's intercession will suffice," he said. "I've been told Colonel Price is being especially careful about access to Durán. I suspect he's concerned Don Agustín will conspire with his co-revolutionaries to render the planned court martials useless by colluding in their testimony. Or, even worse, escaping." He grinned. "Our colonel is rather protective of the prerogatives of his military process."

Jessie's shoulders slumped and she nodded. Dick Green gave her a sympathetic look, but Vigil put his hat back on his head. "And now, señorita, we truly must bid you good day."

The men stepped off the portal and into the plaza. Jessie watched them bleakly. So, even if she could somehow convince her father to ask Colonel Price for permission for her to speak with Durán, it was unlikely he'd grant it. She blew out a breath of frustration. All she wanted to do was talk to the man. And she wasn't a co-conspirator. The colonel had no reason to keep her from seeing him. Surely Don Donaciano was mistaken.

"Miss Milbank?" a voice said behind her. She turned to find Private Fitzgerald and the lieutenant. She wasn't sure she was ready yet to speak to her distant cousin, but then again, he was a military officer. Maybe he would know how she could accomplish her goal. She forced herself to smile politely.

They chatted for a few minutes, then she steeled herself. "I have a dilemma, gentlemen," she said. "I wonder if you could give me some information?"

The lieutenant studied her, but Fitzgerald jumped in eagerly. "We are at your service, señorita," he said gallantly.

She smiled slightly, glanced at the lieutenant's wary face, then plunged in. "I'd like to find a way to visit someone in the military jail."

The men exchanged looks. Fitzgerald pursed his lips. "A prisoner?"

"One of the conspirators."

The lieutenant frowned. "I'm not sure that would be allowed."

She forced herself to give him a pleading look. "Even if you interceded for me?"

"Unfortunately, I will be returning to my grazing company early tomorrow. I had hoped for a word—"

She turned to Fitzgerald. "Would it be possible? A private interview? I have money."

He gave her an alarmed look. "I have no contacts in the jail. Even if I did, it would be strictly against regulations to smuggle you inside."

"Even for a sufficient sum?"

"Especially for that," the lieutenant said. "I'm surprised you would even think such a thing."

Her head jerked up, eyes sharp, but his face had changed again, from disapproval to something almost pleading about it. "May I call on you this evening?"

She didn't meet his gaze. "My father will be home." She glanced up the street toward the Sena compound. "I have an engagement."

"I see." He stepped back. "There are arrangements to make before I leave tomorrow, so I must bid you good day." He nodded to Fitzgerald, directed a small, formal bow in Jessie's direction, and walked off.

"I'm sorry I could not be of service to you in this matter," Private Fitzgerald said. "I fear I also must be on my way." He bowed formally, then smiled apologetically. "Buenos días."

He moved toward the palacio entrance, but Jessie didn't watch him go. Instead, she stared after the lieutenant, whose stiff back was just passing the plaza flagpole. Somehow, the lieutenant's disapproval had cut her more deeply than her father's opposition to her plan. Yet why should she care what he thought? Rain began to mist down again and she turned and headed for home.

CHAPTER 21: Wednesday, January 6, 1847

Jessie didn't tell her father where she was going the next morning. She simply put on her cloak, left the hood down, wrapped her rebozo around her head and shoulders, and went out. Yesterday's sullen clouds had persisted. They lay low over the town, hiding the eastern mountains from sight.

She lifted her chin against the grayness and moved firmly toward Government House. The massive double gates to the interior courtyard stood half open. Men and wagons moved sluggishly around the big space beyond. Jessie veered right, to the portal, then stopped to flatten her palm against the nearest pillar. The wood was cracked, battered, and sun bleached, but thick and tree-like, as if still rooted in its mountain soil. She straightened her shoulders, lifted her chin, and moved to the palacio entrance.

She found herself in a narrow room with blood-hardened floors. A guard stood in front of a closed door at the far end. He was young and slender, with reddish-brown hair, anxious hazel eyes, and a nose too large for his face. He shifted slightly as she marched toward him, and, when she stopped, wet his lips with his tongue and said something in mangled Spanish. The only part she understood was "señorita."

She gave him a confused look, then realized he thought she was New Mexican. "Please," she said in English. "I'm here to see Colonel Price."

Now he looked confused. "You are American?"

"Yes. I'm here to see Colonel Price."

"I apologize, miss. I mistook you for a local." When she didn't respond, he shifted again, stabilizing himself. "Your name, miss?"

"I am Jessie Milbank. I am the daughter of the merchant, Hubert Milbank." She paused, waiting for him to respond. When he simply looked at her, she said impatiently, "I'm here to see Colonel Price."

"Do you have an appointment, miss?"

"It will only take a minute."

"I'm sorry, miss. The colonel is a very busy man. Perhaps if you returned with your father."

She stared at him. It was true then. But surely—

She threw a note of indignation into her voice. "If I return with my father?"

He shifted uncomfortably. "Yes, miss." He gave her a pleading look. "I have my orders, miss."

She opened her mouth, then shut it again. After all, he was only a guard. And he had his orders. "Of course," she muttered. She turned away.

"I'm sorry, miss."

She raised her hand in acknowledgment as she went out the door.

She was too full of words to go home. One look at her face, and her father would want to know where she'd been and what she'd been doing. And she would tell him. She wouldn't be able to help herself.

But it was starting to snow. Small sleety flakes stung her cheeks. She headed toward the Sena compound and was almost to the gate when she realized Juanita would not sympathize with her efforts to talk to the jailed gambler. After all, Narciso Beaubien believed Don Agustín had nothing to do with Raúl's death. Jessie turned and headed across the street to la parroquia.

The church's dimness, the faint scent of incense and candles, settled her at once. There was no one else there except a man sitting cross-legged on the right side, facing the altar. She stayed toward the back on the left, sank to her knees, and stared blindly in the same direction.

How would she ever find out who killed Raúl? How could she live with herself if she didn't? First the man in the plaza, and then Juanita's cousin. To the military authorities, the two men were merely Mexican greasers. To her father, their deaths were unfortunate but too dangerous to investigate. And Juanita seemed to have given up on finding out what happened.

Jessie closed her eyes. She needed to know. There had been no way to go after the men who killed her mother. She knew what at least one of them looked like, but they weren't local. She'd never seen them before. And Missouri was awash with strangers back then, most of them in pursuit of runaway slaves. No doubt the men who'd attacked the cabin had moved on soon after, hunting elsewhere.

But people in New Mexico weren't that prone to mobility. The locals had business to attend to: farms, animals, children. Unless Raúl's killer was a member of one of the military troops that had already left Santa Fe, it was likely he or she was still in the city. Jessie stiffened and blinked. He or she? She? Was that possible?

There were simply too many questions. Were Vidal and Raúl killed by the same person? The only thing linking their deaths was the similar weapon, but there were plenty of knives just like them in New Mexico, at least two in the Milbank kitchen.

The Americans seemed to think the note in Raúl's pocket linked him to Agustín Durán. But Don Agustín might not be the killer. He might simply care about Raúl and be willing to tell her something. After all, he had been friendly with the young man.

But then there was the question of whether Don Agustín would tell her if he did know something. He could be protecting someone else. She tilted her head, considering. Perhaps not, but he might inadvertently provide a clue to the mystery, something that would help her find out the truth. If only she could speak to him! The idea that she was forbidden to talk to someone, or even ask permission to do so, was infuriating. It made her want to do it simply because she'd been told she couldn't.

And Durán might actually have some answers, if she asked carefully enough. Her chin lifted. If she didn't do it, who would? Certainly, no one else seemed to care.

Jessie's awareness returned to her surroundings as the man on the other side of the church rose, turned, and moved toward the doors. As he drew level with Jessie, he hesitated and she looked up. "Mr. Green!" she said with delight.

"I wasn't sure if you wanted to be greeted," he answered softly. He glanced toward the altar. "This being a place of prayer and all."

She followed his glance. "I think I'm through." She got to her feet and walked with him toward the exit. "Do you come here often?"

"Sometimes, just for a spot of quietness. The padre don't seem to mind, even though I'm not Catholic."

"I'm not either." She looked back at the altar. The painted saints behind it gazed calmly at her. "I find it peaceful, though," she said. "It's a good place to sort out my thoughts."

He cocked his head at her. "Is something troubling you?"

"Despite the advice of Don Donaciano and Señor Saint Vrain, I tried to get permission from Colonel Price to visit Agustín Durán. They were right. Colonel Price won't see me without an appointment, and my father has to request the appointment."

Green nodded, then shook his head. "It does seem mighty unchivalrous of the colonel not to give you even a moment."

"Unchivalrous is the kindest of the terms that spring to my mind."

Green chuckled as he pushed the left-hand church door open. "It seems to me like you might want to take another look at your sight lines."

She stepped outside. The sleet had turned to large steady snowflakes, blurring the edges of the buildings ahead. Jessie gave Green a puzzled look.

He smiled and gestured toward the church. "You're not Catholic but you use this here building to get what you need from it."

"That's true."

"You're not in the military, neither."

She studied his brown face. He grinned. "There's a saying they have here. Dios aprieta pero no ahoga."

"God squeezes but does not choke." She studied the street again, the hotel at the far end, the plaza beyond, hazy in the falling snow. "It's true," she said slowly. "All problems do usually have some sort of solution." Her lips twitched, then she found herself smiling broadly. "I do like the way you think, Mr. Green." She dropped him a curtsy. "Thank you, kind sir."

He smiled back at her, then his eyes darkened. "Just you be careful now, you hear?"

But she wasn't listening. She was already well into the street, striding through the snow toward the plaza and home.

CHAPTER 22: Thursday, January 7, 1847

The snow stopped falling during the night, but began again early the next afternoon. As Jessie moved up the slushy street toward the plaza, she bent her head to keep the flakes out of her face, then stayed under the shelter of the portal roofs as she worked her way toward the palacio. The big wooden gates to the Government House courtyard stood open. She knew from store gossip that the americano military jail was somewhere in there, in the old Mexican calabozo. She swallowed, lifted her chin, and tightened her fingers around the little bundle under her rebozo.

The snow was icy and uncomfortable, but it also kept almost everyone indoors. Jessie peered through the gates into the passageway created by the buildings on either side. A dappled gray horse attached to a wagon stood at the far end, gazing at her mournfully. Then a male voice, also mournful but closer, said, "May I help you, señorita?"

A pimply faced young man with straw-colored hair, a scrawny mustache, and a disheveled uniform rose from a narrow adobe seat built into the left-hand wall. A door at the near end of the bench opened into a hallway in the building beyond. She glimpsed the pale face of a prisoner behind stout wooden bars, then turned to the guard and smiled brightly. "¡Buenos días!" she said.

He smiled back at her. "Buenos días yourself." Then he paused, his face twisted in concentration. "Cómo puedo—" He chewed on his mustache. "Service," he muttered. Then he brightened. "Utilidad." He looked into her face "¿Cómo puedo utilidad?" he asked slowly.

She tried not to smile. After all, he was making an effort. But continuing in Spanish would be too painful. "I bring necessities for Don Agustín," she said in English.

His face brightened. "By golly, you're an American!"

She nodded and smiled. "Yes. And I bring necessities for Don Agustín."

"I'll take them to him for you."

She shook her head and kept smiling, throwing entreaty into her gaze. "No, please. I need to give them to him myself."

He frowned slightly and she shrugged. "It's only a few twists of tobacco. It's in payment for a debt, so it's important that I give them to him myself. I need him to sign a receipt."

The soldier grinned. "I've done heard about his gambling debts, but I thought he only owed them."

She looked down, trying to look embarrassed. "Some of us have found ourselves in debt to him, instead." Then she flashed an alarmed look into his face. "Not me, of course. But others who are dear to me and would prefer to remain nameless."

"And you must give it to him yourself in order to keep their secret."

"You are very intelligent, sergeant."

He blushed, the spots on his face turning dark red. "I'm a mere private, miss." Then he sobered. "However, I will need to inspect the goods."

She lifted the edge of her rebozo to reveal the bundled tobacco, then untied the strings enough to pull out a twist of tobacco. "Please, take a bit. I'm sure Don Agustín won't object."

The yellow-haired guard pulled out a horn-handled knife and sawed off a small piece. "It smells mighty nice." He returned the remainder of the twist to Jessie, tucked his portion into a pocket, glanced from one end of the little tunnel to the other, then waved her toward the door. "He's at the far left on the end. The cell with the window. Don't take too long, now."

She smiled, dipped him a curtsy, and stepped through the door, then stopped abruptly and blinked at the lack of light. The pale-faced man she'd seen earlier looked at her blankly, then disappeared from the window. He was replaced by a prisoner with tousled red hair, a blanket around his shoulders, and a belligerent expression. Jessie moved quickly left, toward what appeared to be an open door. Light flickered in the space beyond, as if from a candle.

Jessie turned her head away politely as she knocked on the battered doorjamb. There was a rustling sound, the crackle of folding paper, and then Agustín Durán was there, holding a candle shoulder high and peering quizzically at her. He didn't look nearly as well-groomed or self-content as he'd been in Doña Tules' gambling salon, but he smiled politely, stepped back, and waved a welcoming hand.

"Ah, señorita," he said. "Welcome to my humble abode." Then he looked at her more closely and said in English, "I think I do not have the pleasure of having already made your acquaintance, señorita, though I believe you may be the pretty daughter of Señor Milbank."

She smiled in spite of her anxiety. "Yes, I am Hubert Milbank's daughter. My name is Jessie. I don't believe we have ever formally met." She paused, then held out the bundle of tobacco. "I brought you a gift."

"You are very kind." He took it and sniffed the cloth appreciatively, then looked at her quizzically. "And this is from you, not tu padre?"

She nodded, not quite knowing how to proceed. He stepped back, placed his candlestick on the table, and waved a hand at the only chair in the room. "Please, seat yourself."

She did so, and Don Agustín perched on the edge of the bed, the package of tobacco beside him. He looked down at it, then at her. "I am old enough to be your father." He smiled mischievously. "Perhaps even your grandfather. Therefore, I suspect this is not a visita social. Have you come in reference to a debt? I must confess I have no funds readily available. Colonel Price has done his best to keep me in the most possible of reduced circumstances."

He gestured at the table, which contained the candle, two newspapers, and a plate of bread and cheese. "These are all gifts from mis amigos." He nodded toward the tobacco. "And now I have the luxury of smoking, as well. It was most kind of you. I have missed mis cigarillos."

She smiled at him. "I thought you might. I have seen you once or twice and on each occasion you were smoking. In fact, the first time I saw you, you were seated at Señora Barceló's monte table—"

He nodded. "Sí, I recall that event. I had lost yet again, and stopped to speak to the young Cabeza de Baca on my way out of the room. You were standing nearby." He gave her a quizzical look. "And tu padre approves your frequenting of such places?"

Her face tightened and he smiled apologetically. "Forgive me, señorita. It is no business of mine where you go or what your father thinks of your choices." Then he straightened. "But I return to the question of why you have honored me with a visit." He ran a hand through his hair. "I would be flattered beyond measure to believe you sought my company for my good looks or mi conversación vívida, and I can think of no legitimate request I can make of you or tu padre. So—" He spread his hands and smiled at her quizzically.

She looked away. "It's about Raúl." She looked into his face, steeling herself. "About his death."

"This is the young Cabeza de Baca? The one you spoke to that day? The one who was killed in November?"

She nodded. "The authorities found a note on his body. A promissory note for a debt to you."

He put a hand on his chest. "To me? I wish it were so. I am in need of funds." Then his expression sobered, became slightly bitter. "The young man in question was making money, not losing it. His future mother-in-law saw to that."

"So there was no reason for him to have borrowed money?"

"Certainly not from me. I had none to lend." He smiled wryly. "Doña Tules also saw to that."

Jessie frowned, hesitating, then plunged in. "Do you know of any reason someone might want to kill him?"

His eyes narrowed. "Who sent you?"

"No one sent me. I came on my own."

His eyes narrowed further.

"I tried to get permission from Colonel Price, but he wouldn't speak to me."

Durán's lips twitched and he nodded, but his eyes didn't blink. "¿And tu padre?"

She shook her head.

"He doesn't know you are here? Or the Lieutenant Milbank? That americano dragoon who has been courting Juanita Sena?"

She glanced at him in surprise. He spread his hands. "It is a small town, this Santa Fe." He leaned toward her slightly. "Did one of them send you?"

She felt a tremor of something close to fear, then reminded herself that the pockmarked guard was within call. "No one knows I am here."

He leaned back, his fingertips just touching the bundle of tobacco. "And this is why you came? To ask me this question about the asesinato of Cabeza de Baca?"

She nodded wordlessly. He studied her. "Why do you think I would know something of this event?"

"Because of the note."

"As I already said, if he owed funds, it was not to me."

"His prometida—"

"His promised one? The little Guadalupe Barceló? What of her?"

"She says he was part of the conspiracy."

"And if he was?"

"We thought—"

His face smoothed then, became a clean slate upon which nothing was written. "I know nothing of such things."

She stared at him, remembering the scene on the palacio portal, when Donaciano Vigil confronted him. He stared back. "What was it you thought?"

She looked away. "Guadalupe wanted him to go to her mother and ask her advice."

"About whether he should report la conspiración to los americanos?"

When Jessie nodded, his tone hardened. "And that one of los insurrectos learned Cabeza de Baca intended to betray them and so killed him before he could speak?" He leaned toward her. "As I already mentioned, I know nothing of such things. However, if the young man did intend to inform on the actions planned for Christmas Eve, to turn against his compañeros patriotas, if that is what happened, then his death was well deserved."

Then he pulled back, frowning, the intensity dropping from his face. "But why do you come to me with this question? Doña Tules could have told you el pagaré was not mine. She knows my handwriting well enough." He narrowed his eyes at her, then broke into a broad smile. "You think it was I who killed him!"

"No, I—"

His lips flattened. "Because of the note? Why would I kill a man who owed me money? If he refused to pay, I would simply go to Doña Tules, and that would be the end of his engagement to the sweet little Guadalupe. He would not take such a risk." He studied Jessie's face. She dropped her gaze. He chuckled mirthlessly. "You think I was of los insurrectos, learned he planned to betray them, and took action."

She glanced at him, then away again.

"After all, no mexicano is to be trusted," he said drily. "Either we are too hotly tempered because of our pure Spanish heritage, or we are of the mongrel race, with untrustworthy native blood in our veins. In any case, we greasers are quick with a knife, especialmente in dark alleys."

She looked up, eyes blazing.

He spread his hands, palms up. "It is a common enough perception of us among los americanos."

"I do not hold to such thinking! Just ask Juanita Sena!"

"And I was quick to ask questions of los americanos the morning after young Cabeza de Baca died." He touched the packet of tobacco and looked at her from the corner of his eyes. "Because I was concerned for a friend and knew they would do nothing in particular about his death. They would make a quick judgement based on little evidencia and be satisfied that another greaser had been removed from their path."

Jessie looked at him. What could she say? Whether or not Don Agustín was telling the truth about his own motivation, the military's response to Raúl's death did seem to reflect the attitude he had just described.

He sighed and shook his head. "You have not pursued any further ideas about how this death may have come about?"

She made a helpless gesture. "I don't know where else to look."

He nodded and leaned back on the bed, staring at the diagonal peeled poles that formed the ceiling. Outside the window, an American soldier called to a friend. Jessie swallowed against the lump in her throat.

Then Durán blinked, pushed himself upright, and placed his hands on his thighs. "I fear I have no advice to give you in this matter. However, I do know that once a blow is struck, not even God can take it away. Life must go on." He rose to his feet. "Please accept my sincere thanks for both the gift and the visit, señorita. I regret that I can be of no use to you in your quest."

Jessie was suddenly overcome with weariness. She forced herself to nod politely, rise, thank Don Agustín for his time, and go out. The guard stepped forward eagerly, but she barely acknowledged him as she moved through the dark passage to the plaza.

She crossed to the palacio portal and touched the thick post again, leaning into it this time, her head bowed. She had learned nothing. Except to confirm there was no debt, at least to Durán.

And that she was a fool. If the man had killed Raúl, he was not going to tell her so. What had she been thinking? Did she herself harbor an unacknowledged assumption about the trustworthiness of these people who had been so universally kind to her?

She jerked away from the pole. She had told Durán that Guadalupe knew about Raúl's involvement with the conspiracy, had wanted him to inform on them. Would that put the girl in danger? Surely not. Jessie moved blindly across the plaza toward home. The snow was heavier now, but she did nothing to protect herself from it.

She didn't tell her father she'd been to the jail, but Santa Fe was a small city. At noon the next day, he met her in the entrance to the kitchen, his face tight with anger. "I asked you not to visit Durán."

She looked away.

"Jessie!"

"I should have listened to you," she said wearily. "There was no debt. And he said that if Raúl did plan to betray the conspiracy and someone found out and killed him, then he got what he deserved."

Her father blew out a breath of frustration. "I asked you not to go see him."

"And I should have listened to you. I learned nothing. Well, except that it seems unlikely Don Agustín would kill anyone. He's more likely to use words as a weapon than a knife."

He jerked away from her. "You thought he was Raúl's killer? And you still went to see him?"

Jessie pulled up defensively, then let out a breath of defeat. "I'm sorry, Papa. I should have listened to you and done as you said."

His face softened. "Apology accepted. However, in future please remember that I am not only your father, but I have seen more of the world. I know your mother taught you to protect others, to think of them before yourself, but there are limits." He touched her cheek. "And you are now all I have, Jessie girl."

She leaned into him, her head on his shoulder as his arms went around her. "Oh Papa, I am truly sorry."

CHAPTER 23: Thursday, January 14, 1847

It was another week before Jessie spoke to Juanita. She'd been to la parroquia to pray and was returning home along the south edge of the plaza when she saw the other girl entering it from the direction of the Sena casa, alone for a change. Jessie changed course and headed to the flagpole to wait for her.

It had snowed the night before and the resulting melt made the ground damp and a little slick. Juanita's head was down, watching her feet, but her slumped shoulders under the blue-and-white rebozo indicated that the weather wasn't her only concern. She was so preoccupied she didn't notice Jessie until the American girl said, "¡Buenos días, mi amiga!"

Juanita looked up. "Oh, Jessie. I was on my way to you."

"Are you all right?"

"As good as it is possible to be when one's sweetheart has left them."

"Left you?"

"Narciso has gone to Taos with Governor Bent. He did not need to do so. His father will be en la ciudad next week. Cisco could have waited and then returned home with him." Juanita shook her head and looked away. "He was in a great hurry to lay eyes on his mother. As if she occupies a place more important in his heart than I." She looked at Jessie, hazel eyes anxious. "It is an ill omen."

"Perhaps he wanted to tell her about you."

Juanita shrugged. "Perhaps. However, su padre will undoubtedly leave Taos before the arrival there of the group of el Gobernador, so he cannot speak to him until after Judge Beaubien returns home." She sighed heavily.

"If Governor Bent's party left here about the same time Judge Beaubien left Taos, they may meet on the road."

Juanita's eyes brightened. "Perhaps they will join camps for the night at Las Trampas or Santa Cruz de la Cañada or Los Luceros. Cisco could speak with him then."

"And then he can go on to Taos to speak to his mother."

"Sí, it is posible." She smiled at Jessie. "Gracias mi amiga." Then she frowned again. "I hope that is what happens and they do not encounter insurrectos of some sort. Governor Bent was in a great hurry and did not wish to be encumbered by a large number of compañeros. He took no soldiers with him."

Jessie chuckled. "You are determined to worry, aren't you?" She put a hand on Juanita's arm. "Charles Bent has lived in New Mexico many years and is married to a Taos woman. He knows the people here well. I'm sure he has a good sense of when additional men are needed and when it's safe to dispense with their services."

"I am sure you are correct and I worry foolishly." Juanita shivered. "I have felt so anxious all the morning." She looked away. "And I miss him."

"When did they leave?"

"At sunrise."

Jessie suppressed a smile. So much for taking the courtship slowly. "You need some exercise," she declared. "Let's go see if Guadalupe is available for a walk along the river." It would be a good way of allaying her own worry about the fourteen-year-old's safety, but she couldn't tell Juanita that. Her friend had enough on her mind.

Juanita brightened. "I was coming to see you and suggest a walk. Inviting Guadalupe is an excellent idea." Then she sobered. "She will serve to remind me that there are other people with sorrows much greater than my own."

"I didn't suggest Guadalupe for that reason, but it is true enough." Jessie took Juanita's arm. "Let's go find her."

They turned toward the northwest side of the square. "But that is enough about me," Juanita said. "I want to think of something other than Cisco." She glanced sideways at her friend. "Have you received a visit from your lieutenant recently?"

Jessie twitched her rebozo closer to her head. "He is not my lieutenant."

Juanita grinned, but Jessie ignored her. She would have called the man a thoughtless, presumptuous bigot a week ago. But now, after her interaction with Agustín Durán, the words felt too close to home.

They reached the palacio and swung left. The guard at the end of the courtyard passage nodded to Jessie as they went by. Jessie nodded in response and his shoulders straightened, his head turning to follow them toward the street to the Barceló casa.

Juanita raised an eyebrow. "Is this un hombre nuevo who has caught your interest? I must say he is not as tall or good looking as Lieutenant Milbank."

Jessie smoothed her rebozo over her chest. "I met him when I went to see Señor Durán."

Juanita stopped abruptly. "You paid a visit to Don Agustín? In el calabozo?"

"I wanted to question him about Raúl's death."

Juanita let out a breath. "And what did he say?"

The guard had left the passage and was coming toward them. Jessie took Juanita's arm. "Let's find Guadalupe and then I can tell you both at the same time." She shook her head at her friend's hopeful look. "I didn't learn anything of much use."

CHAPTER 24. Thursday, January 21, 1847

Jessie was still mulling over her conversation with Don Agustín a week later as she stood on a small stool behind the store counter and stacked cans of peaches onto the shelves. Some of her self-recrimination had died down and she was once again wondering who had killed both Vidal and Raúl. "Will we ever know?" she muttered as she positioned one tin on top of another.

Her father looked up from the other end of the counter, where he was carefully folding lengths of brightly colored cotton. "Pardon?"

"Nothing of importance."

He raised an eyebrow at her. "I know the weather has been miserable, but you've seemed out of sorts for the last month or so." He tilted his head at her. "Would you like to tell me about it?"

He wasn't going to want to hear what she had to say. That Raúl's murder still tortured her. That the dreams about her mother's death had returned. She placed another can on the shelf, starting a new row. He watched her. She sighed, turned toward him, and opened her mouth.

Then the street door opened and Dick Green rushed in, his eyes wild. "They've done killed him!"

Jessie's breath caught. The lieutenant?

Her father dropped the red-and-white cotton in his hands. "Dick? Who's been killed?"

The Bent slave reached the counter and hung onto it as he gasped for breath and shook his head.

Jessie stepped down from her stool. "Mr. Green? What is it?"

"News from Taos. Just now." He looked from her to her father. "They've all been killed."

A fist clenched her stomach. "They?"

"The Americans in Taos." His face twisted. "A rabble broke into Guv Bent's house and scalped—" He gulped, shook his head as if he couldn't believe what he was about to say, and went on. "They killed him in front of his wife and her sister and the young ones. Shot him with an arrow and then cut off—" He shook his head again and turned to Jessie's father. "Sheriff's dead, too. Murdered in his own jail. I reckon that's what started the rampage." He took a deep breath and looked at Jessie, his face grim. "And the Sena girl's young man, that Beaubien boy. They got him, too."

Jessie felt the room tilt. She reached for the counter, fingers digging into the worn wood. "Narciso?"

As Green nodded, her father asked, "Who did all this?"

"Rebels. More of those insurrectos who were plotting in December. And men from Taos Pueblo with them."

"Are you sure about this? It's not just a rumor?"

Green shook his head. "One man escaped with the news, but just barely. He was almost scalped himself. I was at the palacio when he arrived." He turned to Jessie. "I feel so bad about the Beaubien boy. He was so young."

Nausea bit Jessie's throat as she nodded agreement. Then she shuddered. "Juanita," she said. "Oh, poor Juanita." She looked at her father. "I must go to her."

He had barely nodded before she was across the room and grabbing her rebozo from its peg. She ran out the door and down the street, flinging the long shawl over her head and shoulders as she went. The plaza was filled with people, mostly soldiers. Their voices were shrill as they called to each other and barked orders. Horse teams strained to pull cannon into position at each corner of the square.

She skirted around the men and animals in the northeast section and hurried up the street. The Sena big gate and the little sliding window in its center were both shut tight. Jessie slammed the wood with the base of her palm over and over until a frightened voice called, "¿Quién es?" and the porthole opened. Juanita looked out.

"Jessie! In only a rebozo! What are you doing here?"

"You haven't heard."

Juanita stepped back, eyes suddenly huge, freckles dark against her pale skin. "What is it?" she said again.

Perhaps it wasn't true. For a brief moment Jessie had a wild hope that it was all a horrible rumor. But then Juanita's uncle appeared on the other side of the courtyard, his face grim. He headed their way.

Juanita saw Jessie's eyes shift toward him and turned.

"There's been some kind of uprising in Taos," Jessie said to the back of her head. "Killings."

Juanita looked at her, then her uncle, then back to Jessie. Her hand went to her mouth. "Cisco," she whispered. As Jessie nodded, Juanita swayed and dropped to the ground.

Later, when Jessie had slipped through the gate, the two girls huddled on the adobe seat built into the wall beside the kitchen fire. Juanita's aunt had administered smelling salts, and her uncle had broken out the El Paso brandy, and Juanita's tears and shivering had finally stopped.

She rested her head on Jessie's shoulder and stared at the little mica-covered window on the other side of the room. Its thick white surface glowed as if under water. "The sun has come out," she said dully. "Even after this. First Raúl and now Cisco." She began to shiver again and Jessie pulled her closer.

The light behind the window slowly dimmed and was the dull gray of dusk when Dick Green arrived with Jessie's winter cloak. "Your father thought you might want something a mite warmer than your rebozo for going home," he said. "I've come to escort you, if you're willing."

She nodded dully, submitted to being wrapped up, kissed Juanita's cheek, and allowed the Bent slave to lead her out of the compound.

In the plaza, just past the cannon that now blocked the northeast outlet, they met Henry Fitzgerald on his roan mare. The dragoon greeted Jessie with a broad smile. "Revolt!" he said. "Finally, we will see battle!" He patted the dispatch bags behind his saddle. "I go to Albuquerque with the orders to march. At last!" Then his smile dropped. "That is, if I'm not left in Santa Fe to guard against the possibility of attack here." He gave her a flirtatious look. "If that happens, I'll at least have the pleasure of your proximity."

Jessie blinked, trying to form a response, but he didn't seem to expect one. He touched a finger to his hat in a semisalute. "And now I'm off. I hope to see you soon. Glory awaits!"

He turned the horse and trotted off, the mare transitioning into a gallop as it left the plaza.

Dick Green pushed back his hat and shook his head. "That there is one right foolish young man. To think glory comes in moments of blood."

"He wants to avenge his brother," Jessie said dully. "It's why he came to New Mexico." She pulled her cloak closer. So much death. "His brother Archibald was one of the Texan prisoners in 1841. The men Armijo captured and sent south."

Green nodded. "I know who they are. And I reckon what they went through was a right painful thing. I can see how he'd want some justice. Me, I'd like to avenge Guv Bent. But revenge isn't the same as glory, and both carry a price."

A group of soldiers moved toward them, heading to the palacio. Green and Jessie stepped out of their way, careful to avoid the steaming evidence Fitzgerald's horse had left behind. The sky was darkening toward night and clouding over as well, a thick pale gray that threatened snow.

"I reckon we'd better get you home before that storm comes barreling in," Green said. Jessie nodded and gratefully tucked her hand into the crook of his arm.

CHAPTER 25: Friday, January 22, 1847

As soon as the Milbank store opened the next morning, men crowded in to buy weapons, stock up on ammunition, and swap news about what was now being called "the revolt." If the rumors were true, it had spread. Cattle had been run off in the Cimarron area east of Taos, and half a dozen American merchants and traders had been killed farther south, outside Mora.

"And there's fightin' north of Taos at Arroyo Hondo," a voice said from the far end of the counter. "Up at Turley's gristmill and distillery. Simeon was havin' a regular confab with some old friends of his, but now they'll be fendin' off rebels 'stead of talkin'. I hear tell none of the locals are comin' to his rescue."

"If anyone can make it out, Turley can," a voice said from the direction of the stove.

"I wouldn't count Turley's chickens just yet. These savages are out of control."

"So it's the injuns?" someone else asked.

"Naw, it's the greasers, too. They've all gone crazy. Did you hear about Mora?"

"I heard. And a couple of trappers on the way back from Bent's Fort were bushwhacked up near Red River. Shot in the back, both of 'em."

"You don't say. What happened?"

Jessie moved away from the counter, finding goods to rearrange near the door to the kitchen, so she could assist her father without hearing the mixture of ghoulishness, anger, and fear in the voices around her.

Then they all left at once. Silence fell.

Jessie's father stood behind the counter, his hands flat on the scarred wood, staring at his knuckles. The window shutters were wide open, though the day was cold. Jessie knotted her rebozo around her shoulders, found the broom, and began sweeping the floor. The customers had left an unusual amount of grit and other debris behind them.

The sound of men's voices drifted from the plaza, punctuated by occasional shouts. Then suddenly, there was a triumphant roar. Jessie's father looked up. "I expect that's Saint Vrain's group gathering itself."

Jessie swept her little pile of dirt closer to the door. "Saint Vrain?"

He moved around the counter and peered out the window on the left. "The man who bought that last rifle said Ceran was forming a group to go north to help the Army punish the rebels. After all, Bent was his business partner." He craned his neck, trying to see around the building on the corner and into the plaza. "They're calling themselves the Avengers."

She opened the door and swept the dirt into the street. Avengers. It sounded like something Henry Fitzgerald would come up with. Not justice. Revenge. Her stomach was a dull knot of pain.

Her father moved toward the pegs beside the door and reached for his coat and hat. "I might as well go take a look."

He glanced around the room. "I expect we won't be getting any more customers for a while now."

Jessie frowned. If anyone did come in, she certainly didn't want to deal with them. "I think I'll go with you."

When they got to the plaza, they found most of the city there, watching the Avengers organize themselves. Ceran Saint Vrain sat on a big chestnut stallion in front of the palacio, speaking to a motley square of men who'd arranged themselves beside the flagpole. There were about seventy in all, each with a gun on his shoulder. Mountain men in shaggy fur coats and bedraggled beards, clerks in fine wool and stovepipe hats, even a few Mexicans.

And men with darker skin. Dick Green stood firmly in the middle of the pack, next to a broad-shouldered man with a long craggy brown face and a curly, neatly trimmed black beard.

Saint Vrain paused. Wind whipped the flag, snapping it impatiently. The stallion moved restlessly as Saint Vrain raised his hand. "Consider yourself enrolled in the United States Army!" he bellowed.

A cheer went up from the men. Dick Green waved his battered hat. Jessie turned to her father. "I thought people of color couldn't join the American military."

"At this point, I suspect Colonel Price will take anyone who can shoot," he said absently. Jessie studied him. He looked the way he had in the store. Preoccupied. Unhappy. "What is it?"

He shrugged, still not looking at her. "I expect I'd be joining them if I could."

Jessie stared at him. This was the man who didn't want to get involved in anything. Yesterday's news had affected him more than she'd realized. "Then you should."

He shook his head, eyes still on the men in the square. They turned clumsily right, then left, following Saint Vrain's commands. "I won't leave you alone."

"I wouldn't be alone. Manuelita would be with me. And I know how to shoot."

He turned toward her, eyes glinting in amusement. "You are so much like your mother." Then he sobered. "But I will not leave you like I did her."

"Papa—"

"The rebellion isn't only in Taos."

"I know. I've heard the news. Taos, Red River, Mora." She looked away, feeling the weight of all the death, but her father didn't seem to notice.

"This outbreak isn't just a few people angry with the governor and taking it out on the sheriff and whoever else happened by," he said. "This was planned, just like the conspiracy that was uncovered in December. Only this time no one reported it." His eyebrows tightened. "And it's likely to spread. Several people told me this morning that a call to arms is circulating among the villages. A declaration of war with los americanos. Since Santa Fe is the capital, I expect the next step will be to seize it."

Jessie glanced involuntarily toward the northwest corner of the plaza and the street to Guadalupe's house. Her father's gaze had returned to the men in the square, marching more or less neatly now. "It started in Taos, so I expect they'll be coming south from there," he said. "Gathering villagers as they come. With all the snow in the mountains, they'll have to stick to the roads. If they do, Colonel Price and Saint Vrain's Avengers can stop them well before they get here."

He looked around the square, at the people watching the Americans in its center, and lowered his voice. "However, there's always the chance they'll swing east to Mora and Las Vegas and come in through Apache Pass."

Jessie frowned. "There are American troops stationed out that way," she said. "The grazing companies around Las Vegas will block anyone trying to approach from that direction."

Her stomach tightened. Grazing companies. But Lieutenant Milbank was stationed south toward Galisteo, not Las Vegas. She took a breath and turned back to her father. "If you want to sign up with the Avengers, I think you should do so. I will be perfectly fine. Besides, I heard someone complaining this morning that the army teamsters have been ordered to stay behind. I'm sure they all know how to use weapons."

Her father's face set. "I did that once, went off adventuring. And it cost me more than dearly. I can't lose you, as well."

"I could go with you."

He turned to her, his mouth open in surprise. She stared back at him, almost as equally shocked. Where had that suggestion come from?

But it felt right. She could go, could help with all the camp things that needed to be done. There would be men in need of nursing. She could do that. And she found that she wanted to go. Not only because it would free him to do so, but for herself. When her mother was killed, she'd stood helplessly by. Then Vidal and Raúl died, and still she did nothing. She needed to do something, anything, to conquer this sense of pervasive inadequacy.

She opened her mouth to try to explain, but then, on the other side of the square, Saint Vrain gave a shout. The Avengers roared back at him, then broke apart, men streaming in every direction. The tall one next to Dick Green clapped him on the shoulder and loped off toward the nearest drinking house. Green stayed where he was, turning slowly, studying the plaza. When his gaze reached Jessie's, she waved at him.

He maneuvered toward her, his face grim and tired, and she reached to greet him properly. He patted her hand and turned to her father. "I hope you have enough ammunition to keep us all well supplied."

"I plan to do my best," the merchant responded. "I take it you've joined the Avengers."

"Yes sir, I sure did. I plan to get some justice for Guv Bent."

Jessie's forehead furrowed in confusion. "But you—" She stopped, not knowing how to say it.

Green's lips twitched. "Were his slave." He glanced around the square. "I reckon Charlotte and me belong to one of his brothers now. Or Don Ceran, depending on what the will says."

Jessie frowned, but Green shook his head at her. "I may be a slave, but I'm a man first. And Guv Bent was always good to me and mine, even if he did hold papers on us. Whatever his faults, what was done to him was wrong and it should be put right. His brothers are too far away to do it, so I aim to try as best I can." He hefted his rifle and turned to her father. "I reckon I'll need more ammunition for this thing,

Don Hubert, if you're willing to put it on the Bent account." Humor flashed in his eyes. "I tried to get into your place this morning, but you were a mite busy. I hope you have some left."

The other man nodded. "I expect we can find some for you, even if I have to dig into my personal stores." He looked across the square toward Government House and his jaw hardened. "But there won't be a charge. Consider it my small contribution to the cause."

They turned toward the store and Jessie followed, knowing she'd lost her chance, that both she and her father would stay in Santa Fe. She wasn't sure if she was relieved or saddened by that fact. She felt so helpless, so unable to do anything. So confused and full of energy at the same time. There were so many things in her life that she couldn't knit together, couldn't bring into a clear whole. She pulled her rebozo closer and tried not to think about it.

The men of Santa Fe had found themselves short on tobacco as well as ammunition. Jessie was replenishing the pile of twists at the end of the counter late that afternoon and debating whether it was dark enough to light the lamps when the street door opened. Lieutenant Milbank came in, taking off his hat. His blond hair was longer now, touching the collar of his coat, but it still gleamed in the gathering dusk.

Jessie's hands stilled. She looked down at the tobacco in her hands and breathed in the rich smell, concentrating herself.

"Good afternoon," he said.

She placed the twist on the little pile, smoothed her skirt, and looked up. "Good afternoon." At least her voice was steady. "My father—"

He moved toward her. "I hoped to speak to you alone." Even in the half dark, she could see his face redden. "That is, I had hoped we could have a conversation." He looked around the room.

"He will return shortly," she said. "Until he does, I must mind the store."

The lieutenant glanced at the outer door as if willing it to remain closed, then turned to her, his face grave. "My company will be marching north with Colonel Price. I didn't want to leave Santa Fe with any sense of disagreement between us."

He paused, studying her, but she could think of nothing to say. She touched the tobacco lightly, then smoothed her skirt again.

The lieutenant turned away. He moved toward the little stove. "I came to town as soon as word of the events in Taos reached Galisteo. I suppose it wasn't necessary. All sorts of men are flocking to join Ceran Saint Vrain." He shook his head at the chimney, a slight frown marring his face. "I wish the colonel didn't find their services necessary. Revenge and vengeance aren't useful emotions on the battlefield. Yes, men have been killed and justice should be administered in consequence. But revenge is a dangerous sentiment."

"Yes," Jessie said quietly.

He swung toward her. "Battle is also dangerous. The outcome is always uncertain." He looked down at his hat and ran a finger around its brim. "I've been expecting an outbreak. In the area around Galisteo, I and my men have encountered numerous New Mexicans who are polite, but not welcoming." He moved toward her and bent slightly, as if to peer into her face. "That's what I was referring to when I said what I did that day on the plaza."

She looked down at her hands, still on her skirt, and nodded. "Yes, I realize that now." She forced herself to meet his eyes. "It was unfair of me to be so upset with you. I know not everyone here was delighted when the army arrived."

His expression lightened, then became grave again. "I had hoped the bad feelings would fade in time. That it would not come to outright rebellion and the need for violent suppression. Fighting doesn't tend to accomplish a great deal, if anything."

Her lips twitched. "You don't sound much like a soldier. A professional one, I mean."

He took a step toward her, his free hand out, then stopped. It dropped to his side. "Your friendship means a great deal to me. I didn't want to leave without speaking to you. Without apologizing. Whatever I meant, my words were badly put and offensive."

Her fingers smoothed her skirt as she looked up at him.

He took another step forward. "Will you accept my apology?"

She nodded wordlessly. She could think of nothing to say. After a long moment, the lieutenant made a small helpless gesture, then said quietly, "I hope we meet again," and went out.

Jessie put a hand on the counter, just to feel the wood under her palm. She stared at the gloom beyond the windows, waiting to know what she felt, to understand it.

She was still there when her father came in the street door. "Standing in the dark?" he teased. "Are you hoping everyone will think we've closed up for the day?" When she didn't answer, he took the lamp from its shelf and carried it to the stove. "I saw Lieutenant Milbank in the plaza just now," he said as he reached for a sliver of wood to use as a taper. The stove door creaked open. "He said he's been ordered north with Colonel Price."

Jessie nodded without speaking and hurried out of the room.

CHAPTER 26: Saturday, January 23, 1847

Jessie was in the kitchen Saturday morning, peeling potatoes for Manuelita and thinking about Lieutenant Milbank, when Juanita arrived. "They have marched," she said as she removed her rebozo. "I watched them out of la plaza." She shook her head. "I wish I could go with them. I feel so helpless."

Manuelita moved away from her soup pot, picked up a bundle of carrots and a horn-handled knife, and handed them to her.

Jessie chuckled in spite of her preoccupation. "Manuelita holds the same philosophy my mother did. Activity keeps one sane."

Juanita smiled. "Mi tía is of the same mind. Her activity is to clean la casa."

"My mother's was baking." Jessie looked at her friend. "By 'they' I assume you mean the colonel and the men going north with him."

Juanita nodded and selected a carrot. "Saint Vrain's Avengers is a grupo mixto, but they still look very dashing on their horses. And fierce." She stared down at the vegetable in her hand. "I hope they succeed in bringing los hombres who did this to justice." Her shoulders hunched. "It still seems absolutamente imposible."

Manuelita pointed her wooden spoon at the carrot. "Peel and cut."

The girls exchanged a smile and Juanita turned to her task. They were almost through both piles of vegetables when Jessie's father came in. He moved to the fire, sniffed appreciatively at the pot of soup, then turned toward the table, his hands behind his back. "I just had a visit from the army sutler," he said. "He had a proposition for me."

Jessie looked up. "A proposition?"

"Colonel Price's expedition was arranged so hastily that the sutler had little time to acquire supplies, and he doubts what he has will be sufficient. He's asked me to go along with a wagonload to supplement his goods. Colonel Price is expected to order up the dragoons in Albuquerque as well, and they're unlikely to bring supplies with them."

Jessie put her knife on the table. "I want to go with you. Please."

He shook his head.

"I will be just as safe with you as I would be here," she said. "Maybe safer. You said yourself that the rebels could attack Santa Fe." She heard Juanita's breath hitch at this and thought of Guadalupe, but kept her eyes on her father. "I want to be useful. I can help with the merchandise and the mules. Please let me go, Papa."

"Then Manuelita would be alone."

The cook gave him a sharp look and turned back to her soup.

"She can go with us." Jessie turned to her. "It would be safer than being here by yourself."

Manuelita's spoon stopped moving. She studied the two of them, her face inscrutable as always. But then she nodded. "I go."

Juanita leaned forward. "Don Hubert, would it be possible for me to accompany you?"

He shook his head, his face troubled. "I could not agree to such a thing without explicit agreement from your uncle and aunt. Even then, I would be concerned that your parents might object. Even if the rebels do reach Santa Fe, I expect you would be safer in your uncle's casa than in a supply caravan behind Colonel Price and his men."

Juanita's face fell. She nodded politely and looked away. He turned to the others. "I will need time to collect the necessary goods and pack the wagon. Can you be ready to leave Monday morning?" When Jessie and Manuelita nodded, he headed for the door. "I expect I'd best bestir myself."

He'd only been gone a few minutes when Juanita pushed away from the table. "I must return home," she said. "Mi tía will be wanting me to assist with the cleaning." She bent to give Jessie a goodbye hug, flung her rebozo over her head, and slipped out.

Jessie's eyes followed her. "I wish it was possible for her to go with us."

"Dinner now, then bread," Manuelita said.

Jessie grinned and went back to work. They were stoking the fire in the horno, the courtyard adobe oven, two hours later when Juanita returned. She carried a note from her aunt which politely inquired whether Señor Milbank could find it within his power to extend his protection to her niece on his journey north, thus enabling Juanita to visit and provide assistance to the Beaubien family in their time of grief. The note was accompanied by a formal document from Juanita's uncle which authorized Don Hubert to act as the girl's protector during the journey.

"I would consider it a great kindness if you will agree, Don Hubert," Juanita said, her hazel eyes wide with supplication.

He looked up from rereading the second document. "Your uncle has done me a great honor." Then he frowned. "I only hope your father will approve of his decision. And that I can live up to the responsibility he has vested in me."

"More wood," Manuelita said.

Jessie turned toward the woodpile. Behind her, Juanita asked hesitantly, "Am I to understand that you agree, Don Hubert?"

As Jessie gathered up an armful of split piñon pine, her father chuckled, looked from her to Juanita, and carefully folded the two pieces of paper together. "I expect you went to a good deal of effort to gain your aunt and uncle's permission. How can I possibly deny you?"

"¡Gracias, Don Hubert!" Juanita said as Jessie beamed at him. She placed the wood beside the horno and Manuelita began inserting it into the oven. Jessie moved to Juanita, who gave her a sideways hug. "I go with you!" she crowed.

Jessie's father shook his head at them. "This is not a pleasure trip. It's the middle of winter, and we will be following military troops to what may very well become a series of battlefields. We are carrying mercantile goods, so there won't be much room in the wagon. You will need to carry everything you need in a single knapsack." Then he frowned at Jessie. "In addition, I expect you both to do as you are told. No haring off on campaigns to save the world or anyone else."

"Yes, Papa," she said meekly.

"I mean it, Jessie. You will do as I say and stay close to Manuelita. Consider her your chaperone."

The cook straightened from the horno. "If you don't mind," he told her apologetically. "Try to keep them from doing anything foolish."

Jessie could have sworn the cook smiled as she turned to add more fuel to the fire. But Juanita was kissing her father's cheek and making his face redden. Jessie laughed in delight as Juanita said, "¡Gracias, Don Hubert!" yet again.

CHAPTER 27: Wednesday, January 27, 1847

The first two days out of Santa Fe were relatively comfortable, but by Wednesday, Jessie had begun to feel the cold. Even her heavy wool cloak and the blue-and-white rebozo couldn't counteract it. The Milbank wagon was at the end of the sutler's train, and the slushy road grew worse as it turned up the Santa Cruz river east toward the town of Santa Cruz de la Cañada. The track's well-churned ruts looked as miserable as the low snow-splotched hills which huddled along the edges of the valley under menacing gray clouds.

Jessie shivered, tugged on the cuffs of her buckskin gloves, and flicked the reins at the mules' broad brown backs. "I don't remember this trip taking so long when we went to Taos last spring," she said.

Her father, riding beside the wagon on Saturn, grinned. "I expect that may be because on this trip we have to keep pace with everyone else."

"Also, it was sunny. And green in the valleys."

He chuckled. "Well yes. These hills are made of sand and any water they get drains away pretty quickly."

"Into los valles to nurture the cottonwoods," Juanita said. She was on Jessie's left, one hand firmly on the end of the bench seat, the other clutching her thick muted-yellow wool cloak closer to her chest. She nodded toward an arroyo up ahead. Massive thick-barked cottonwoods lined the far side, the wind rattling their pale copper leaves.

Jessie shivered again. "There seems to have been a good deal more snow here than in Santa Fe."

"I expect so," her father said. He studied the hills to their right and the craggy white-capped Sangre de Cristos beyond. "The snow may be a blessing, though. If it's heavy enough, the rebels won't be able to get through the mountains and hit Santa Fe."

Jessie breathed a prayer for Guadalupe, but then Manuelita, on her right, sniffed audibly. Jessie glanced at her. The cook was staring straight ahead, her face expressionless.

Jessie turned to her father. "Didn't the messenger Colonel Price sent yesterday say that the rebels were on this road?"

He nodded. "There was an encounter with them somewhere near here on Sunday. We're likely to see evidence of it in the next hour or so." Jessie and Juanita shivered simultaneously. Manuelita glanced at them and went back to studying the road.

An hour later, the town of La Cañada came in sight on its bluff above the river. The travelers could see the big church at its center long before they crossed the half-frozen stream and came upon remnants of the battle three days before. A small house lay to the right. There was a large gap in the wall facing the road. The retablo of a smoke-marked saint gazed at the travelers from the other side of the room.

Beyond the house, broken corn stalks stuck up from muddy snow. One held the remains of a battered hat. Jessie felt a tremor deep inside and took a steadying breath, pulling herself up. This wasn't Missouri. Her father rode beside her.

The wagon moved steadily on, the mules doing the work while Jessie's eyes returned unwillingly to the remainders of war. A crow called from the trees. A cluster of buildings lay just ahead. One part of the adobe wall surrounding it had collapsed completely. A coyote appeared in the gap and stared at the Milbanks as they went by.

Jessie took another deep breath and tightened her grip on the mules' reins. Her father leaned toward her. "Are you all right?"

She nodded, but they both knew it wasn't true. The first house had been the worst. That corn field. The silence. The gazing saint. Juanita squeezed her arm. Jessie took another deep breath and flicked the reins on the mules' backs.

The one on the left snorted impatiently, and she saw that the wagons ahead had begun to pull over as far as they could without leaving the road. A two-wheeled Mexican cart came slowly down the resulting gap, its ungreased cottonwood axle squealing angrily. An old woman wrapped in black sat in the wagon bed, her head down. The shaggy donkey pulling the carreta looked equally somber. A man wearing a broad-brimmed straw hat walked beside it, shoulders hunched against the cold.

As Jessie maneuvered the Milbank wagon to the side, her father rode forward and positioned Saturn in front of the mules. "Buenos días," he said as the carreta reached him.

The other man's head jerked up, his face startled, then he rattled off a series of questions in Spanish so rapid that Jessie couldn't follow. Her father leaned toward the man and said something in a low voice. A question of his own.

The man glanced down the road, saw that they were the last in the train, and spoke to the donkey, who halted instantly. As his owner stepped toward Jessie's father and began speaking again, his face twisted with bitterness, the old woman lifted her head and stared at them with dull eyes.

Jessie leaned forward, trying to understand what the man was saying, then turned to Juanita. "I can't follow his Spanish."

The other girl nodded. "He's speaking rapidly, but it's also the northern dialect. It's different from how we speak in Santa Fe." She frowned a little, listening, then said, "I think he asked where los soldados americanos went and if they were coming back. Also, how many more people they were going to kill." She took a breath and leaned forward again. "He says los americanos came and los insurrectos attacked them with great fervor, but not on the open field. They used the houses. His casa was one of them."

Manuelita shook her head and grunted.

"Those poor people," Jessie said. She looked at the old woman, who had closed her eyes and pulled her black rebozo closer to her face. "I wonder if we have anything that would be useful to them."

Juanita shook her head. "I believe they would find such an offer un gran insulto."

Jessie frowned. "Our soldiers damaged these people's house. The least we could do—"

Manuelita muttered something and Jessie gave her a startled look. Had she just said "Go home"?

But the men had ended their conversation. The old man spoke to the donkey, and the cart began moving again, edging past the wagon. Jessie leaned to speak to him, but he looked away. The woman's eyes were still closed, her lips moving as if in prayer.

Jessie took a breath, straightened, flicked the reins, and spoke to the mules. They tossed their heads and strained against the harness. The wagon wheels slipped in the ruts, then caught, and the Milbanks followed the rest of the little train up the hill into Santa Cruz de la Cañada. The public square, with its massive brown church on the left, was strangely quiet, as if the buildings had withdrawn along with the rebels.

By the time the Milbank party reached the square, the first of the sutler wagons had already left the plaza. Jessie's father frowned. "I thought we might stay here tonight," he said. "But it seems the wagon master believes we won't be welcome, and I expect he's correct." He looked at the women apologetically. "I'm afraid we'll have another night of sleeping in the open."

Manuelita grunted again. "Tent," she said. Jessie turned to her and she shrugged. "Not open. Tent."

Don Hubert laughed. "Yes, I suppose the tents are a little more luxury than strictly necessary. If we were truly roughing it, we would have to do without." He cocked his head at the cook, eyes twinkling. "Would you prefer to sleep in the snow?"

Manuelita scowled and Jessie laughed. The cook looked away, and Jessie and Juanita exchanged a puzzled glance. He'd clearly been joking. Did she think he was serious? Jessie flicked the reins again. "Come on, mulies!"

When the little train did stop for the night, the wagons were well spread out along the road. Manuelita dug out the food while Jessie and Juanita got a fire going and Jessie's father attended to the animals and set up the tents. They'd brought dried meat and fruit and a supply of bread, so the fire was for warmth and coffee only, and they soon retired for the night, the women in one tent, Don Hubert in the other.

As tired as she was, Jessie couldn't sleep. She lay staring at the pale canvas, seeing instead the blasted walls, the forlorn retablo, the bitterness in the old man's face, the black-clad woman's slumped shoulders and blank gaze.

A hand touched her arm. "Is it too much?" Juanita whispered. "Do these things bring back las memorias?"

Jessie nodded. There was a lump in her throat. She swallowed it, but still she couldn't speak.

"I too," Juanita murmured. "I see Raúl's face." The intake of her breath was audible. "Mi pobre primo. He did not deserve what happened to him. Nor did those old ones."

Jessie turned toward her. "Why must people be so cruel to each other?" she whispered. "When will it end?"

Juanita shook her head and put her arm around her friend's shoulders. Jessie snuggled into her warmth and somehow they drifted off to sleep.

CHAPTER 28: Thursday, January 28, 1847

They woke early the next morning to a clear blue sky and sunlight that gleamed on the snow beside the road. They all moved a little more briskly than usual and were soon breakfasted, reloaded, and ready to pull out. Jessie had just turned the mules toward the road when there was a shout on the track behind them and a horseman appeared, trotting briskly.

"Why, it is Private Fitzgerald!" Juanita exclaimed.

Jessie's father, on his big black, could see further than the others. "There's a troop of dragoons behind him," he said. "They must be the men from Albuquerque."

As he got closer, the dragoon raised his hand in recognition, then reined in beside Don Hubert. "I hardly expected to see you here," he said, his eyes on the wagon. "I didn't have time to go by the shop as we came through Santa Fe. I'm glad now I didn't. I would have been quite concerned to find you were not there."

"My aunt would have informed you of our whereabouts," Juanita said.

Fitzgerald's gaze jerked toward her. "To be sure, to be sure." Then it moved back to the wagon and the barrels and boxes just visible under the canvas top. He looked at Jessie's father. "I take it you've come along to assist with our supply issue."

Jessie's father glanced at the troops marching up the road behind them. "I have, yes. At the sutler's request."

The dragoon nodded, then turned to Jessie. "We collected the Texan six-pounder as we came through Santa Fe." He straightened as he said it, and touched the two pistols tucked into his belt. "The snow and rough terrain here make it quite difficult to maneuver the larger artillery. They were of little use on Sunday and, if we must go all the way to Taos, getting them through the mountains may prove difficult." He grinned. "My brother and his friends knew what they were about, bringing that smaller piece." Then his blue eyes darkened. "I hope we get to use it decisively against these traitors."

Jessie's father glanced ahead at the sutler train. "You'll be wanting to get past us all."

The dragoon nodded. "I'm on my way to the wagon master to arrange that." He smiled at the girls. "You'll get a bit of a rest while we march by."

Rest in the cold. But Jessie didn't respond, just flexed her hands in their buckskin gloves and spoke to the mules, turning them back to where they'd been. The dragoon waited until they were off the road, then bowed politely and went on. He returned in a flurry of galloping hooves and flying snow, and rejoined his companions. The dragoons were all on foot, except for Captain Burgwin, the tension in his long thin face offset somewhat by the way his curly brown hair stuck out from the edges of his black hat. He nodded politely to Jessie's father as he rode by, then the troops trudged past, doing their best to keep their eyes focused straight ahead.

Jessie and Juanita exchanged amused glances. "They must wonder what it is we are doing here," Juanita said.

Jessie moved her feet, twisting her toes against each other. "I'm beginning to wonder that myself. I hadn't expected it to be this cold."

The little six-pounder cannon rolled past on its two-wheeled carriage, pulled by a brace of horses who nickered at the Milbank mules. When Jessie gave the signal to follow, her team seemed a little more enthusiastic about the chore ahead.

Her father grinned and shook his head at the animals. "Don't go getting in too much of a hurry," he told them. "We still have a good way to go before we stop for the night." He smiled at Jessie. "The sutler tells me we will be staying at Los Luceros."

Jessie tugged at her gloves and wiggled her fingers inside them. "Isn't that where we stayed last spring?"

"Yes, that's the place."

"It is truly a lovely site," Juanita said. "Although I have never seen it this late in the year. The acequia madre there is one of the oldest in all of Nuevo Méjico."

"The irrigation ditch?" Jessie asked. She flicked her reins at the mules. "I didn't realize that. It's a beautiful stream. The irrigation methods here seem so connected to the land. As if they really are streams and only incidentally the conveyors of water to the fields." She turned to Manuelita. "Have you ever been there?"

The cook shook her head.

"You're in for a treat," Jessie said. "Well, it will be different from when I saw it, of course. It's not going to be green. But the orchards are quite extensive and there's a nice little chapel."

"Ah," Juanita said. "How could I have forgotten la capilla?" She turned to Jessie's father. "Do you think there will be time for me to visit it and light a candle?"

He gave her a troubled look. "I expect the troops will be camped in the fields around the hacienda. I doubt they'll be better behaved here than they were in Santa Fe. In fact, I expect they're keyed up and therefore even more unpredictable."

She nodded reluctantly. Don Hubert's lips twitched. "If you must stray beyond our fire, I advise you to exercise caution." He looked at Jessie. "You should go nowhere alone. In fact, I would prefer that you girls not go anywhere without Manuelita."

Jessie opened her mouth to protest, but then glanced at the cook and saw her scowl. She looked at Juanita, who was already nodding meekly to Don Hubert and saying, "As you wish, señor."

They continued slowly on, then suddenly they were there, moving carefully down a snow-mucked hill and across the wooden bridge over a ten-foot-wide irrigation channel, the water flowing sluggishly beneath two-inch-thick ice.

Clusters of bare-branched fruit trees stretched out on their left, sheep nosing the snow beneath. On the right, fields of harvested corn and other crops had been taken over by the soldiers. They had no tents, but they did have fires. Men moved purposefully back and forth, collecting dead stalks and other plant debris. Captain Burgwin and his dragoons swung off to join them and the supply wagons went on. Los Luceros' walled hacienda lay ahead, its big double gates open to the road opposite a small chapel.

The little church was a simple structure, perhaps twenty feet wide and fifty long. As the Milbank wagon drew closer, the bell in the small tower rang out, clear and sweet in the late-morning air.

Juanita stirred. "Ah, how could I have forgotten that sound?"

Jessie chuckled. "You live across the street from the Santa Fe parish church and hear its bells daily. How is this different?"

Juanita looked away. "It has a special meaning for me."

"I'm sorry," Jessie said. "I didn't realize."

Juanita turned to face her. "It is a memory most preciado. I visited here with my parents five years ago. Mi padre had business with Señor Lucero and we remained several days. During that time, Señor Carlos Beaubien and Narciso arrived."

The wagon was almost to the little building now. The bell fell silent. "It is where we first truly spoke with one another," Juanita said softly.

Jessie reached for her friend's hand.

CHAPTER 29: Thursday, January 28, 1847

They were well settled in a grove of cottonwoods near the river, alongside the other supply wagons, when Private Fitzgerald appeared. He swung down from his roan mare and doffed his hat to them. "And now it begins!" he said exultingly. "Archie will be avenged."

Don Hubert looked up from grooming the mules. "I hope you seek justice, rather than revenge."

The dragoon scowled. "I have had neither. When the December conspiracy was discovered, I began to think this moment would never arrive." He shook his head. "It's so difficult to ascertain whether someone will turn out to be truly trustworthy."

Jessie frowned. Trustworthy? What an odd thing to say. But then Manuelita crossed to her holding a mixing spoon and a bowl full of batter. "Grid cake," the cook said. She pointed to the fire and the spider-shaped cast iron skillet she'd already placed on the coals. "Pan hot."

"What an excellent idea," Don Hubert said approvingly. He turned to Fitzgerald. "Have you heard anything about the condition of the roads ahead? Or does Colonel Price expect to use this as a base camp?"

The dragoon smiled. "I carry dispatches, I'm not usually apprised as to their contents." He glanced at the other wagons under the big trees and lowered his voice. "However, I can tell you that there is every indication the colonel hopes to learn more about the rebels' movements before we march on."

Jessie ran the spoon through her bowl of batter. "So we're likely to be here at least a day?"

"I would surmise that. But of course I'm a mere private." He smiled at her. "I go where I'm sent and do as I'm told." He looked at her father. "I suspect we will march all the way to Taos and beyond. Are you aware of the outcome of the events at Turley's mill?"

"There at Arroyo Hondo?"

Fitzgerald nodded. "The gristmill and distillery were destroyed by fire and none of the defenders escaped."

Jessie's spoon stopped. "None of them?"

When the dragoon nodded, her father shook his head. "I'm sorry about the others, but I'm not surprised that Turley had upset a few people," he said. "The man was cutting timber on the Arroyo Hondo land grant. More and more of it. He completely cleared the hillside behind the mill and was moving outward from there. No amount of talking could make him stop. His distillery required firewood and he had a ready market for as much liquor as he could produce. I expect he intended to make the most of the opportunity while he could."

Jessie tucked her rebozo out of the way, bent over the fire, and ladled the first spoonful of batter onto the hot griddle. "But to kill him—"

"And the others," Fitzgerald said. "The bastards must be punished."

"Surely there are less violent ways to deal with disagreements of that sort." Jessie straightened and looked at her father. "Even if Mr. Turley wouldn't listen to the locals, couldn't the other Americans have spoken to him?"

He shrugged. "I expect they didn't feel it was any of their business. And getting between parties in a conflict like that doesn't tend to be healthy."

She stared at the bubbling batter, then absently took the turner Juanita proffered and flipped the griddlecake over. "And now half a dozen men are dead."

Her father looked away. Private Fitzgerald glanced from her face to his, then at the griddle, gave the company a stiff little bow, and went to his star-blazed roan. No one spoke. He mounted, bowed again, and rode off.

They ate in silence. After they'd cleaned up, Juanita turned to Jessie. "I would like to visit la capilla now. Not only to pray for mi amor, but also these other men."

Jessie glanced at Manuelita, who was stowing dishes in the box. She didn't look like she was in the mood to go anywhere.

Juanita had seen it also. She turned to Jessie's father. "The camp is very quiet," she said. "Everyone seems to be taking una siesta."

His lips twitched. "And you will be perfectly safe."

She dimpled at him. "I believe so, señor."

Don Hubert chuckled. "I suppose it is unfair to ask Manuelita to follow you two around. And the chapel is directly across from the hacienda." He turned to Jessie. "But you must promise me to go only to the chapel and to be extremely careful. These January days are short. I want you back here well before dark. Can you do that?"

"Yes, Papa."

"I mean it, Jessie. These troops aren't in Santa Fe any more, and they were bad enough there. I'd accompany you myself, but I promised to join Colonel Price as soon as we arrived, and it's already long past that time."

Juanita flung her rebozo over her head and moved toward him. "Perhaps you can escort us as far as the chapel."

He smiled and held out his elbow. "It would be my great honor."

Jessie suppressed a laugh, adjusted her own headgear, and took his other arm. When they reached the chapel, he went inside briefly to ensure it was empty, reminded the girls to return to the wagon before dark, and crossed the road to the hacienda.

The girls watched him enter the courtyard, then Jessie turned to Juanita. "I know you would like to be alone," she said. "I'll stay out here and make sure no one interrupts you."

"You also must wish for the comfort of prayer."

"I don't believe as you do. And I have not lost a sweetheart."

Juanita closed her eyes. "It still seems absolutamente imposible."

Jessie touched her shoulder. "Go. I will stand guard."

Juanita leaned in to kiss her cheek. "You are una buena amiga."

As Juanita slipped in through the whitewashed chapel door, Jessie tucked her hands inside her rebozo and studied her surroundings. The hacienda was the typical sprawling compound. Beyond the open gate, she could see the usual beehive-shaped oven, stacked firewood, strings of dried red chili suspended from the roof of the interior portal, and scratching chickens. The courtyard even had the luxury of a well.

Soldiers began to stir in the fields beyond the chapel as siesta came to an end. A small boy emerged from the hacienda carrying a basket filled with steaming corn tortillas. He stopped in front of Jessie and held them up. "¿Dos por un peso?"

She smiled. Two tortillas for one peso was an outrageous price, but they smelled good and he was so bright-eyed that she couldn't resist. "I hope you make lots of money," she said as she handed him the coin.

He grinned at her, clearly not understanding. "¡Sí, señorita!"

She laughed and he went on toward the field of men. She finished the last of the treat and bent forward to brush the crumbs from her skirt. When she looked up, Lieutenant Milbank stood in front of her. "Señorita," he said gravely. "I hope I find you well."

"Señor," she said formally. "I am well enough. And you?"

"It is good to feel useful," he said. "I had hoped the encounter with the insurgents outside La Cañada would bring an end to this outbreak. However, it appears that we will be marching onward." He turned a little, as if looking for something to lay his eyes on, then back to her. "I'm surprised to find you here. I assume you're with your father."

Jessie nodded. "He was asked to bring supplemental goods, because the sutler didn't have much time to prepare and was worried he wouldn't be able to meet the needs of the troops."

He nodded, then smiled knowingly. "And you couldn't resist coming along."

"He was worried about leaving me behind in Santa Fe," Jessie said stiffly. "When we left, it was believed the rebels might attack the city."

He glanced at the chapel behind her. "And you have come to pray?"

"Juanita wanted to pray. She's going with us to Taos so she can provide support to Cisco's family."

"This is Narciso Beaubien? The son of the judge? The young man who just came back from college in Saint Louis?"

"The one who was killed, yes."

"I understand he and Kit Carson's brother-in-law were assassinated at the same time."

Her breath caught, in spite of her annoyance. "Another one?"

"Yes." He frowned. "I can understand the rebels' anger at the American-appointed officials, but this killing of boys—"

"Yes."

"The Beaubien boy's death in particular seems to have fueled a good deal of anger amongst our troops." He studied her, his brows furrowing. "Are you absolutely sure you want to be in the middle of what may be coming?"

She stiffened. "Want? You truly think I want to be here? That I came along in order to poke my nose where it doesn't belong?"

Lieutenant Milbank took a step back. He raised a hand, palm out to block her anger. "No, I—"

Behind her, the chapel door opened. Juanita came out. She looked tired and her eyes were puffy, but she smiled bravely when she saw Jessie's companion. "Lieutenant!" she said. "¡Buenos días!"

He looked at her with an air of relief. "Good day to you, too," he said. Then, more gently, "I wish to offer you my deepest condolences on the death of your amigo."

"Gracias." She turned to Jessie. "And thank you for waiting for me." She glanced apologetically at the lieutenant, then back to her friend. "I'm a little tired. If you don't mind, I'd like to return to the wagon."

"Of course." Jessie took her arm. When the lieutenant raised an eyebrow, she said, "We promised my father to stay together and to be back before dark." She glanced at the sky. "Which seems to be coming on rather quickly."

He looked up as if startled to see the sky existed. "Yes, I suppose it is." He turned to Juanita. "May I have the pleasure of escorting you safely back to your protector?"

Jessie's jaw tightened as Juanita took his arm. Then she gave herself a mental shake. The man had virtually accused her of being a busybody, thirsty for excitement, not having the sense to stay at home. Why should she care if he offered to escort Juanita, rather than herself, back to the fire?

The lieutenant didn't stay for supper. After the meal, the women cleaned up, spread sheepskins on the floor of the little tent, then wrapped themselves, fully clothed, into thick Navajo blankets with a buffalo robe on top.

But Jessie couldn't sleep. Juanita lay soundlessly beside her and Manuelita snuffled near the door while Jessie stared at the shadows the cottonwood branches cast on the canvas tent. She couldn't stop thinking about her conversation with the lieutenant.

What he'd said was so similar to things her father used to tell her mother when they argued. "You simply want to be in the middle of things," he would say. When she responded, "I want to help," he'd shake his head and leave the room, his shoulders stiff with disapproval.

Her mother would be tightlipped long afterwards. And defensive. Days later, even after he left for Santa Fe, she'd still be justifying herself. "I'm not looking for excitement," she'd grumble as she rattled pans on the cookstove. "I want to help people. If that puts me in danger, so be it."

Remembering this, Jessie closed her eyes. Her mother's actions had indeed put her in danger. In fact, they had cost her life.

Jessie turned, pulling the covers closer. Somewhere, a coyote yipped, was answered, and fell silent. Jessie stared into the darkness. Just why was she here?

Her father wouldn't have come without her, and he definitely wanted to do so. She sighed. She really didn't know why she'd come along. She didn't seek revenge for Governor Bent's death or even Narciso Beaubien's, as tragic as that was. Yes, she'd like to see justice done, but not vengeance. She'd heard Raúl's perspective too often to be completely unsympathetic to the insurrectos. After all, the American army had marched into New Mexico as if they held a God-given right to possess it, as if the entire region naturally belonged to them.

And there was a kind of arrogance in the way General Kearny headed to California as if the war here was over and there was no danger of resistance. He'd treated the New Mexicans like a bunch of placid peasants with neither the courage nor the initiative to fight back. It was downright insulting. She could understand why Raúl and his friends had gathered, conspired, and organized. Why the resistance had apparently not evaporated after the plot was discovered in December, but simply moved north.

What she didn't understand was why the rebels would kill a nineteen-year-old boy who was not part of the administration, not a threat to anyone in any way. The argument could be made that Cisco died because he was more americano than nuevo mexicano. After all, he was half French and he'd just returned from three years of American college indoctrination. And he was the son of Carlos Beaubien, who General Kearny had made Justice for the northern court district.

But Pablo Jaramillo. His ancestors were Spanish and no one in his immediate family held positions in the new government. Why did he die? Did he just happen to be in the way? Jessie pulled the blankets closer. It all seemed so senseless.

But then, a mob had killed them, not a single person. So the only thing to do was punish the rebels as a group. She shivered. Where would it lead?

And her father wanted to participate. The wagon load of goods was merely an excuse. He longed to be part of Ceran Saint Vrain's Avengers. Jessie stared into the darkness, her body suddenly stiff. If he did join them, and there was a battle, he could be injured. Even killed.

Suddenly she couldn't breathe. She pushed at the covers, shifting the weight off her chest, fighting the panic.

Then she stopped moving. Was this how he felt when she put herself in what he saw as harm's way? Why he became so upset? Yet she was only following her mother's example.

Following her conscience. Trying to do what she thought was right.

Her mother. All her causes over the years: the woman's vote, land reform. Most importantly, helping slaves get to freedom. Yes, she was doing what she felt was right, but at the points of highest action, her mother carried herself differently. Stood straighter, lifted her chin higher.

Jessie smiled, remembering, and took a deep breath, knowing that if her father joined the Avengers, she wouldn't protest. After all, how could she? She'd given him a way to be here. And she was here herself. For whatever reason.

The coyote yipped again and was answered. Cottonwood branches scraped together, their dry leaves rattling. Jessie stared sleeplessly into the shadows.

CHAPTER 30: Friday, January 29, 1847

The Milbank wagon moved out late the next morning, the little supply train now surrounded by ammunition transports. The road did not return to the hills, but ran straight north through snow-covered fields. On their left, a line of gnarled cottonwoods marked the course of el Río Grande del Norte, the rocky ridges beyond the river outlined in snow.

More snow was coming. The damp heaviness in the air presaged its arrival even more than the low gray sky.

Jessie felt as heavy as the atmosphere. She shivered inside her thick wool cloak and pondered her conversation with Lieutenant Milbank. Yes, she was here to support her father. Perhaps, if she was honest, to be in the middle of things. But perhaps she would also discover who killed Raúl and why. There was also the question of Vidal, the man who'd died in the plaza. No one seemed to care about what had happened to him.

Or maybe she was just making excuses, trying to justify where she was, what she was doing. She pushed impatiently at her rebozo, nudging it away from her face. Had she allowed the rebellion and the American response to it to sweep the other questions aside? What kind of friend, what kind of person, was she, to drop those particular searches for justice in favor of a new one? One she could only observe?

Jessie blinked back sudden tears, flicked the reins at the mules, and shuffled her feet closer to the hot stones Manuelita had wrapped in wool cloth and tucked between the bench and the footboard. Juanita, on her left, stared bleakly at the snow-covered landscape. Beyond her, Jessie's father dozed in his saddle.

Of the four of them, only the cook seemed awake. She studied the ammunition wagons ahead of them, but looked away when she saw Jessie watching. "We go slow," she said irritably.

Juanita roused slightly. "It is true," she said. "I begin to think we will never arrive."

They went on, snow crunching under the wagon wheels, mules huffing, an occasional shout from a teamster. Jessie had little work to do. The mules followed the wagons ahead and needed no guidance. Her shoulders slumped and her eyes drifted into the half gaze of almost sleep.

Then cannon boomed in the distance. Jessie jerked upright. Her father stood in his saddle, staring ahead to where the river valley narrowed between rocky cliffs. He spurred Saturn forward, then sawed on the reins. The big black pranced back to the wagon, head swinging irritably.

"Can you find out what's happening?" Jessie asked.

Her father frowned anxiously.

"There are wagons and teamsters all around us," she said impatiently. "We'll be perfectly safe." The mules had stopped, responding to the proximity of the wagon ahead. She looked at the team, then her father. "You see? We're not going anywhere, at least not any time soon."

He nodded, gave her another anxious look, and set off.

There were more thumping sounds in the distance, louder now. And gunfire? Jessie leaned forward and Juanita put her hand on her arm. Manuelita squinted at the cliffs ahead. "Battle," she said.

She sounded strangely pleased. Jessie frowned at her, but was distracted by Juanita, whose grip tightened on her arm. "Dios mío," she said. "How many will die this time?"

The image of Lieutenant Milbank's grave face rose in Jessie's mind. She half stood, straining to catch a glimpse of her father. Along the line of wagons ahead, men crowded together, peering at the cliffs and sharing speculations. Then she spied her father returning, tossing bits of news to the others as he rode.

"You remember this route," he said as he reached her. "The road swings east from the river and up Embudo Creek to the village. Remember how narrow that valley is, with the cliffs on both sides? I'm told the rebels have set up in the rocks. That sound we heard was the Texas cannon." He shook his head. "I expect it won't accomplish much against men holed up in the rocks, but that's Colonel Price's business." He looked over his shoulder at the milling teamsters. "It's likely to be a good while before we know anything or can move forward. You might as well get down and walk around a bit."

Jessie peered down at her feet in surprise. "My toes are numb. I hadn't noticed until now."

He chuckled. "That's because you were asleep."

She and Juanita clambered down while Manuelita climbed off the other side. Jessie's father looked up at the sun. "We might as well go ahead and get a small fire going and cook up some coffee." He cocked an eyebrow at the cook. "And maybe some hot food?"

She stared at him, then nodded brusquely and turned away.

Jessie frowned. "I thought we were going to eat jerked meat at midday."

"I expect we'll be here a while. We should take advantage of the opportunity while we have it."

The contents of the cook box rattled as Manuelita pulled it out of the wagon. "That seems like a lot of work," Jessie said.

He gave her a puzzled look. Manuelita appeared with the box and his face cleared. "Oh," he said. "Yes, I see. And there will be dishes to clean."

"And we don't know for certain how long we'll be delayed."

He turned to the cook. "I apologize, Manuelita. Jessie's right. It makes no sense to try to prepare an entire meal on the spot."

She stopped and looked at him, then glanced down at the box.

Jessie moved forward. "I'll put that back."

"Though perhaps we have time for hot coffee?" her father asked.

She grinned at Manuelita and got an answering glimmer from the cook, who handed her the box, then dove into it to pluck out the packages of ground coffee and matches. Juanita moved to the side of the wagon to grab a pot for the water.

Jessie's father sniffed the air. "We aren't the only ones with this idea."

They were savoring the last bit of the coffee an hour later when the men assigned to the ammunition wagons began moving around again. Jessie's father went to see what was happening and came back with a satisfied air. "We should get some answers now."

Jessie gave him a questioning look and he jerked his chin toward the front of the line. "I expect you'll see in a minute. I know he saw me."

"¡Un misterio!" Juanita chuckled.

Then the star-blazed roan mare appeared, and Private Fitzgerald rode toward them, a triumphant gleam in his eye. "We've achieved a definite victory this day," he announced, reining in. He nodded to Don Hubert, then bowed to the girls. "I'm pleased to see you all well." His face clouded. "I hope you are indeed well? This weather is somewhat brutal."

"What of la batalla?" Juanita said.

"Quite a number of rebels were wounded or killed. Colonel Price is still counting them." He turned to Jessie's father. "We weren't doing too well until he sent my company in. We dragoons did quite a business today."

"And the troops?" Jessie asked. "Was anyone hurt?"

He sobered a little. "Yes, unfortunately. Two of Saint Vrain's Avengers. I'm told one man died and another was wounded."

She frowned. "I'm sorry to hear that."

He looked at her father again. "I believe the injured man is a friend of yours. The Bent family slave they call Green."

The carelessness in his tone made Jessie's fingers twitch. "How serious is his wound?" she asked.

"I didn't see him myself. The colonel dispatched me with revised orders for the supply transport." He turned back to Jessie's father. "Our scouts have reported that the road directly north along the river is virtually impassable."

The older man nodded. "I expected as much. Even in summer, that route is best with pack animals. It's far too rocky and narrow for wagons."

"So Saint Vrain and the others told us, and it turned out to be true," the dragoon said. "In consequence, Colonel Price has ordered all the wheeled vehicles, both the artillery and supply wagons, to swing east and use what the locals call the mountain road."

Jessie frowned. "Won't we need to backtrack all the way to La Cañada to do that?"

Fitzgerald shook his head. "Our scouts say there's a small canyon just south of here which provides a natural path due east to the mountain route."

Jessie's father looked doubtfully at the eastern foothills. The snow was thick and icy under the trees, a dull crust that reflected the gray sky. "We're going up an untraveled arroyo?"

"A dry creek bed that's apparently firmer and wider than the road north of Embudo." The dragoon's roan tossed her head impatiently and he reached to stroke her neck. "It's also less susceptible to ambush."

Jessie's father's brows furrowed, but Fitzgerald went on. "Colonel Price has ordered most of the troops to swing back this way and take their place in front of the artillery. They'll march in front of you, packing down the snow and creating a surface stable enough for wheeled vehicles, hopefully even the gun carriages." He glanced at Juanita. "Of course, while you're doing that, we dragoons will head straight east and forge a path across the mountains to connect to the wagon road north of where you'll come in."

Juanita looked away.

"And what of Dick Green?" Jessie asked. "Where will he be and who will care for his wounds?"

"I'm afraid I can't tell you anything certain," Fitzgerald said unapologetically. "I didn't see the man, and Colonel Price dispatched me to you all before a decision was reached regarding his situation. I did overhear a discussion with the military doctor. Although Green was sworn in as an Avenger, men of color cannot legally join the U.S. military, so his status is unclear. In addition, a surge of frostbite cases among the enlisted men is requiring a great deal of medical attention."

"Enlisted men who happen to have the appropriate color skin—"

But her father interrupted her. "Please inform the colonel that we'll be happy to provide a place for Mr. Green in our wagon," he told the dragoon. "I will jettison goods if I need to."

"I'm sure that won't be necessary—"

"No man should be subjected to medical treatment from someone who doesn't wish to provide it." He looked at Jessie, then the cook. "We have two competent nurses who can provide Dick Green with better care than a doctor who doesn't wish to do so."

"Tres enfermeras," Juanita said.

He smiled at her. "Three nurses." He turned back to the dragoon. "If the colonel doesn't send Green to us, I will come for him myself."

"I'm sure that won't be necessary." Fitzgerald bowed stiffly. "I will inform the colonel of your kind offer and request I be allowed to escort the wounded man to you." He rode off.

"Thank you, Papa," Jessie said.

He tossed the dregs of his mug into the snow. "I may be only a merchant and have obligations which prevent me from fighting, but I am damned if they will treat that man as if he is a mere piece of property." He stomped off to tend the mules.

Jessie turned to Juanita and the cook. "Let's see if we can rearrange the wagon so we don't have to leave anything behind. I wonder if we can lash the tent to the side." She looked at Manuelita, who shrugged and turned away. Jessie frowned. The older woman didn't seem very happy about helping the Bent slave. Which was odd, because she'd never demonstrated any antagonism toward him in the past. In fact, she'd almost seemed to like him.

But Jessie didn't have time to worry about Manuelita's attitude. They had a wagon to rearrange. Juanita was already inside, going through the bedding to identify what could be set aside for the wounded man's use.

The troops marched by well before Green arrived. He lay on the bare boards of an old cart, blood seeping from a chest wound below his right shoulder. His eyes were glazed with pain, but he was still conscious.

"Kind of you, Don Hubert," he muttered. Jessie's father nodded as he and the orderly lifted Green into the wagon. Then they twisted to set him on the pallet the girls had arranged, and his breath caught. Jessie, reaching in from the other end, grabbed his shoulders, and helped to ease him onto the blankets. He smiled up at her and closed his eyes.

The orderly jerked Green's legs, straightening them, and Jessie shot him an impatient look. "Be careful!"

"He's just a slave. Too damn stupid to get out of the way."

Green's eyes opened and he half-smiled. "Didn't get killed."

Jessie chuckled in spite of her anxiety. "That's right, you were smart enough to stay alive." She patted Green's shoulder. "And we're going to do our best to keep you that way."

The orderly eased out of the wagon, shaking his head.

Manuelita appeared, carrying a bowl of hot water and looking angry. "Wash first," she said.

Jessie slipped into the wagon and reached to unfasten Green's shirt, but he batted feebly at her hands. "No, miss," he whispered. "Cookie—" Then his eyes rolled up and he fainted.

"Out," Manuelita ordered.

"I can help," Jessie said.

"You girl. I woman. You go."

Jessie straightened, ready to argue, then thought better of it. Green clearly didn't want her to see him uncovered. She should respect that. "All right," she said. "But I'll be right outside if you need me."

"More water," Manuelita said. She began rolling up her sleeves. "Stupid," she muttered. "Idiot."

Jessie, not sure if the cook meant her, Dick Green, or people in general, slipped out of the wagon.

Juanita had gathered clean snow and placed it in a pot on the fire. She stood over it, waving smoke away from the simmering contents, and watching the artillery and supply wagons move out.

"What's happening?" Jessie asked.

"They are moving on without us," Juanita said. "Tu padre, he has gone to speak to the sutler." She looked toward the wagon. "I saw the blood. The pain, is it strong? How can he endure it?"

"He fainted. Manuelita is washing the wound, but she needs more water."

Juanita gestured at the pot. Jessie turned to the wagon. "I'll get a dipper and bowl."

When she came back, her father had reappeared. "We're going to stay here tonight so we can make sure Green's wound is properly cleaned," he said. "Colonel Price has detailed a small guard to remain with us. They'll come with us when we follow the other wagons and the artillery in the morning." He looked at Jessie. "Is Manuelita with Dick?"

She nodded. "He didn't want me to see."

He smiled. "He's a good man." Then he sobered. "I hope she can get that wound cleaned thoroughly and keep it that way."

"We have plenty of water and rags, and a good fire. We'll do our best."

The rest of the day and evening was a blur of melting snow, turning some of the jerked meat into broth for Green, and preparing a simple supper. The sick man needed to be monitored constantly.

Jessie took the first night watch. The men Colonel Price had detailed to guard them stayed off to one side and didn't interact with the Milbank camp. She could hear low voices through the wagon's canvas cover, but then even they settled. Finally, there was only the yip of a distant coyote and the low breath of the man in the blankets.

Jessie allowed her muscles to relax for the first time since they'd heard the initial cannon fire. She closed her eyes. The explosions hadn't sounded like gunfire, not like the night her mother had died. But they'd certainly been more ominous than the curfew signals in Santa Fe. And sent arrows of anxiety into her spine.

However, she hadn't let go. And she hadn't let her father see how she felt. She was proud of herself for maintaining control, for not letting her fear out. It would only upset him, make him feel guilty for bringing her along.

She took another deep breath and straightened her shoulders. Other girls her age had suffered what she had, or much worse. At least the men who'd attacked the cabin hadn't found her, done what they did to her mother.

Her stomach twisted. Jessie took a deep breath, forcing her mind away from the images, and looked down at the sleeping Green. At least she wasn't a slave. Or wounded. Or a wounded man's wife, going on with her duties, not knowing he was in danger. His poor wife, to not have any idea what was happening to her man. Could she feel it? Sense something was wrong? That would be even more horrible, to feel that something wasn't right, but not know for certain. Or know what it was.

Inexplicably, Jessie's mind flickered to Lieutenant Milbank. Where had he been today during the battle of Embudo?

She shook herself. The other man who'd been injured— the one who died—was a member of Saint Vrain's Avengers, not the regular military. And the lieutenant was merely a friend. And not in any danger, as far as she knew. She should be worrying about Private Fitzgerald. He was the one with

Captain Burgwin's dragoons, forging the way across the mountains toward the next encounter with the rebels.

Jessie forced her mind onto more pleasant things: a new way to rearrange the mercantile to show off local produce, speculation on what this year's snow levels might mean for the summer crops, the way the mules flicked their ears at her when they were irritated. By the time Manuelita came to relieve her, the girl felt in control again. She went to the tent and snuggled, fully clothed, in beside Juanita.

But then she dreamed: the cabin in flames, the men wrestling her mother out the door, down the steps, and into the yard. Jessie cowering in the outhouse, smoke from the burning house mixing with the stench of the pit and coating the back of her mouth. She tried to pull her face away from the knothole, to force herself not to see, but she couldn't move.

And then she was crying out, despite her best intentions, despite her mother's many past admonitions. "Mama!" she shouted, her throat thick with grief. A gun blasted, then someone grabbed her from behind. From the outhouse pit itself. She whirled to confront them.

"Jessie," a soft voice said. "¿Amiga? It is I, Juanita. Are you well?"

Jessie flailed, her chest heaving, and found herself awake. Juanita leaned over her. "Pobrecita," she murmured. "You had a bad dream, I think."

Jessie sat up and wiped her face with her sleeve. She could still taste the smoke. She swallowed against it. "I dreamed of my mother," she whispered. "Of what happened." Her hands scrabbled at the blankets. "I'm so cold."

"Let us go sit by the fire."

Juanita located their cloaks, and they threw them on and slipped outside. The clouds had dropped lower, so the night air wasn't as icy as it might have been. The heat from the flames felt good on Jessie's face and shoulders, and she gradually relaxed. Neither girl spoke. They watched the flames and the sparks flying into the muted darkness, and fell into a kind of meditative state which wasn't disturbed until Manuelita suddenly appeared.

"You watch now," the cook told Juanita. She jerked her chin at Jessie. "Then you."

Jessie nodded.

"Can you sleep now?" Juanita asked her.

Jessie shivered and shook her head. "I'll watch with you."

"And yours," Manuelita said.

Juanita smiled at the cook. "I will stay with her. We will not disturb you."

Manuelita turned away and the girls headed for the wagon. Green was sleeping peacefully. Juanita touched his forehead. "No fever," she said softly.

"That's good. I hope he heals quickly, for his wife's sake, at least."

"Si." Juanita settled herself on a cushion beside Green's head. "What is she like?"

"Charlotte? She's one of those people who's always busy but never cross. She has a kind word for everyone and loves a good entertainment. I don't think that I've ever seen anyone dance with such enthusiasm."

"A woman que vive plenamente."

"Who lives fully? Yes. In many ways she reminds me of my mother. That same energy. The gift for engaging fully in life." Jessie sobered and looked away. "At any risk."

"¿Tu madre?"

Jessie nodded. "I miss her so much," she whispered.

"You have it also, la pasión."

Jessie looked up in surprise.

"You see a wrong and you must set it to rights. Especialmente if the wrong has harmed another human being."

Jessie looked away. "I betrayed my mother."

Juanita studied her, waiting.

"We were harboring a young man, an escaped slave on his way north. There was a sort of cellar beneath the barn. I was there with him when they came." Jessie studied her hands. "He was a very good-looking young man, a few years older than me, and gentle in his speech. I—"

The man on the bed twitched and the girls swung toward him, but then he settled. Juanita turned back to Jessie. "Es natural to find others of interest," she said. "To be—how do you say it? —attracted to them."

"I—" Jessie stopped, then went on, more slowly now. "We only talked. But I stayed too long. When I came out of the cellar, it was full dark. I didn't have a lamp with me, so the men on the porch didn't see me at the barn door." She picked at the edge of her cloak. "I knew who they were. They had visited us two days before, threatening my mother. When I saw them, I ducked behind the door. I didn't know where to go. They were banging on the cabin door and I could see their long guns. I turned to go back inside the barn, but then I realized that if they caught me, they'd find the runaway as well, and there would be no hope for him."

She paused, staring into the past, that yard, the attacking men. "So I waited until they broke the door down and were focused on my mother, and I ran for the outhouse," Jessie said. She shuddered. "That's where I was in my dream. Watching her." She closed her eyes. "Watching what they did to her."

Juanita reached for her hands. "Mi pobre amiga," she said softly. "You have told me of this before, but I see it now with new eyes. How you have suffered. And the men? They escaped la justicia? Is it not so?"

Jessie nodded bleakly. "Because I didn't come out. I hid instead of confronting them or the man who led them. He was the only one I saw clearly, and he wasn't anyone I knew, anyone I could put a name to. He had a scar on his right cheek—" She made a small, hopeless gesture. "I doubt my mother's killers will ever be identified and brought to justice. I suppose that's why I keep trying to discover who killed Raúl and the man Manuelita says was named Vidal. I want to balance the scales. At least a little."

Juanita reached to give her a sideways hug, then they sat in silence, watching over the sleeping man.

CHAPTER 31: Saturday, January 30, 1847

The sun rose eventually, filling the space inside the wagon with a soft glow and dissipating the last remnants of Jessie's dream. Manuelita appeared, looking sour, but the girls greeted her cheerfully.

Dick Green roused and tried to push himself into a seated position. The cook growled at him and motioned for the girls to climb out. "I need—" he said.

"Quick!" she snapped at the girls, then turned to him. "I got gourd."

He nodded and fell back. "I sure do wish my Charlotte was here."

"I don't look."

Jessie and Juanita grinned at each other as they jumped to the ground and shook out their skirts. Jessie's father came toward them. "I've roused up the fire. Jessie girl, once you've tidied yourself, do you think you can mix up some griddlecake?"

They headed out after breakfast, following the track laid down by the artillery and supply wagons, their escort swinging in behind. Manuelita stayed in the wagon with Green, whose wound was still seeping. When Jessie's father dropped back to ride alongside the foot soldiers, Juanita turned to Jessie. "Are you feeling better now?"

Jessie smiled at her. "Yes, thank you."

"No, I must thank you."

Jessie gave her a surprised look.

"You, among all mis amigos and family members, are the only person who believes it is possible to find the killer of mi primo."

"My father and Lieutenant Milbank would say that I simply don't know when to mind my own business." Jessie nodded toward the wagon interior. "Manuelita probably agrees."

"Ah, but I know this is not so." Juanita squeezed her arm. "I know your heart."

Jessie shook the reins at the mules and they went on for a long while in silence. The snow was thick enough to absorb the voices of the men behind them. The only sounds were an occasional snuffle from the animals, the creak of wheels against snow, and the huff of raven wings as the big black birds lifted from the pine trees beside the road.

Then Juanita said, "There could be any number of reasons someone might wish death to un hombre such as Raúl."

Jessie gave her a quizzical look.

"Jealousy, for example. Or perhaps a gambling debt."

"But we know Raúl didn't owe anyone money."

"Perhaps someone owed him and was unwilling to pay."

"I suppose that's always possible." Jessie brightened. "Or maybe someone robbed him."

"He had already taken his winnings to Guadalupe."

"Whoever attacked him wouldn't have known that. They might have stabbed him because they were angry he didn't have money on him."

Juanita nodded. The wagon moved past a downed log. The snow on it was crisscrossed with tiny bird tracks. She turned to Jessie. "Un soldado americano would not have known he took his money to her each day."

Jessie frowned "If it was a soldier, we'll never find out who did it."

Juanita sighed. "Mi pobre primo. If only he had given us a name. Instead, he said to say to Lupe 'no warning'."

"Yes." There was a slight incline ahead. The mules looked at it suspiciously and bobbed their heads. Jessie leaned forward. "Hiya!" she said. "Come on, mulies!" She leaned back and moved her shoulders up and down, easing the tension. "After Guadalupe told us she encouraged him to go to the authorities, I thought maybe Raúl meant he hadn't been able to do so."

Juanita nodded. "I thought the same. But now I wonder. Perhaps he meant el ataque came with no warning."

"But why would Lupe need to know that?"

Juanita grinned. "He was un hombre. To think he could be attacked and not defend himself—" Her smile dropped and she looked away. "Mi pobre primo."

The slope was steeper now. The mules' ears twitched. Jessie flicked the reins. "Come on, mulies. You can do it!"

Juanita leaned over the side to peer at the snow. "It built up a crust in the night," she said. "That is why they struggle as they do."

Jessie's father trotted up on Saturn. "Let's get them to the top of the hill and stop for a breather," he said. "Then I'll ask the guard to move ahead of us so they can break down the surface a bit more." He rode forward, level with the mules' heads. "Just a little farther now, team," he said encouragingly. "I expect you're almost there."

When they reached the summit, Jessie reined in and her father dropped back to their escort to explain what he wanted to do.

Juanita jiggled her feet on the floorboards, then stood to stretch her legs. "Is it possible the person who murdered Raúl was an official in la administración americana?" she asked. "Someone who wanted to ensure there was no warning?"

"Do you mean a current government official who wanted rebellion?" Jessie frowned. "But why?"

"They may have thought a little fighting might—how do you say it—clear the air? Certainly it would cause great happiness for hombres such as Señor Fitzgerald." Juanita shrugged. "Also, una confrontación outright would enable the identification of those who oppose the new regime. Those identified could then be placed in el calabozo or watched more closely."

"They put people in jail in December when the conspiracy was exposed."

Juanita shook her head. "Not all those involved were detained. If that had happened, perhaps Narciso—" Abruptly, she sat down on the bench seat and stared at the snow-laden pine trees.

Jessie started to reach for her, then drew back her hand. The guard was still marching past. She waited for the last of them, then spoke to the mules. The wagon creaked forward. "Who would do such a thing?" she asked. "Kill a man because he was trying to prevent violence?"

Juanita shook her head. She stared at the sky overhead, still laden with gray clouds. "I only wish to know why," she whispered.

CHAPTER 32: Sunday, January 31, 1847

Late the next day, the Milbanks and their escort passed through the village of Las Trampas. The sun had reappeared, and the straw in the grand old church's adobe walls glinted cheerfully at the travelers. Dick Green was on the mend, and Manuelita was back on the wagon bench, more silent than ever. She'd wrapped a blue-and-gray-striped wool blanket over her head and shoulders, hooding her face.

Jessie's father had returned to riding beside them, though he seemed puzzled by the lack of conversation. After a particularly long gap, he bent toward the girls. "Did you know that we are still on the original land grant given to the man who founded Los Luceros?"

Jessie looked up at him, playing along. "This far away? How large was the grant?"

"Something like fifty thousand acres. We're about twelve miles from the original homestead, as the crow flies. Las Trampas is on the eastern edge."

Jessie studied the little valley ahead of them. It was pretty, but snow lay everywhere. Narrow paths restricted movement between the houses, and there were no animals in sight. Were they all inside? "It must be nice in the summer," she said. "But the winter conditions seem overwhelming. Why would anyone choose to live up here?"

Manuelita stirred. "Free land, genízaros," she said from her blanket.

Jessie frowned. "What do you mean?"

"After los cautivos from the savage tribes reached adulthood, they were sometimes given land," Juanita explained. "Generalmente, their villages were beyond those of los españoles, to serve as a buffer against attack by the wild tribes."

"Free slaves, make shields," Manuelita said.

Juanita stirred uneasily. "They were given the land."

Manuelita's head swiveled. "Big cost."

Jessie peered at her. "Do you have family in one of those settlements?"

Manuelita turned away.

"I don't know that everyone here in Las Trampas was genízaro," Jessie's father said. "One of the original settlers was an African man who came as a drummer boy with the Spaniards in 1692."

Jessie was about to ask for more details when a member of the guard came floundering back through the snow, wiping at his dripping nose. "The sergeant says we ain't gonna catch up with Colonel Price and the rest of 'em tonight," he told Jessie's father. "There's a likely wide spot up ahead where we can stop, if you're willing."

Though the mountain tops still glowed with reflected sunlight, the valley ahead was sinking into darkness. The path Colonel Price's dragoons had beaten north through the snow was a black stripe which disappeared up yet another pine-covered slope. Jessie breathed a sigh of thanks as her father agreed to the sergeant's suggestion.

Their escort also seemed glad of the respite. Several wandered over to the Milbank fire after the evening meal and hunkered down to complain about the cold, the snow, and what appeared to be the never-ending mountain range.

"I'm beginning to think this Taos place don't truly exist," an older man groused.

"I'm beginning to think green grass don't exist," a scrawny younger one with greasy brown hair said. "My feet feel frozen permanent-like."

"Bite of frost," Manuelita said with a twinkle. Jessie frowned in confusion. It had been a long, cold day, and she herself was beginning to feel as if the journey would go on forever. The cook had spent most of the last ten hours wrapped in her blanket and looking sour. Why was she suddenly almost cheerful?

CHAPTER 33: Monday, February 1 to Tuesday, February 2, 1847

The next day was more of the same. The sun was out but that only made it colder, an iciness that numbed the mind as well as hands and feet. There was nothing to see but an endless succession of snow-burdened pine and the backs of the mules as they huffed up the slope, then switchbacked around a curve and down yet another ravine only to climb up again.

The only bright spot was Dick Green, whose wound was mending nicely. Unfortunately, this made him restless and prone to complain about having nothing constructive to do. His grumbling seemed to amuse Manuelita, who ordered him to stay under the blankets, but kept turning around to check on him.

The wagon and its escort dropped into yet another valley, this one wider than the last, and moved steadily north, past the little village of Chamisal. As they began climbing again, the snow grew steadily deeper. This slope was longer than any they'd attempted to this point, but they were all too tired and road-weary to comment on it. Not even the blueness of the sky could lift the general exhaustion.

Then they reached the summit and the world opened up. Jessie reined the mules in and they all gazed at the Taos valley, stretching before them like a great snow-covered platter. A broken one. The deep black gash in its center broke the flow of the land abruptly, its cliffs falling toward a thread of water far below. West of the gorge, the flat lands started up again, extending toward a range of more mountains, purple-blue in the distance.

"At last!" Juanita said.

"It doesn't look much like a valley," Jessie said. "It's so wide."

"I expect it's twenty miles, at least," her father agreed. "Less than the distance we still have to travel to get to it." Then he grinned. "Though the road's all downhill from here."

"That won't make the mules very happy," Jessie said.

"Need my help keeping them in line?" a man's voice asked from the wagon bed.

They all turned. Green smiled back at them, his battered brown hat on his head.

"Mr. Green!" Jessie scolded. "Manuelita told you to stay under the blankets."

He grinned at her. "I reckon they might need some airing. They're beginning to take on a mite of smell."

Manuelita sniffed as Jessie shook her head and her father chuckled.

Up ahead, their escort was milling restlessly and watching the wagon. "Those young ones seem to be in something of a hurry," Green observed. "Wanting to get in on the fight, I reckon."

"We're not going anywhere until you lie down again," Jessie said, smiling to take the sting from the words.

"You sure you don't need help with those mules?"

"I'm sure. And that wound of yours doesn't need to be reopened."

Jessie's father chuckled. "You might as well do as she says, Dick," he said.

Green grimaced and touched the right side of his chest. "I reckon I should listen to this here, as well. It's a bit sore." He looked at Jessie, then Manuelita, who scowled at him. "I suppose I'll just have to go on and do what I'm told." He grinned at them. "At least for now, anyway." He withdrew into the wagon and Jessie signaled the team to go on. Her father raised a hand to the guard and they formed up and moved down the slope.

The switchbacks were many and steep, and took longer to navigate than seemed reasonable. There were occasional gaps in the pines, though, enough to reveal the long narrow east-west valley below. A line of massive cottonwoods ran along the river at its center, their copper leaves clinging to gray branches. "That's certainly a welcome sight," Jessie said.

Juanita smiled, her lips stiff with cold. "Not pine."

Manuelita sniffed disapprovingly. Her sour mood had returned in full force. "Pine has nuts."

"That is true," Juanita said. "But they are so monótonos to observe. Especialmente when I am this cold."

There was a sudden shout from their escort, and Jessie's father spurred Saturn ahead to learn why. When he returned he looked aggravated and amused at the same time. "We've almost caught up to the ammunition and supply wagons," he reported. "Unfortunately, they're moving more slowly than we are. We're going to have to camp short of the valley." He smiled at Juanita. "But we'll reach it tomorrow and then follow it north. We might even reach Don Fernando de Taos!"

CHAPTER 34: Wednesday, February 3, 1847

Everyone seemed to move a little faster the next morning, as if even the animals could sense their destination was within reach. The Milbanks and their escort moved out of the foothills and up the narrow valley. When they came in sight of the supply wagons, the soldiers went on ahead, moving quickly through what was left of the snow.

Manuelita watched them go with a sour look, but everyone else felt more cheerful now. It was warmer, there was less ice on the road, and the track was flat compared to what they'd just traveled.

"It's an interesting little valley," Jessie's father said, playing tour guide. "This stream flows year round and there's a hot spring up ahead of here somewhere." He raised his voice, tilting his head towards the wagon interior and Dick. "That would be just the thing for a chest wound."

Green poked his head out from the space behind the bench seat. "I'm not sure my nurses would allow me that luxury."

Manuelita shrugged. "Good medicine."

He frowned. "But we'd fall behind and miss the fight."

Jessie turned. "You want to participate in the fight?"

"I surely would like to."

Manuelita scowled. "Hot spring better."

"Justice for Guv Bent best," he retorted.

Jessie opened her mouth to reiterate her argument about what, in her opinion, slaves owed to masters, but her father gave her a sharp look and she subsided. They rode on, passing quickly through the little town that lay at the junction of the river and the río Chiquito, bright in the midday sun.

Then they heard the guns, a periodic dull thump Jessie recognized from the fight at Embudo. Dick Green and Jessie's father looked at each other.

"That's too far away to be at Don Fernando de Taos," her father said. "The rebels must have retreated northeast to the pueblo. What is that? About three miles?"

Green nodded. "Right around that. Though it seems like a whole lot of shelling for a few pueblo walls. Those buildings are real old, too."

"Thousands of years," Jessie's father agreed.

"I reckon some of them are mighty thin by now."

Jessie's father nodded, but Manuelita moved restlessly. "Over soon," she muttered.

Jessie glanced at her, but the cook tucked her chin to her chest and turned her head. Juanita placed an anxious hand on Jessie's arm. Jessie smiled at her. "I'm all right." She realized with surprise that she actually was, that the sound of the cannon didn't send an echoing shiver up her spine. She sat a little straighter. Perhaps the fight at Embudo had inoculated her fear, and the worst was over.

Her father studied her speculatively, then said, "I'd best go on ahead to speak to the sutler and find out where we'll be camping."

Jessie nodded, but he was already trotting off. She suppressed a smile. He just wanted to know what was happening. She turned to find Green behind the bench seat, his hat on his head and a blanket around his shoulders. His eyes were fixed on the northern horizon, although the hills bounding the valley blocked his view.

What was it in a man's makeup that created such an interest in gunfire and war? Jessie forced her focus back to her surroundings. The houses beside the stream, the big cottonwoods, the chickens scratching a thin spot of snow, pecking delicately. A woman paused in a doorway, a basket on her hip, watching the little caravan pass. The weather had broken, and the sky was a deep blue, with puffy white clouds pushed by a breeze Jessie couldn't feel.

The clouds had moved on and the sky become a luminous purple before the wagon reached the mouth of the little valley and turned north toward the village of Don Fernando. Beside the road, the snow on the pastures and fields glowed golden in the dying light. The top of the mountain that bulked ahead on the right was a blinding white. Off to the left, between the fields and the setting sun, lay the black gorge, only seen in glimpses now, but still somehow ever present.

"It is a truly una vista maravillosa," Juanita said.

"I feel as if I'm caught between two worlds," Jessie told her. "The river at the bottom of that canyon and the mountains above us, the houses and fields suspended between."

Then the peaceful mood was broken by another blast of cannon fire. There was a pause, then another thud, then silence.

"That just don't sound right," Green said.

Jessie looked up at the mountain. Its broad snow-laden top lay in darkness now, as gloomy as the slave's tone. Yet he clearly wanted to be with the big guns, participate in the battle, if that's what it was.

But when the lieutenant showed up at the Milbank campsite outside Don Fernando that evening, Jessie had to admit that not every male of her acquaintance was enthralled by warfare. He looked tired and unhappy. He accepted a mug of coffee from Juanita and came to stand by the fire, where Jessie was stirring the pot of soup Manuelita had prepared. He nodded hello, then stared morosely into the flames.

Jessie kept her head down, moving her carved cottonwood spoon carefully through the thick liquid. Finally, she faced him. "I want to apologize for the way I reacted when we last spoke," she said.

He gave her a puzzled look, then his expression cleared. "Oh, at Los Luceros." He shook his head. "It is I who should apologize. I spoke without thinking, with greater freedom than I'm entitled to." He studied the fire. "Though we don't know each other well, I find that I feel remarkably comfortable with you." He lifted his gaze and grinned at her. "Even when you're angry." He turned back to the fire. "Then I forget myself and speak out of turn." He looked up at her. "Will you forgive me?"

Suddenly tongue-tied, Jessie nodded, and concentrated on moving her spoon through the soup. The lieutenant looked at the fire. Jessie cast around for another topic. "We heard the cannon," she said. Her father and Green came around the wagon, and she nodded toward them. "They both thought it sounded as if it came from the pueblo."

The lieutenant nodded, then went to greet the two men. When he returned, Jessie asked, "Is the battle over?"

He shook his head. "I wish it was. Colonel Price opted to deploy the Texan six pounder, but it was apparently too far from the walls. The adobe simply absorbed the shells." He shook his head. "My understanding is that the natives were forced by Spanish missionaries to build the church. That the building constructed by them under duress should become their place of refuge seems ironic indeed."

Her father frowned. "The rebels are in the pueblo church?"

Lieutenant Milbank nodded, his brow furrowed with concern. "Yes, not only people from the pueblo, but also from Don Fernando de Taos. There are women and children with them. If and when we breach the walls, I fear for the lives of the innocents."

Jessie shivered. "They must have thought they'd find sanctuary there."

"Colonel Price shows no signs of offering it."

Private Fitzgerald strode into the light. "Why should he? They killed and scalped Governor Bent in his own home." He turned toward Juanita, sitting by the wagon and nursing her own mug of coffee. "And others. The truly innocent."

She stared at him without speaking. He turned back to the fire, his face bitter. "We wasted over two hours and a good deal of powder this afternoon. In fact, we ran out of artillery rounds and have nothing to show for the expenditure. If Colonel Price continues in this way, the rebels will all simply slip out the back of the pueblo and disappear into the mountains."

Green had crossed to a small sawed-off stump and seated himself gingerly. Lieutenant Milbank nodded to him. "How are you doing?"

The Bent slave smiled at him. "Well enough for a little fighting, I reckon."

Before Jessie could remonstrate, the lieutenant had turned to the dragoon. "I'm sure the colonel is spending his evening reconsidering our approach." He looked at Jessie's father. "We did use up all the ammunition on hand. The rest of it came in after nightfall with you all." He turned to Green. "I suspect we'll get plenty of action tomorrow morning."

Green nodded in satisfaction as Private Fitzgerald said, "I certainly hope so. I refuse to once again be denied the vengeance due me."

The lieutenant turned away. "I, for one, hope we can bring this to a speedy resolution without the death of the women and children who've fled into that church for protection."

Fitzgerald sipped his coffee. "They chose to be there and must suffer the consequence." His eyes drifted toward Juanita. "Other innocents have also died. Murdered along with the governor and the sheriff and all the others. Evil doers who commit such deeds should receive the requisite punishment." Then he smiled as if mocking himself. "And the resolution to the conflict ahead should not be so speedy as to deny me an opportunity for glory."

"I pray for all of it," Juanita said somberly. "Justicia for the men who died. Protection for those who caused no one harm. And for you—" She paused, studying the dragoon. "Que tendrás la gloria y la venganza you seek and it will be sufficient to ease the pain in your heart."

He lifted an eyebrow. "Que tendrás?"

"That you will have." Then she translated all of it. "That you will have the glory and the vengeance."

He stared at her for a long moment, the only sound the crackling flames. Then he tossed his remaining coffee into the fire, said, "I thank you for your concern," tipped his hat to Jessie, nodded to her father, and walked away into the darkness.

Jessie lifted the soup pot from the fire, placed it on a nearby stump, and crossed to the wagon. As she settled in beside her friend, their shoulders touching, the lieutenant and her father moved off, speaking in low voices. Green stared at the burning logs.

CHAPTER 35: Thursday, February 4, 1847

They were startled awake the next morning by more artillery fire, the crash of it reverberating from the hills to the northeast. Jessie took deep, calming breaths, telling herself her nightmares had ended. Then her mind jumped to Lieutenant Milbank and she forced herself into occupation, rolling up blankets, reorganizing food stores, and generally getting in Manuelita's way. The cook seemed as edgy as she was.

Jessie's father was also distracted. The sutler had sent a runner to ask for canned goods, which were stored in the bottom of the wagon bed. Everything had to be taken out to get to them. Dick Green helped as much as he could, but his injury slowed him down, and it was clear that he didn't really want to be there. Every time there was a particularly loud cannon burst, he jerked upright and stared longingly north.

Only Juanita seemed unaware of the guns. She had been to the Beaubien casa early that morning and was now absorbed in gathering her clothing and personal items to return there. It was early afternoon before everything was finally arranged. The canned goods were loaded into the small cart the sutler had sent, Juanita bade Jessie a tender goodbye and Manuelita a more restrained one, then set off with Jessie's father for the village square. He would deliver her to the Beaubien household and go on to the army camp north of town with the supplies.

Manuelita, Jessie, and Green replaced the remaining goods and supplies in the wagon and settled around the fire. The big guns pounded steadily in the distance. Jessie, braced both against the sound and her reaction, found she was much calmer than she might have expected to be. Manuelita looked grim and Green anxious. "I sure do wish I knew what was going on up there," he said.

When Manuelita nodded, Jessie looked at her in surprise. "You, too?" Manuelita shrugged and looked away, but when Jessie's father returned and Green broached the idea of finding a vantage point from which to watch the fight, she made it clear she wanted to go with them.

Don Hubert nodded and looked at Jessie, who hadn't participated in the discussion. "I'm uncomfortable leaving you here alone," he said. "Would you like to go to the Beaubien casa instead?"

Jessie shook her head. It was a house of grief. She couldn't bring herself to either experience that or to inflict the weight of her presence on its inhabitants. She looked at Green, then her father and Manuelita. They all wanted to see what was happening at the pueblo. "I will go with you." Then she frowned. "But surely Mr. Green shouldn't be walking that distance."

Her father nodded. "He can ride Saturn."

They saddled and bridled the big black horse, and Green climbed carefully aboard. Jessie wrapped herself in her cloak and rebozo, and they set off, skirting the village plaza and the buildings beyond: the jail, the Bent casa, and others Jessie couldn't bring herself to examine too closely. The gates and doors of the houses they passed were all shut up tight, as if the town's inhabitants had lost interest in interacting with their fellow human beings. Jessie shuddered. Given what had happened the previous week, the reaction was understandable.

The big guns roared again in the distance and her father turned toward her. Jessie shook her head at him and concentrated on taking her buckskin gloves off so she could rearrange her rebozo closer to her face. "Even though we're walking, it's still a little chilly out here," she said as she tugged the leather back over her hands.

He eyed her, but then nodded, and they went on up the rutted track toward the pueblo. Behind them, the sun began to drop, sending shadows across the land and refreezing the muddy road.

They were within sight of the pueblo's church towers when Dick Green leaned down to speak to Jessie's father and gestured toward a field on the left. Don Hubert studied it, then nodded agreement, and they veered off the track, the women following.

Others had been here recently. The churned up snow marked them path of marching men who had then turned east toward the pueblo and the low walls surrounding it. In the center of the field, soldiers and artillery horses clustered around a large cannon on a two-wheeled gun carriage. As Jessie watched, the animals were led off to the side. Then the gun carriage suddenly jerked backward, and the cannon roared and belched smoke. A shell flew toward the pueblo church. Jessie clenched her fists to keep herself from covering her ears like a child, and looked elsewhere. Anywhere but there. There was a dull thud.

"It fell short," Green said in disgust. "They're bringing the horses up again."

Jessie forced herself not to look. Directly ahead, an outcropping of rust-colored rocks rose perhaps twenty feet above the snow. It was crowded with people: men, women and children sitting and standing wherever the rocks allowed them purchase and a view. Not all of the residents of Don Fernando de Taos were holed up inside their houses. Many were here, watching the American army do its best to subdue their neighbors.

Dick Green and Saturn led the Milbanks to a less-crowded section of the hill, and Jessie tucked her cloak closer to her skirts and followed her father and Manuelita up into the rocks. They turned to face the pueblo. The little Texan cannon was positioned between the big gun and the pueblo wall. The church, its associated graveyard, and an upright-pole corral filled the left-hand corner of the pueblo compound, which was enclosed by a waist-high adobe wall that swept past it, then curved west and out of sight.

To her right, a team of army horses strained across the churned-up snow, pulling the big cannon toward the church as rifle flashes danced from the slits in its side. The adobe-brick bell tower above, outlined against the deep purple-blue of the darkening sky, seemed unaware of what was going on below. Its top glowed with light reflected from the setting sun.

The rifle flashes slowed, then increased. Jessie glanced toward the road. A troop of American soldiers had massed near it and were firing steadily at the church without moving forward. Jessie frowned, wondering why. Then a man near the front crumpled into the dirty snow and mud. Another one fell farther on. A slim man wearing a lieutenant's hat moved among the men, shouting orders. Lieutenant Milbank? Bile burned her throat.

Then he moved toward the other side of the troop, closer to the road. Jessie steadied herself and turned back to the pueblo. Behind the church, facing the central open area, was a massive structure, over a hundred feet long and half again as wide. And tall. Five stories, each stepped back from the one below to create a wide terrace. Ladders led to each level, though she could see none from the ground. Another building, just as gigantic, filled the other side of the plaza. A small river ran between them, flowing toward the road to Don Fernando. The ice along its edges gleamed in the dimming light.

"Those are some buildings, aren't they?" Jessie's father asked. She nodded, taking them in. Watchers stood on the topmost roofs, but otherwise there was no evidence of the pueblo's inhabitants. Except for the church, where rifles continued to lay down a steady fire. Were they all inside the one building?

Jessie took a breath and looked at the far end of the square and the low wall that ran between the two buildings along the back of the pueblo and separated it from the mountains beyond. She could just make out movement in the area between: men on horseback, including Ceran Saint Vrain's big chestnut.

Below her, Saturn danced with impatience. "They've moved that little six-pounder up just about as close as they can get it," Green said. They all watched as soldiers unhooked the gun's horses and led them toward the road.

"Walls still stand," Manuelita said.

Jessie's father frowned. "That gun looks to be less than sixty yards from the church now."

"I reckon you're right," Dick Green said. "That there's one risky position." A man beside the little cannon crumpled as he spoke. Jessie's fingers bit into the leather of her gloves.

An American man perched on the rocks behind them took off his moth-eaten beaver hat and bent toward her father. "They've been throwin' shells at that church most all day," he said. "Tried to storm it earlier, but all that got them was Captain Burgwin bein' shot up." He glanced over his shoulder at the setting sun. "If Price don't break through pretty soon, the light's gonna be completely gone and he'll have to start all over again t'morrow." He pulled a handkerchief from his hat and blew his nose on it as a nearby woman wrapped in a faded rebozo said, "Por favor Dios, it is so. Then los pobrecitos can escape during the night."

Manuelita looked at her. "Or attack."

The man shook his head as he replaced the handkerchief and then the hat. "They're holed up in that church the way they would be if the wild tribes was after 'em. That thing's built for defense and protection, not much else. Can't really attack from there without exposin' themselves to our guns."

The cook turned away. The little cannon started up again, its sound not as loud as the bigger artillery piece, but somehow sharper. More intense. Jessie's shoulders jerked.

"They're throwing grapeshot at it now," the man behind her said. "That should tear up that adobe nice and sharp."

Jessie's father reached to put an arm around her shoulders, but she moved away, afraid that if he touched her she'd crumble. "I'm all right," she said.

But she couldn't keep her stomach from clenching as the gun sounded again and then again, the grapeshot slapping against the church walls, pieces of adobe flying as it hit. The gun went on and on: six, seven, eight volleys. The tenth one hit with a different sound, a hollow crunch. A dark spot appeared in the wall as the adobe gave way.

"They've broke through," the man in the hat said. He pulled a spyglass from his pocket and put it to his eye. "Looks like they used a shell for that last round. It made a hole big enough for a man to crawl through."

"A very brave man," Jessie's father said. "I expect the current building occupants will be waiting for him."

Manuelita turned and looked at him, her eyes glittering. Jessie shivered. He reached for her shoulders again, and this time she didn't pull away.

Five American soldiers, two of them dragoons, ran toward the church and crouched in the snow next to the pueblo wall. Near the road, someone bellowed an order and the men there began moving forward, firing as they went, though the flashes from the church had almost stopped.

The Texan cannon belched again, and another shell landed directly inside the earlier break, widening it. This had a different sound, an echoing hollowness. As the soldiers moved closer, rifle fire exploded from the slits in the side of the church. Another American fell.

The five men crouching below the wall by the church suddenly surged up and over it to the gaping hole. But they didn't plunge through. Instead, the dragoons stepped away to stand, one on each side, with their backs against the pitted wall, while two of their comrades scrambled into the breach.

After a long pause, a third followed, then the dragoons turned and plunged in after them. A ragged cheer went up from the soldiers in the field.

Jessie's father shook his head. "Brave men, one and all." He looked at Green, still on Saturn. "You can be proud to be part of that group."

"I'd be prouder to be down there with them."

"You've done your part."

Green shook his head, his eyes fixed on the church.

"Now what's goin' on?" the man with the spyglass asked, moving it to the right. "There's a man on a horse just boilin' around that corner there."

They all swung to look where he pointed. A buckskin-colored horse careened toward them, its rider waving an arm and yelling something about mountains and rebels.

"They're getting away!" Green said. He kneed Saturn forward, then reined in and turned back to Jessie's father. "They're getting away!"

Jessie's father grinned, nodded and raised his hand, waving the other man on. Green lifted his hat, swung it in the air with a whoop, then urged the gelding toward the buckskin.

Jessie frowned. "He's going to tear that wound open if he's not careful."

Her father chuckled. "I expect he can't even feel it at the moment."

Jessie looked at him. "Do you want to go with him? Help them fight?"

He stared past her at the battered church. Smoke drifted from the empty rifle slits. Below the building, dead and wounded soldiers lay in the dirty, blood-spattered snow. A lone medic moved among them. "No," Jessie's father said. "There's been enough killing."

Above him, the man with the spyglass exclaimed, "Look at 'em go!"

Jessie glanced back at him. The little telescope was now trained on the space between the pueblo wall and the mountains. "I can't see much," he said, "But it looks like Saint Vrain's Avengers are goin' after anyone fool enough to try and escape." He clicked his tongue in admiration. "They're slaughterin' 'em."

Jessie's knees buckled. Her father grabbed at her. "Jessie! Jessie girl! Manuelita, help me!"

The cook turned with a scowl, then her face smoothed and she reached to steady the girl, then assisted her from the rocks. They headed toward the road, Jessie's father following with his hands in his pockets and eyes on the ground. A phalanx of soldiers went past, toward the church.

Then, on the far side of the pueblo, a horse screamed in pain. Jessie bent forward, clutching her sides as she vomited into the snow. Manuelita yanked on her arm. "Come!"

Jessie fumbled clumsily for her handkerchief, the buckskin gloves getting in the way. "In a minute."

"Now!" the cook snapped.

Jessie frowned and wiped at her face. She took a deep breath, steadying herself.

"Come," Manuelita said again.

Jessie turned to locate her father, who stood watching the pueblo. The big church doors stood open. American soldiers poured in, rifles at the ready, while others marched toward the housing complexes. The sun had dropped below the horizon, leaving gray twilight behind. There were no rebels in sight.

Another horse screamed in the distance. Jessie's knees collapsed and she fell into the snow, retching up nothing but thin yellowish bile.

The sound got her father's attention. He came to her and reached for her arm. "Jessie girl," he said tenderly. "I'm sorry I brought you to see this." He turned to Manuelita. "And you as well. It isn't a sight for women's eyes."

The cook sniffed. She turned toward the road and the others followed.

Jessie had begun to recover by the time they reached the outskirts of Don Fernando. She walked close to her father, but she no longer needed his arm for support.

As they reached the edge of the village, they saw Juanita coming toward them. A slim young woman with long brown hair, large brown eyes, and a bitter face walked regally beside her. When Juanita spied the Milbanks, she rushed ahead and grabbed Jessie's hand. "Is it really true? Someone told us the battle is over; los insurrectos are crushed." She turned to Jessie's father, asking again. "¿Es realmente cierto?"

"Yes, it's true."

"Oh, I am so glad. And the rebels, they are defeated definitivamente? Well crushed?"

"It seems so."

"¡Gracias a Dios!"

"You weren't there," Jessie said. "You didn't see." Her breath hitched. "So many gone. And for what purpose?"

Juanita stared at her, then looked at the young woman with her, who stood at the side of the road gazing into the middle distance. "Yes," Juanita said sadly. "That is so. The dead don't return to us, except in our dreams."

She moved toward her companion. "Luz?" she asked tentatively. "Please, come and meet mi amiga, Jessie Milbank. Jessie, this is María de la Luz Beaubien. Narciso's sister."

The two young women nodded to one another, then Jessie said, "I was so sorry to learn of your brother's death—"

Luz's eyes flashed. "His murder!" she spat. "He did not simply die. He was asesinado!."

The others stared in surprise. Narciso's sister lifted her chin. "Perdóname," she said. "My grief makes me a poor companion. Juanita, I will leave you with your friends and return to la casa." She nodded to the others, then turned and stalked toward the Don Fernando plaza.

"Pobrecita," Juanita murmured. "It is very hard for her." She turned to Jessie. "On the morning her brother was killed, Luz and the sheriff's daughter were almost caught by los insurrectos. The girls ran to la casa of Padre Martinez and hid there until it was safe to return home." She glanced toward the retreating figure, then in the direction of the pueblo. Her face hardened. "Los insurrectos who died received all they deserved. I hope los soldados americanos catch the remaining ones and hang them all."

"So death should be followed by more death?" Jessie asked. "What good will that accomplish?"

Juanita's face darkened. "You do not understand." Then she turned and hurried after Narciso's sister.

Jessie stared after her, her eyes filling. Her father put an arm around her shoulder. "Give it time."

She nodded and they plodded on past the village plaza toward their campsite south of town. Jessie tugged her rebozo closer but the cold crept in anyway, making the freezing temperatures of the mountain journey seem like a mere chill. By the time they reached the wagon, she was shivering so violently she could hardly stand.

Her father guided her to a seat beside what remained of the fire and hurried to his knapsack. "More wood!" he snapped at Manuelita.

Jessie closed her eyes and pulled her cloak and rebozo closer. A log thumped onto the coals and flames snapped in response. But she couldn't feel any warmth. Her teeth knocked into each other, hurting her jaw.

Then something heavy touched her back and shoulders. Fur. The buffalo robe. Manuelita bent over her, tucking it in. Jessie tried to thank her, but her lips refused to cooperate.

The cook moved away, and Jessie's father appeared, proffering a bottle of whiskey. Jessie gave him a confused look. The cook huffed with impatience, moved to the box of kitchen supplies, and returned with a mug. Jessie continued to stare at them both.

Her father hefted the bottle. "It's Taos lightning."

Jessie tried to shake her head, but she was shivering too hard. "Mama—" she managed.

"In this case, I expect even your mother would think this a suitable remedy." He took the mug from Manuelita, filled it halfway, and gently lifted it to Jessie's mouth. "Just a sip."

Somehow, she managed to still her wobbly chin long enough to get her lips to the edge of the cup. The liquid bit her throat, and she coughed violently, but then the shivering eased, and she was able to whisper, "I understand now why it's called lightning."

Her father laughed, more loudly than strictly necessary, and proffered the mug again. "See, it's good medicine. Drink a little more and then let Manuelita help you to bed. I think you'd better sleep in the wagon tonight."

The cook turned away and threw another piece of wood onto the fire, as if making a point, but Jessie and her father didn't notice.

CHAPTER 36: Friday, February 5, 1847

Jessie's muscles were sore the next morning, but she wasn't cold anymore. She lay under the blankets, thinking about all that happened, then firmly moved her interior gaze from the men lying in the blood-spattered snow and replaced it with Juanita's pain-filled face. Her friend had only expressed what others felt. Dick Green. The spyglass man on the rock. Perhaps even Lieutenant Milbank, though she doubted it. But even her father—

She pushed back the blankets and began to dress.

When she reached for her cloak, she found the edges streaked with vomit and dirt. Jessie wrinkled her nose. It also smelled. She stood, noting the sunlight filtering through the wagon's canvas top, the hint of warmth in the air. Her rebozo would have to do.

Her father looked up from the fire as she climbed stiffly from the wagon. "How are you feeling?"

"Much better." She turned to Manuelita, who was tending a pot of cornmeal mush. "Thank you for taking care of me last night."

The cook barely looked at her, but she did nod. Jessie and her father exchanged glances, and he shrugged slightly and shook his head. When Manuelita dished up the food, he thanked her. When she didn't respond, he looked at her quizzically, but said nothing more.

After they finished eating, Jessie said, "I think I will go find Juanita. It would only be polite to extend my condolences to the Beaubien family as a whole."

He nodded. "Please express mine as well."

"I wonder how the men who were wounded yesterday are being cared for."

"We don't know that the fighting is over."

"I don't hear any cannon."

"They may still be mopping up. When Dick Green brought Saturn back this morning, he said there was still quite a lot of activity in the mountains east of the pueblo. They're searching for the one leader they know is still alive, a man named Tomás Romero."

She looked up. Señor Romero? "I can't simply sit," she said.

"You should." His eyes narrowed. "Please restrict yourself to visiting the Beaubien casa."

"There were men injured yesterday."

"The army has people to take care of them."

"You were happy to assist Mr. Green."

"We know Dick Green. And his people. Besides, he was unlikely to get the treatment he deserved."

"He deserves to be free."

Her father's jaw tightened. "Green has made it clear that he is content with his condition. In fact, he has already returned to the Bent household. Apparently, the governor's wife was delighted to see him and anxious for his assistance." Jessie frowned, but he barreled on. "It's none of our business."

She opened her mouth to argue, but he cut her off. "Don't get involved!" Then his expression softened. "It will only end in heartbreak."

Jessie sighed, nodded, and turned away. She was simply too tired and sore to discuss it.

Her body had limbered a little by the time she arrived at the Beaubien casa on the south side of the Don Fernando plaza. She stopped just inside the interior courtyard, where half a dozen injured American soldiers lay on improvised pallets. Juanita, aided by a young girl who looked remarkably like Luz Beaubien, was at the back of the space, moving from man to man with water, food, and kind words. There was a new dignity about her friend, though her face was still touched with sorrow.

Juanita looked up and saw Jessie, put her water pitcher to one side, and came toward her. "Buenos días," she said.

"I came to apologize for speaking so harshly."

Juanita smiled, tears glimmering in her eyes. "I planned to come to you as soon as I could break away."

Jessie looked at the men. "Were there many injured?"

"A good number. And some dead." Her voice was so sad that Jessie felt a stab of alarm.

"Anyone we know?"

"Private Fitzgerald's captain, Captain Burgwin. He led the original charge at la iglesia, the one that failed."

"It saddens me to hear that. And Private Fitzgerald?"

"I do not believe so. And el teniente?"

"I don't know."

Juanita nodded and was about to speak again when Luz Beaubien appeared on the far side of the courtyard.

Juanita put a hand on Jessie's arm. "Come and greet her," she said. "She is not always as full of bitterness as she was yesterday. In fact, her company can be most agreeable."

Jessie shook her head. "Perhaps tomorrow." She gestured toward the men on their pallets. "This is not a time for social calls." She pressed Juanita's hand. "I simply came to say I was sorry."

The two girls embraced again and Jessie went out. She turned right, toward the gate on the plaza's south side that would take her back to the campsite, but then found herself hesitating. She wasn't ready to return just yet. She moved left instead, along the east side of the square. She was halfway to the gate when Lieutenant Milbank came through it, leading a small band of soldiers. In its center was a tall man in traditional Taos leathers, his hair in neat braids on his chest. His hands were tied together, but he held his chin high.

It was Tomás Romero. Jessie jerked to a halt. The prisoner and his guard moved on, angling toward the southwest corner of the plaza. Then Colonel Price emerged from a building on the west side, his broad shoulders tight under their epaulettes and a scowl marring his handsome face.

Lieutenant Milbank and the others stopped abruptly, and the lieutenant snapped a salute.

"What's this?" the colonel demanded.

"Señor Tomás Romero, sir." The lieutenant's voice was clear in the morning air. "The rebel leader whose surrender you required in exchange for a cessation of hostilities. He came of his own accord."

Colonel Price gave the prisoner a contemptuous look. "In his best finery, I see." He glowered at Lieutenant Milbank. "I demanded two. The only two left alive. Where is the other one?"

"He has already surrendered, sir, and is being held in the jail."

"Where they killed the sheriff. How very fitting. Take this one there, too." The colonel spun on his heel and stalked away. The lieutenant snapped a command, then led Romero and his escort toward the plaza gate directly opposite the one they'd entered by.

"¡Señorita!" someone said in Jessie's ear. She turned to find Henry Fitzgerald, the wide belt around his waist looking less pristine than usual. It now held a single pistol and a new-looking horn-handled knife.

"So they have all surrendered?" she asked.

He nodded, his eyes on Lieutenant Milbank and his men. "A delegation came from the pueblo early this morning to treat with Colonel Price. He told them withdrawal of our guns was conditional on the surrender of the remaining rebel leaders." He jerked his chin toward Tomás Romero's back. "Those still in the vicinity, at any rate. Apparently there's a third man, but the coward escaped south as soon as we began shelling the church."

The little procession had stopped again, just short of the northwest plaza exit. The soldiers seemed to be waiting while Romero spoke with a truculent-looking young man in traditional pueblo clothing.

"Shall we see what the fuss is about?" Fitzgerald asked Jessie, offering his arm.

She nodded and they moved forward. "I find it hard to believe that Tomás Romero instigated the violence here," she said. The dragoon gave her a sharp glance. She shrugged.

"He seemed like such a nice man when I met him in August."

She turned her head to ask his own opinion, but Fitzgerald was focused on Romero and his guard, his lips pursed. They paused a few yards away, as the Taos leader frowned at the young man he'd been speaking to. "You were not there," he said firmly.

The boy's chin lifted. Romero stepped toward him, one hand out, but the nearest guard moved to block him. The big man's hand dropped. "You were not there," he repeated. "Go home to your mother. See to your family. Our people need you."

The boy stared at him for a long moment, then dropped his eyes, and nodded. "I will do as you say."

Romero turned to Lieutenant Milbank. "Please accept my apologies, señor."

The other man nodded and the little group moved on. Jessie and Private Fitzgerald followed them, joined by other interested bystanders.

The dragoon touched the pistol nearest his right hand. "And now the rebellion has been fully suppressed," he said. "It was quite a battle." He shot her a look. "I imagine the cannon fire sounded momentous even from here."

She winced and nodded. "And from the rocky outcrop west of the church."

"You were watching?"

"For part of it," she said, her throat suddenly tight.

The dragoon didn't seem to notice her discomfort. "Did you see the assault itself?"

She gave him a puzzled look.

"I'm referring specifically to the final successful assault on the church. That was the point at which we finally broke through their defenses." His shoulders straightened and his chin lifted. "I was there at the breach. The smoke inside was tremendous!"

They were out of the plaza now and moving around the buildings behind it toward the little jail. Jessie searched for something to say that would keep Fitzgerald from reliving the attack on the church. Then Tomás Romero and his escort stopped again, this time to allow him to speak to a stocky young woman around Jessie's age.

She stood in the middle of the street, her rebozo falling from her head. Her curly black hair looked as if it hadn't been combed in days, and her splotchy dark skin was streaked with tears.

"What of your father and grandfather?" the prisoner asked her.

She shook her head.

"Both of them?"

She nodded.

"Forgive me, señorita," he said. "It was not what I intended."

"And yet it happened." She looked around, at the jail just ahead and the battered wooden bench beside its yawning door. At the soldiers guarding him. The onlookers. Her gaze rested on Jessie, then returned to Tomás Romero. "Is this how we are to live now? Hating each other? In constant fear?" She shivered and turned to look at the house directly across the wide street.

"That's the Bent home," Fitzgerald murmured in Jessie's ear.

She nodded absently, her eyes on the girl, who had turned back to the Taos leader. "My father and grandfather came to Nuevo Méjico to be free." She pushed her dark curls away from her forehead. "To be treated like other men. They should have stayed in Missouri. They would probably be in chains, but at least they would be alive." Her voice broke then. She bent her head and pulled the edge of her rebozo up over her mouth.

Tears welled in Jessie's eyes. She moved forward impulsively, but Private Fitzgerald put a restraining hand on her arm. "She has someone with her," he murmured. "That little greaser there behind her."

Jessie gave him a sharp look. Greaser? When would the man learn? But now was not the time to remonstrate. A thin, careworn New Mexican man old enough to be the curly haired girl's grandfather stepped forward and took her arm. As they turned away, Luz Beaubien came out of the Bent casa. She looked haughtily at Romero and reproachfully at the lieutenant, then came forward and took the girl's other hand. She and the old man led her up the street.

Jessie's eyes followed them, but Fitzgerald's attention was on the prisoners and soldiers. "They're going into the jail now," he said, jiggling Jessie's arm. "If we're not quick about it, we'll miss the show."

Jessie gave him a puzzled look, but allowed him to maneuver her through the still-growing crowd to the little building.

As they entered, the men who'd been escorting the prisoner pushed past them and into the street. Jessie blinked, her eyes adjusting. On her left, Lieutenant Milbank sat at a scarred wooden table, filling out paperwork. Two blond guards, one very tall and one very short, leaned against the scuffed adobe wall by the door. Tomás Romero stood in the center of the room, looking through a waist-high half door into another room. It was crowded with dark-skinned prisoners.

"And here we are," Fitzgerald said. "The illustrious and infamous Taos jail."

The lieutenant looked up and Romero turned toward them. They both frowned when they saw Jessie, but she couldn't leave. Other people had come in behind, blocking the way.

Fitzgerald jerked his chin toward the half door and the men behind it. "We captured the worst of them," he said. When Jessie didn't respond, he added, "We arrested the one who speared your friend's sweetheart, too. The boy who was killed as he cowered in a shed." He snorted contemptuously. "They're all cowards in one way or another."

Romero scowled and turned away, moving toward the far wall. Fitzgerald dropped Jessie's arm and went after him.

A man appeared at the door to the room beyond and leaned out, his left arm stretched toward Lieutenant Milbank. The dirty rag around the man's bicep was spotted with fresh blood. The lieutenant rose and went to him. Jessie followed.

She pushed her rebozo away from her face and was leaning to ask how she could help when she heard Romero's voice at the other end of the room. "¿Gloria? Honor? ¡Bastardo! You lie!"

She turned. Fitzgerald's pistol was in his hand now. "¡Tendré gloria, honor y venganza!" he shouted. As Jessie registered his Spanish, the right gun roared and Romero's head exploded. A spray of blood hit the wall behind him, and thick whitish-gray brain matter fell onto his shoulders as he crumpled to the floor.

Jessie clutched at the lieutenant, but he was already moving toward Fitzgerald. She reached blindly for the half door, and the bandaged prisoner's hand met hers. "Manténgase firme, señorita," he said. She could barely hear him past the ringing in her ears.

Hold steady. Yes. Jessie squeezed his hand, then released it and moved numbly to the table and dropped into the chair. The room seemed to tilt. She grabbed the table edge and it righted itself. The doorway was crowded with staring faces, all watching the other end of the room.

Fitzgerald had dropped the pistol and pulled out his knife. Lieutenant Milbank moved toward him, hands up as if placating the man. The two guards appeared beside him and they all moved steadily forward, forcing the dragoon into the corner to the right of Romero's body.

Then they stopped, facing each other. There was a long pause, then the guard on Fitzgerald's left said something in a jeering tone. As the dragoon's head swung toward him, the lieutenant lunged for the knife. Fitzgerald stepped back and Lieutenant Milbank followed. Jessie's breath stopped. She closed her eyes, fighting the darkness. Then the crowds at the inner and outer doors exhaled, and her chest expanded.

As she opened her eyes, Fitzgerald's horn-handled knife spiraled through the air and onto the floor in the middle of the room. The guards grabbed Fitzgerald's arms and shoved him into the corner. Lieutenant Milbank picked up the dragoon's pistol, then crossed to the knife and collected it, too.

Behind him, the guards moved even closer to Fitzgerald. One of them raised a knee, kicking out, and the dragoon yelped and doubled over in pain. The lieutenant turned. "That will be enough!"

"What should we do with him?" the taller guard asked.

"Give him to us," a prisoner in the cell doorway said, flexing his hands.

The man who'd assisted Jessie nodded and grinned. "¡Sí! ¡Dénoslo a nosotros!"

The lieutenant frowned. "I am not going to give him to you. He will have justice, but not by your hands."

The first man laughed derisively. "Americano justice? Same as us?"

Lieutenant Milbank's frown deepened and the man looked away.

Jessie started to push herself away from the table, but then her eyes fell on the blood and brains on the wall above Tomás Romero's body and the sticky mass on his shoulders. She dropped back onto the chair and looked at Fitzgerald, his arms pinioned to his sides by the guards.

"How could you?" she asked.

"He was only an Indian." There was a hiss of anger from the cell door, but he kept his eyes on the girl. "He was a traitorous beast, like all of his kind, like your friend Raúl." Then, bizarrely, his face split into a triumphant smile. "I have accomplished my task."

As she stared at him, processing this, Lieutenant Milbank snapped, "Get him out of here!" at the guards.

"But where, sir?" the shorter one asked.

"Here!" a prisoner called.

The lieutenant ignored him. "The courthouse," he said. "Find a room there and make sure it's secure." He moved toward Jessie. "Are you able to stand?"

"I think so."

"Come."

Her eyes drifted to Romero and the mess around him, then focused on the bandaged prisoner in the doorway. "That man needs—"

"Yes, I know," Lieutenant Milbank said. "He and a number of the others, as well." He gestured toward the papers on the table. "I was making the arrangements."

She nodded, pulled her rebozo closer, rose, and took his arm. The prisoners and other onlookers murmured sympathetically as the crowd by the outer door moved aside to let them through.

They stood for a moment in the clear early February sunlight, then the lieutenant guided Jessie to the bench beside the door. She sank onto it gratefully and put a hand to her chest. Her breath came in short, uneven gasps.

Lieutenant Milbank bent toward her, his face anxious, then he straightened and looked around. A small dark-haired boy with a pointed chin stood nearby. "Water for the lady!" the lieutenant told him.

The child looked uncertainly from him to Jessie. She tried to make herself smile. "Agua, por favor," she whispered. He nodded and took off at a run.

"I'm needed inside," Lieutenant Milbank said reluctantly.

Jessie nodded and gulped back the bile in her throat. "Go," she said hoarsely. "I'll be all right."

Some of the watchers had come outside with them. He looked at them uncertainly and she smiled. "Truly," she said. "I will be fine."

The crowd's gaze followed him back inside the jail, and Jessie no longer felt the need to keep herself together. Her rebozo slipped from her shoulders as she covered her face with her hands. The blood. The—

She bent forward, clutching at her wayward stomach, then shuddered, straightened, and gasped for air.

People filled the street now, streaming toward the jail. News of the shooting had clearly spread. Men, women, and children clustered at the door, trying to peer inside. Crowding her. Jessie stood abruptly and pushed her way into the street, walking aimlessly, eyes squinted against the sun, hands clutching her rebozo to her chest.

That shot. The blood. Her mother's blood. Her knees buckled and she almost fell, then the little boy was there, holding out a gourd dipper filled with water. Jessie forced her knees to straighten and accepted it.

The water felt good. A solid mass of liquid down her center, stiffening her spine. "Gracias," she murmured as she returned the gourd.

"De nada." The boy smiled up at her, then peered into her face, reached politely for her hand, and led her into the tiny courtyard of a house a few doors from the Bent casa. A gnarled cottonwood stood in the center of the walled space, a battered bench beneath it. The boy helped her sit, then brought more water from a nearby bucket.

She smiled at him gratefully.

"¿Descansa ahora?" he asked.

She nodded. "Yes, I will rest now. You are very kind." He smiled shyly and disappeared into the house. Jessie leaned against the tree's rough bark and closed her eyes.

She tried to relax, but her mind wouldn't settle. What did it mean? Why had Henry Fitzgerald shot Tomás Romero? And why had the Taos leader called the dragoon a lying bastard? And made that reference to glory and honor?

She frowned. How had Romero known about the dragoon's obsession with glory and honor? But then, they must have spoken at least once. She'd seen them together just a few weeks ago, leaving the old chapel in the Santa Fe plaza.

So much had happened since then. Had the dragoon actively encouraged Romero to lead a rebellion? Told him the American soldiers were weak and wouldn't fight? Seduced him with the promise of honor and glory, all with the hope that Fitzgerald could get his revenge and his own glory? It didn't seem possible that anyone could be that perfidious. And yet—

Jessie rearranged her rebozo, spreading it carefully over her head and smoothing it around her shoulders. Her mind flicked to the night Raúl died. How shocked Fitzgerald had looked when Raúl tumbled into the street. How oddly angry. And how disappointed he was in December when the conspirators were arrested. That there would be no rebellion, no one to fight.

Jessie's head jerked and she sat straight up. The knife. That horn handle. Yes, the type of knife wasn't uncommon, but the same exact make had now featured in three deaths. Vidal, Raúl, and Tomás Romero. Romero, who had called Henry Fitzgerald a liar.

But wasn't that what the dragoon had called Romero? She frowned, trying to remember. No. He'd said the Taos leader was traitorous. It wasn't quite the same. And he'd said the same thing of Raúl. Before he smiled and declared, "I have accomplished my task."

Jessie shivered. The statement was simply bizarre. His task?

The one thing Fitzgerald had been obsessed with since she first met him was vengeance for his brother's death. Jessie shook her head. Surely, the battles at Embudo and Taos Pueblo had given him enough opportunity to obtain that.

She took a deep breath, considering. Was it possible that the dragoon had actively encouraged rebellion so he would be sure to have his revenge? But what could he possibly accomplish by killing Vidal, Raúl Cabeza de Baca, and Tomás Romero?

Jessie frowned. She didn't know that Vidal or Raúl were part of the plot against the occupying Americans. If they were, the insurrectos must have begun planning their resistance even before the U.S. Army entered Santa Fe. She frowned, remembering that August morning in the plaza. Was the Mexican clothing Raúl wore that day more than a symbol? Perhaps a signal to others that he supported resistance? A message to people like Agustín Durán?

She shivered and pulled her rebozo closer. If they were already organizing, was Vidal part of the plot? Had he been involved, then thought better of it? Been killed to keep him from reporting those early discussions? Had he made the mistake of reporting to the first soldier he saw, who just happened to be someone with a deep personal interest in encouraging battle and bloodshed?

Had she and Juanita been befriended by a murderer? Her spine stiffened. A murderer who'd shouted "Tendré gloria, honor y venganza". I will have glory, honor, and vengeance. In Spanish. Not English. Using the proper tense for "I will have." Fitzgerald knew a good deal more Spanish than he'd let on. Her eyes widened. Enough to write a promissory note in Spanish? It seemed likely.

"Are you cold?" A voice asked from the courtyard gate. She looked up to find Lieutenant Milbank.

She shook her head. He moved toward her. "I apologize for leaving you as I did. I didn't want someone in the crowd deciding to try to free all our prisoners. We've had enough bloodshed."

He stopped in front of her, hands clasped behind his back, and looked around the little courtyard. "The boy who brought you here came to tell me where he had deposited you." He grinned. "At least I think that's what he said. We had a little trouble understanding each other. However, I did make out the words for 'small house' and 'street.'"

Jessie smiled. "I am grateful to him. The crowd was a little overwhelming." She slid to the left and patted the bench beside her. "Please sit down." She took a deep breath. "I think I know why Henry Fitzgerald shot Señor Romero."

He sat down, took off his hat, and laid it on his knee. "Private Fitzgerald is an impulsive young man eager for revenge against anyone of Indian or Spanish extraction."

Jessie nodded. "That's true enough, but I believe he acted on more than impulse." She took a breath, not quite believing what she was about to say. "I think he needed to prevent Romero from telling you or Colonel Price that he fomented the rebellions. This one, the one discovered in

December, and one that was in the early planning stages in August.”

He raised his eyebrows at her. “That’s quite a charge.”

“Yes, but I believe that it’s true. As you know, Henry Fitzgerald has been eager since he arrived here not only to avenge his brother but also for what he calls glory and honor.”

He nodded thoughtfully.

“He’s also expressed a great deal of frustration that there’s been no opportunity to do so,” she said. “Remember how disappointed he was when the December plot was discovered and the conspirators were jailed?”

“Yes, I do recall that.” He frowned. “You think he’s responsible for three separate deaths?”

“Murders,” she said grimly. “It started in August.” She began laying it out: the reasons, the timing, the opportunities, the promissory note, the knowledge of Spanish. By the time she finished, Lieutenant Milbank’s expression had turned from disbelief to growing acceptance.

Though he still hesitated. “None of this changes the fact that the people of New Mexico rebelled.”

Jessie nodded. “And they have every reason to want to do so. After all, they see themselves as fighting against an invader. The war hasn’t ended elsewhere in the country. Why should they submit here? But encouraging them to insurrection for private reasons, enticing them—” She shook her head.

He frowned. “I doubt Colonel Price will see that as a punishable offense.”

“That’s not the point,” Jessie said. “Private Fitzgerald didn’t kill Vidal and Raúl in battle. He murdered them. They died to further his plans for insurrection. An insurrection he actively encouraged so he could avenge his brother with even more blood. And then he—"

She paused and looked up at the cottonwood's thick branches, remembering Tomás Romero's proud face, his regal bearing. He'd done what he thought best for his people, and Fitzgerald had made a mockery of him. Had blown the top of his head off.

"Then he killed again," Jessie said grimly. "This time to cover up the fact that he'd actively conspired to foster a hopeless rebellion so he could obtain glory and honor along with his vengeance."

Silence fell in the little courtyard. The lieutenant studied its walls for a long moment, then nodded and rose to his feet. "We need to speak to the colonel."

As they stepped into the street, they encountered Dick Green, coming from the direction of the Bent house, and looking a little dazed. When he saw Jessie, he broke into a huge smile and waved his hat at her. "Miss Jessie, you need to congratulate me!"

She gave him a confused look.

The lieutenant's eyes glimmered in amusement. "And what is it we're to congratulate you for?"

Green was still beaming at Jessie. "The Bent family gave me my freedom papers. Charlotte's, too." He laughed exultantly and swung his hat if he didn't know what to do with himself. "We're free!"

"That is definitely cause for congratulation." The lieutenant extended his arm. "Let me be the first to shake your hand as a free man."

They shook, and Green turned to Jessie. She smiled at him in spite of her preoccupation. "I'm so glad for you, Mr. Green."

He grinned at her. "Thank you!" Then he settled a little. "The guv's wife said it was to express their gratitude for my fighting against los insurrectos." He shook his head. "And I was just doing it because I was mad. I can tell you I sure wasn't expecting anything like this here." He looked up and down the street. "I feel like I could tell the entire town."

The lieutenant laughed. "I can understand that."

Green nodded and grinned, then looked at Jessie. "I think I'll find your Pa and give him the news."

"He'll be glad to hear it. Come by this evening, and we'll celebrate." She grinned. "I'm afraid we don't have an oven for Manuelita to bake bizcochitos, but I can make griddlecake."

He laughed, shook their hands again, and headed off. Jessie and the lieutenant continued up the street and around the corner into the plaza.

They found Juanita outside the courthouse door, pacing under the portal. When she saw Jessie, she rushed toward her. "Private Fitzgerald!" she gasped. "I have heard what he did and I now understand—"

"What happened to Raúl," Jessie finished.

The other girl nodded grimly. "And the friend of Manuelita." She turned to the lieutenant. "Tres muertes all for the same reason. Gloria y venganza."

"He used that very phrase before he killed Señor Romero," Jessie said. "He yelled, '¡Tendré gloria, honor y venganza!'"

Juanita's eyes widened. "In Spanish? He knows 'tendré'? He said it in that way? Properly?" When Jessie nodded, her lips flattened. "He wrote el pagaré."

Lieutenant Milbank studied her, then nodded toward the building's iron-studded door. "It is time we spoke to Colonel Price."

CHAPTER 37: The Same Day, Friday, February 5, 1847

They found the American military leader in a large dimly lit room behind a desk covered with paperwork. A guard stood just inside the door.

The colonel looked up rather crossly when the lieutenant ushered Jessie and Juanita in, then ran a hand through his thin gray hair and rose politely to greet them. After the introductions were concluded, he turned to Jessie. "And just how may I be of service to you, señorita?"

Jessie looked at the lieutenant, who said, "Miss Milbank and Señorita Sena have evidence regarding the reason Private Fitzgerald shot and killed Tomás Romero."

"To save us the trouble of hanging the traitorous bastard," Colonel Price growled. He glanced toward the documents waiting on his desk.

"We believe he's responsible for the murder of two other men," Jessie said.

He frowned at her. "Romero? He's responsible for the deaths of a good many more than that!"

"It is Private Fitzgerald of whom we speak," Juanita said.

He made an impatient gesture at them both. "Go on."

"A man was knifed to death in the Santa Fe plaza two days after your army arrived in August," Jessie explained.

"He was genízaro, a man named Vidal. Private Fitzgerald was on duty that night and appeared only moments after the corpse was discovered."

He raised his eyebrows. "How is it that you know about this death and the events leading to its discovery?"

"Miss Milbank and two friends found the body," the lieutenant said.

Jessie nodded. "That's right. Almost immediately after we stopped to see what was wrong, Private Fitzgerald appeared and arrested Señorita Sena's cousin, Raúl Cabeza de Baca, for the murder, apparently because he was the only male present!" She paused, realizing how indignant she sounded, then went on more calmly. "Private Fitzgerald apologized later, after it became clear Raúl wasn't responsible, but it was very—" She paused, searching for the right word. "Precipitous of him to take a man into custody in that way."

The colonel looked from her to Juanita and back. "And now the two of you have put your heads together and concluded Private Fitzgerald killed the man himself and sought to pin the crime on Miss Sena's cousin."

Her chin lifted. "We came to the same conclusion quite separately."

The colonel made a disbelieving sound and circled the desk to return to his chair.

Juanita stepped forward. "Please sir, you must understand. The death of the man en agosto was but the first."

Jessie nodded. "In late November, the man who had been falsely arrested for the August death was murdered."

"We found mi primo in the dark street with a knife in his chest," Juanita said, her voice trembling.

Jessie shot her an anxious glance, then turned to the colonel. "We learned much later that Raúl—Señor Cabeza de Baca—had participated in the initial planning for conspiracy which was discovered in December. His sweetheart convinced him to go to the authorities, but he didn't have a chance to do so." She paused, then went on, her voice grim. "He was killed before he could do so. Murdered with the same type of knife that was used on the man in the plaza."

"That is not proof," the colonel said.

"Since our arrival in New Mexico, Private Fitzgerald has been quite open about his desire to see action," Lieutenant Milbank said. "In fact, he expressed anger when the December conspiracy was brought to light. He was upset that he wouldn't be able to revenge his brother as he wished."

Colonel Price's eyebrows went up again. "His brother?"

"His brother, Archibald Fitzgerald, was among los tejanos captured and taken south six years ago by la milicia de Nuevo Méjico," Juanita explained. "He is said to have died in consequence. Private Fitzgerald told us he came here in search of vengeance for his death. He has many times expressed una profunda frustración regarding the lack of opportunity to complete his mission."

Jessie nodded. "When Governor Bent was killed and it was clear that you would march against the rebels, his only fear was that he would be left behind."

"None of this is proof," the colonel said. He turned to Lieutenant Milbank. "Has the man confessed?"

The lieutenant shook his head, the reluctance clear on his face.

"When I asked him why he shot Tomás Romero, he smiled and said that Senor Romero was a traitorous beast like Raúl," Jessie said. "And then he said he had accomplished his task."

"A comparison isn't a confession." The colonel waved an impatient hand. "The fact remains that there is no evidence this dragoon murdered the two other men you claim he killed. The only thing we know for certain is that he shot the rebel leader Tomás Romero, a man who was going to die anyway." He looked at the lieutenant. "I understand you ordered Fitzgerald to be confined."

"Yes, sir." He glanced at Jessie, who felt a glimmer of hope at the determination in his eyes, then turned back to the Colonel. "We believe the promissory note found on the young Cabeza de Baca may have been forged by Fitzgerald."

"Based on what evidence?"

"The private demonstrated this morning that he is fluent in the Spanish language. Prior to this point, he went to great pains to conceal that fact. It was he who reportedly found the promissory note in the dead man's pockets."

Colonel Price's frown deepened. "If you have firm evidence that Private Fitzgerald committed such a dishonorable action, I will be happy to hear it." He raised a questioning brow at Jessie. When she hesitated, then shook her head, he nodded. "I thought as much." He looked at the lieutenant.

"I'm afraid I know nothing definite," he answered. "If I could question him—"

Jessie's eyes widened. He was willing to do that? She reached involuntarily for his arm, then caught herself.

"You will do no such thing," Colonel Price snapped. "And unless you have sufficient evidence to support a formal accusation, you will remain silent on this matter. I will not have his name dirtied. After all, his action today will make him a hero in the eyes of many of our troops. He saved us the bother of a trial and the cost of a hanging rope." He glanced toward the guard at the door. "I suspect his cell won't be guarded too closely."

Jessie and Juanita exchanged a startled look, and Jessie opened her mouth to protest, but the colonel's hands were shuffling the papers on his desk. He nodded to Lieutenant Milbank. "Good day to you." He reached for a pencil.

Jessie stared, her mouth working, but then the lieutenant offered her one arm and Juanita the other and guided them inexorably out of the room.

They stepped into the Taos plaza and clear winter sunshine. Jessie glared around the square, too angry to speak, but Juanita turned to the lieutenant. "Am I to understand that Private Fitzgerald will not be punished for what he has done this day or in the past?"

His gaze followed Jessie's around the square. "More than likely, Fitzgerald will be confined until he can be discharged and sent back to Missouri." He raised a helpless hand. There was a pleading tone in his voice, wanting it to be enough. "I doubt there will be a further inquiry, but at least he will be removed from New Mexico." He paused, waiting for a response, then turned to Jessie. "I'm sorry I couldn't get permission to speak to him. I can't disobey—"

"The colonel's direct order," she finished. She looked up at him and felt only pity for the pain in his eyes. It wasn't his fault. Yet, when he asked, "May I escort you back to your wagon?" sudden tears blinded her eyes. She shook her head.

"Thank you," she muttered. "I will find my own way back. I need—"

Juanita moved toward her. "I will come with you." Jessie nodded, unable to speak, and they moved into the plaza. When they reached the houses on the other side, she looked back. He still stood there, watching. She raised her hand, he lifted his in response, and she felt oddly comforted.

When they reached the wagon, the girls found Jessie's father opening boxes and pulling out cans of peaches. He dropped what he was doing, hurried across the campsite, and wrapped Jessie in his arms as he reached for Juanita's hand.

"You heard," Jessie said into his shoulder.

"Yes."

"So many dead." She shook her head, feeling the texture of his wool coat against her cheek. "For the sake of some kind of glory." She shuddered and pulled back to look at Juanita. "For revenge."

"And to think I considered him a possible sweetheart," the other girl said.

Don Hubert gave her a startled look.

"It is true." Juanita put her hand on her stomach. "I feel most enferma when I think of it. That I would consider un hombre who would trick others to rebel so he could kill them."

He frowned. "Trick them?"

When the girls nodded, he pulled away and sat down on an unopened box of peaches. "I expect I need to hear this from the beginning." As they explained, he became more somber, and when they had finished, he frowned and shook his head.

"You don't believe us, either?" Jessie asked. "The colonel—"

He held up a hand. "Yes, you told me what the colonel said, and I expect the lieutenant is correct in his prediction. I shook my head because there's something more. Something that will exonerate the dragoon in at least one of those deaths." He gestured toward the far side of the campsite.

The Milbank's cook sat at the base of a large cottonwood, her back to its deep-furrowed trunk. Two soldiers flanked her stiffly, rifles at their sides. One of them had a blood-stained cut in his left sleeve.

"Manuelita!" Jessie exclaimed.

The cook lifted her head, then her hands. They were bound together with rawhide rope.

"¡Dios mío!" Juanita whispered.

Jessie started toward the cook, who scowled and made an impatient gesture with her bound wrists. The girl stopped beside the dying fire. "I don't understand."

Manuelita's face twisted. "You say true. Understand nothing."

"Why—"

"¡Stupido!" the cook spat. The guard on her right shifted and raised his hand, and Manuelita subsided.

Jessie's father rose and moved to the fire, opposite Jessie. "She disappeared this morning after we ate," he said, his eyes on the cook. "She apparently went looking for Tomás Romero and found him en route to Colonel Price. The soldiers assigned to meet Romero discovered her trying to persuade him not to turn himself in." He nodded toward the man with the cut sleeve. "She had a knife."

"I cook!" Manuelita spat. "Sí, knife!"

Jessie's stomach twisted as she stared at the cook. "You killed the man in the plaza. Vidal."

"That traitor! ¡El bastardo!"

Juanita frowned. "He was your amigo."

"No friend me!"

Jessie shook her head. "I don't—" She stopped, not wanting to say it again, be told it was true.

"Pero por qué?" Juanita asked.

"Yes," Jessie agreed. "But why?"

Manuelita flipped an impatient hand and looked away.

"I reckon they were planning an uprising of the genízaros," Jessie's father said. He shook his head. "It doesn't make much sense to me."

Manuelita's chin jutted scornfully. "Better boss ciudad de México, than los americanos here." She looked up at her guards and sniffed contemptuously. "Weak men, strong guns." She shrugged at Juanita. "Vidal say will tell. I stop."

"You killed him," Jessie said.

Beside her, Juanita murmured, "It is at least one sin of which Private Fitzgerald is not guilty."

Yes, Jessie thought bleakly. That particular death was Manuelita's work. The woman she'd thought of as a friend.

The cook lifted her chin to say more, but then a voice just beyond the wagon barked a command. An American sergeant appeared at the head of a small band of soldiers. He nodded respectfully to Jessie's father and the girls and moved toward the tree. The guard with the torn sleeve grabbed Manuelita's arm and hauled her to her feet.

"What will happen to her?" Jessie asked as the newcomers surrounded the cook.

"Under American law, murderers hang," Jessie's father said.

Manuelita and the soldiers were moving past them now. "Not America yet!" she spat. "War not done!"

"Shut up, woman," the sergeant said. The prisoner and her escort marched past the Milbank wagon and disappeared toward the village.

Jessie turned to Juanita. "I had no idea," she murmured.

"Yo tampoco," the Mexican girl answered. "Nor did I."

Epilogue. January 1862

Henry Carr Fitzgerald trudged up the dusty street toward the Geelong, Australia post office, thinking about the cost of firewood. He needed to order more for the bathhouse fires. He shook his head. All those flames in midsummer. But there was no help for it. The scorching January sun made the region's infernal dust even more hellish than usual, and the incoming sheep drovers and Ballarat gold miners gladly paid good money for a warm soak to rid themselves of it before they started their drinking jags.

Henry pushed his hat from his forehead and wiped the sweat from his face. Even after fifteen years, he still found the upside-down weather here and the dust that accompanied it inconceivable. When he finally reached the blessed shade of the post office porch, he stopped beside its rickety bench and beat the worst of the clinging dirt from his clothes before he opened the door.

When he came out a few minutes later, Henry had forgotten the dust. In addition to the usual Melbourne newspaper and two bills, he held a thin missive bearing English stamps. The letter was addressed in his sister Sarah's neat script. Henry pursed his lips. Postage between Britain and Australia was not cheap. She only wrote if there was news, usually something he didn't want to hear.

The paper had been carefully folded and thoroughly sealed. She'd written something on the back, just a few words. He held it up, squinting, then grinned. *This missive contains only good news.* He dropped onto the bench, took the penknife from his pocket, and carefully broke the seal.

First there were the usual family updates. Her youngest son Archie, nine years old now, was doing well. Brother Crofton's oldest, two-year-old Wilfred, was also healthy and full of spirit, anxious to grow up and go to sea like his father. Henry's jaw tightened. Crofton, the British naval officer. Not like the boy's uncle, the bathhouse minder. He shook the letter impatiently and read on.

Sarah was now discussing her recent vacation to Wales. Henry frowned. It wasn't like her to waste paper and postage on mundane events. *I met the most interesting gentleman named Thomas Falconer,* she reported. *He is a former member of Lincoln's Inn and now serves as judge for two counties in Wales and a large section of Radnorshire. Much to my surprise, he told me he knew our brother, Archibald. In fact, they were together on the Texan expedition to Santa Fe. I wish you could have spoken to him, Henry. He recalled Archie with great fondness and reported that he was fascinated by the Mexican people and admired them very much. He also said the men who escorted the Texans to El Paso del Norte did not cause Archie's death. In fact, Judge Falconer has been informed by other Expeditionaries that our brother survived the ordeal of prison in Mexico City and returned to Texas. There, he enlisted in their army and fought the Mexicans at a place called Salado. Unfortunately, Archie and his compatriots were captured during that battle and thrown into prison. Being Texans, of course, (or perhaps*

I should say him being a Fitzgerald man, since they can't abide to sit still) Archie and the others escaped. The Mexicans went after them and he was killed during the ensuing pursuit."

Henry stared at the words blurring on the page, remembering New Mexico and what he had done to avenge Archie's death. How far he had traveled, the lies he had told, the men he had—

He blinked and searched the paper to locate where he'd stopped.

"In other news, the cotton mills here in the north of England are almost entirely at a standstill, due to the scarcity of bales from the southern United States. We watch anxiously for news of their Civil—"

He stared at the hot, dusty street. Archie had been fascinated by those bastards? Admired them? They had tortured him. Killed him, in the end. It might not have been someone from New Mexico, but it was still a greasy Mexican, somewhere.

But the angry phrases didn't rile him the way they once had. The little wooden bench creaked as Henry's weight shifted. Then he shook his head. No, he had been right to do what he did. One way or another, those greasers needed to atone for his brother's death.

Former United States dragoon Henry Carr Fitzgerald stood abruptly, crumpled his sister's letter in his hand, tossed it aside, picked up the rest of his mail, and strode out into the street and the merciless Australian winter sun.

~ ~ **THE END** ~ ~

NOTE TO READER

As with all my fiction, the historical characters in this book are based on what I could find in the records available to me. That being said, there's always something missing, a gap that must be spanned. Therein, of course, lies the fiction.

For several of these people, there wasn't much to go on. If Bent family slave Dick Green hadn't joined Ceran Saint Vrain's Avengers in January 1847, we probably wouldn't know anything at all about him. His wife, Charlotte, was the enslaved person visitors to Bent's Fort noticed and wrote about, both because of her renowned cooking skills and her love of dancing.

However, when Dick joined the Avengers, he won himself a place in New Mexico history and U.S. military records, even though people of color weren't allowed to enlist at the time. Dick Green fought with Saint Vrain's volunteers anyway, was wounded at the battle outside the village of Embudo, and subsequently freed by the Bent family in gratitude for his service. In fact, they freed Charlotte and Dick's brother, Andrew, as well.

The other key character for whom I found little information is the woman believed to have been instrumental in disarming the 1846 Christmas Eve conspiracy.

The sources for this piece of the story are vague and somewhat contradictory. To summarize: a woman associated with Gertrudes Barceló learned of the rebel plans from her conspirator husband or lover. She told Barceló, who then told Donaciano Vigil, who went to Governor Bent. As a result, the planned outbreak was quelled when most of its leaders were rounded up on Monday, December 21, 1846. Three of them were arrested outside the hotel on the southeast corner of the Santa Fe plaza, the location of today's La Fonda hotel.

The historical records are almost unanimous in placing the leak about the planned revolt in Gertrudes Barceló's household. The leap to fourteen-year-old Guadalupe as the person who reported the plans is mine. It is based on the fact that Barceló adopted the infant María Guadalupe de Altagracia in December 1832 and apparently raised her in her Santa Fe household. Guadalupe would have been fourteen in December 1846, making her old enough to have a sweetheart and, in New Mexico at the time, even to be married. I have not been able to locate any other information about this girl beyond her baptism record, so I am imagining a great deal here, including that she had dark skin and lived past babyhood.

While my characterizations of Guadalupe Barceló and Dick Green are necessarily things of fragment and supposition, I was able to piece together more information about Henry Carr Fitzgerald. We know that U.S. dragoon Private Fitzgerald killed Taos leader Tomás Romero in early February 1847. We also have Louis Garrard's report of what Fitzgerald told him a couple months later. According to Garrard, Fitzgerald's brother, Archibald, was killed "while a prisoner in the [1841] Texan expedition against Santa Fe." In consequence, Fitzgerald swore vengeance for the death "and entered the [U.S.] service with the hope of accomplishing it." Fitzgerald also reportedly told Garrard he'd killed three other men besides Tomás Romero.

Garrard doesn't explain why Henry Fitzgerald chose to go to New Mexico to wreak his vengeance instead of heading farther south. Or why he killed Tomás Romero, in particular. After all, Archibald didn't die in New Mexico. He survived the Texan prisoners' forced trek to Mexico City and subsequent imprisonment. When he was released, he returned to Texas and fought at Salado, where he was captured and subsequently died after a mass prison escape.

I can only conjecture that Henry didn't know the details of Archibald's death and assumed it occurred during the march across New Mexico's jornada del muerto, which I've described in my novel *The Texian Prisoners*. This lack of information would explain Henry's decision to seek revenge in New Mexico, though it doesn't provide a rationale for Tomás Romero's death. I have found nothing in the historical record which links Romero to the events of 1841.

I've used this lack of historical report as a springboard to expand Fitzgerald's thirst for revenge to include a desire for glory and honor, as well. This expansion is not pure invention on my part, but is based on the fact that Henry and Archibald were great-grandchildren of Anglo-Irish hero, Archibald Hamilton Rowan. Rowan was celebrated in his time for championing the Irish cause in a period when a more arrogant view prevailed among the British. It seems plausible that early childhood stories of great-grandfather's noble deeds could have fostered a twisted thirst for renown which led ultimately to the little jail in Taos.

Certainly, Henry Fitzgerald seems to have gone to some effort to participate in the American war against Mexico. Born in 1819, he appears to have enlisted in the U.S. dragoons as John Fitzgerald of Cook County, Illinois. While there is no way to know for certain that this is Henry's record, it seems likely, and I've used the military's physical description of John Fitzgerald (5 feet 9 inches tall, blue eyes, dark hair, and a fair complexion) in this novel.

We also don't know for certain that Henry Fitzgerald actively fostered insurrection among the New Mexicans. However, we do have evidence that the American troops in Santa Fe were restless and anxious for some kind of armed confrontation. They'd come for glory and they hadn't found it. It seems logical to extend this hunger to the dragoon who killed the Taos rebel leader.

Whether what happened at Taos in early 1847 was particularly glorious is another question entirely. While Fitzgerald was incarcerated in the Taos courthouse in April and May, the American authorities held a series of trials there. As a result, over twenty men were hung for murder.

Interestingly, only two insurrectos were found guilty of treason and only the first of those two was hanged. The second man's sentence was commuted. In a reiteration of the argument during the January trial of December conspirator Manuel Chavez, the defense argued that a person couldn't rebel against a country to which they had not pledged allegiance. In fact, because the war wasn't over, New Mexico was still part of Mexico and its people were still citizens of that country.

New Mexican resistance to the Americans wasn't over, either. Guerrilla outbreaks continued long after the smoke had settled in the destroyed Taos Pueblo church. They would not cease until late 1847, when word arrived that Mexico City had fallen to the invaders and the Mexican leadership had conceded defeat.

Even then, in the ensuing decades and centuries, the people of New Mexico, both Spanish and indigenous, have continued to find ways to assert their independence and protect their culture from the ever-encroaching americanos. That urge to stand against oppression and its attendant simple solutions to complex problems is something I deeply admire about my adopted state. As Raúl says in the opening scene of this book, Viva Nuevo Méjico!

HISTORICAL CHARACTERS

Armijo, Manuel (circa 1790–1854) The only person to serve as Governor of New Mexico three times. His terms of office were 1827–1829, 1837–1844, and 1845–1846, when he relinquished New Mexico to the invading Americans without a fight.

Barceló, María Gertrudis "Doña Tules" (circa 1800–1852) Female entrepreneur who ran a gambling salon in Santa Fe, invested in New Mexico real estate, and provided loans at interest, including to the U.S. military. Barceló adopted or fostered a number of girls, including María Petra Gutierrez, María del Refugio Sisneros, and María Guadalupe de Altagracia Barceló.

Barceló, María Guadalupe de Altagracia (1832–?) Infant left at the Santa Fe home of Gertrudes Barceló's mother on December 10, 1832. María was baptized in Tomé twelve days later, when Gertrudes Barceló adopted her. See the Note to Reader for my reasons for using this historical character in the way I have in this novel.

Beaubien, María de la Luz (1829–1900) Oldest daughter of Carlos Beaubien and Paula Lobato. She married mountain man Lucien Maxwell in March 1842, three months before she turned 13, although their first child was not born until she was 20. She is 18 at the time of this novel. Luz and Maxwell parleyed the land she inherited from her father into what became known as the Maxwell Land Grant.

Beaubien, Narciso (1827–1847) Oldest son of Carlos Beaubien and Paula Lobato. Narciso was killed during the January 1847 insurrection against American occupation.

He had recently returned from a three-year stint at Cape Girardeau College south of Saint Louis.

Bent, Charles (1799–1847) Member of the family which owned Bent's Fort and business partner of Ceran Saint Vrain. The Americans appointed Bent appointed Governor of New Mexico after they occupied it in Fall 1846. He was killed during the subsequent January 1847 uprising.

Burgwin, John Henry K. (1810–1847) West Point graduate who was captain of the First U.S. dragoons when they invaded New Mexico in 1846. Burgwin was killed during the initial charge on the Taos church following the January 1847 uprising against American occupation.

Cabeza de Baca Family Although Raúl *Jesús* Cabeza de Baca is a fictional character, the Cabeza de Baca family is not. In fact, a captain in the occupying U.S. forces boarded in the home of Raúl *Jose* Cabeza de Baca, one of the December 1846 conspirators.

Durán, Agustín (1792–1874) Santa Fe politician and rico who was its customs house manager in the 1830s and 1840s. A member of the December 1846 conspiracy against the occupying U.S. troops, Durán was arrested and imprisoned following its discovery. One of the best educated men in New Mexico, he also had a well-documented gambling addiction. Although I have not been able to ascertain just how long he was jailed, we do have evidence that Durán held out against American domination for some time. He still hadn't taken the oath of allegiance in 1855, when he served illegally as a Santa Fe County Precinct 4 election judge.

Fitzgerald, Henry Carr (1819–1882) Younger brother of 1841 Texan-Santa Fe Expedition member Archibald Fitzgerald. Henry killed Taos Pueblo leader Tomás Romero in early February 1847. He had reportedly joined the U.S. dragoons in order to avenge his brother's death at the hand of the Mexicans (see Note to Reader). Fitzgerald was incarcerated after Romero's death, but escaped and eventually emigrated to Australia, where he died at age 63.

Green, Dick (circa 1816–?) Slave of the Bent family who fought with the American forces following the January 1847 New Mexico rebellion. Dick was wounded at the battle outside the village of Embudo and he, his wife Charlotte, and his brother Andrew were subsequently rewarded with their freedom.

Kearny, Stephen Watts (1794–1848) Career army officer who led the U.S. forces into New Mexico in 1846. He then marched on to California and participated in its subjugation before serving as civil governor in Vera Cruz and Mexico City. Kearny died of malaria in St. Louis in October 1848.

Mitchell, Lieutenant Colonel David Dawson (1806–1861) Head of the U.S. Army Rangers who entered New Mexico with General Kearny and was subsequently ordered to Chihuahua. To raise the necessary funds, Mitchell borrowed money from Santa Fe businesswoman Gertrudis Barceló, but not before she made him grovel a little.

Ortiz, Juan Felipe (1797–1858) Vicar General of the Catholic church in New Mexico when General Kearny arrived in 1846. Padre Ortiz was also a politician. He served in various New Mexico governmental assemblies between 1825 and 1845 and was its representative to the Mexican Congress from 1837 to 1841. American reports about him always refer to his substantial girth and red hair.

Price, Sterling (1809–1867) Military commander of New Mexico after Kearny departed for California in Fall 1846. Following the war with Mexico, he became Governor of Missouri and then a major general in the Confederate Army. When the Civil War ended, he went to Mexico to establish a colony of Confederate exiles. When it failed, he returned to the U.S., where he died of cholera shortly thereafter.

Romero, Tomás (?–1847) Taos Pueblo leader during the January 1846 uprising against America's occupation of New Mexico. Sterling Price agreed to cease bombarding the Taos Pueblo on condition that Romero give himself up. The day he did so, Romero was shot and killed in the Don Fernando de Taos jail by Private Fitzgerald of the First U.S. Dragoons.

Saint Vrain, Ceran (1802–1870) Scion of French nobility who became a trapper in the Rocky Mountains and New Mexico, then a partner in the Bent brothers' trading enterprise. When news of Charles Bent's death reached Santa Fe in January 1847, Saint Vrain recruited a motley group of trappers, clerks, and anyone else who cared to join and called them the Avengers. They were instrumental in the subsequent battles at Santa Cruz de la Cañada, Embudo, and Taos Pueblo.

Sena Family Although Juanita María de la Luz Sena is a fictional character, the Sena family of Santa Fe and their family compound are not. The house still sits opposite the site of the old parish church (today's Saint Francis

Cathedral), though it has been considerably expanded since Juanita's day. The oldest son of the 1840s Sena family inherited the compound. After his 1868 marriage to Isabel Cabeza de Baca, they gradually added more rooms to accommodate their twenty-three children.

Vigil, Donaciano (1802–1877) New Mexico politician who held various government positions under the Mexican and American administrations, most notably as civil governor following Charles Bent's death. Tall, well-spoken, and educated, he married María del Refugio Sanchez, with whom he had at least eight children.

FURTHER READING

These are some of the resources I accessed during my research process for this book. If you're interested in learning more about this period of U.S. and New Mexican history, I recommend them.

Beyreis, David. *Blood in the Borderlands: Conflict, Kinship, and the Bent Family, 1821-1920.* Lincoln, NE: University of Nebraska, 2020.

Crutchfield, James. *Revolt at Taos: The New Mexican and Indian Insurrection of 1847.* Yardley, PA: Westholme, 2015.

Durand, John. *The Taos Massacres.* Elkhorn, WI: Puzzlebox, 2004.

Gardner, Mark L. and Marc Simmons, eds. *The Mexican War Correspondence of Richard Smith Elliott.* Norman, OK: University of Oklahoma, 1997.

Garrard, Lewis. *Way-to-yah and the Taos Trail.* Norman, OK: University of Oklahoma, 1955.

Greenburg, Amy. *A Wicked War: Polk, Clay, Lincoln, and the 1846 U.S. Invasion of Mexico.* New York, NY: Knopf, 2012.

Keleher, William. *Turmoil in New Mexico, 1846-1848.* Santa Fe, NM: Rydale, 1952.

Twitchell, Ralph. *The History of the Military Occupation of Territory of New Mexico, 1846-1851.* Denver, CO: Smith-Brooks, 1909.

Vidaurre, Alberto. "1847: Revolt or Resistance." *In Taos: A Topical History*, eds. Corina A. Santistevan and Julia Moore. Santa Fe: Museum of New Mexico, 2013.

VOCABULARY

Most of the Spanish words or phrases in this novel are translated in the text or have an English cognate. The list below contains terms that don't fit either of these categories.

adobe - unburnt brick dried in the sun. Common building material in New Mexico in the 1800s.

agua - water

ahora - now

Albuquerque - City south of Santa Fe which is now the largest in New Mexico. The original Spanish spelling included an extra 'r' (Alburquerque). This was changed sometime in the 1800s, after the American takeover and I have chosen to use the later spelling in this book.

amiga/amigo - friend (male/female)

árboles - trees

biscochitos - rolled and cut cookie flavored with anise and cinnamon

bueno - good, very well, all right

buenos días - good day/good morning

calabozo - jail, prison, lock up

carreta - two-wheeled wooden cart

ciudad - city

con - with

conspiradores - conspirators, rebels

de nada - you're welcome, don't mention it

descansa - you will rest

Dios - God

Don - Mister, Sir. Spanish title for gentlemen which is used only before the Christian, or first, name. Used for someone with money and/or family connections.

Doña - title of respect for a lady with money and/or family connections. Used only with the Christian, or first, name.

Don Fernando/Don Fernando de Taos - Over time, what is today known as the town of Taos has been called Don Fernando de Taos, San Fernando de Taos, and also San Fernandez de Taos. In the 1800s, the First Peoples pueblo of Taos three miles northeast of the village was more likely than the town to be called simply Taos. In this novel, I use Don Fernando de Taos or simply Don Fernando to refer to the town.

juego - games, gambling

juegos de azar - games of chance, gambling

enferma - ill, unwell

español/españoles - Spanish

feliz navidad - happy Christmas

gracias - thanks, thank you

hacienda - farm, plantation, large house associated with such an establishment

hombre - man

insurrecto - insurrectionist, rebel

madre - mother

maldito - damned, accursed

malo - bad, evil

mi - my

mi amor - my love

monte - gambling game in which players bet which card will match the suit in the next one drawn

niño Cristo - Christ child

Nuevo México - New Mexico

nuevomexicano - New Mexican, someone from New Mexico

padre- father, priest

palacio - palace, royal residence. In New Mexico, this word referred specifically to the Santa Fe offices and residence of the governor on the north side on the plaza. It is now part of the New Mexico Museum of History complex.

perdóneme - excuse me, pardon me

pero - but, yet

pobrecito - poor little one

por favor - please, literally "if you will"

portal - covered porch or portico. Veranda

primo - cousin

qué - what

qué es - what is it

rebozo - a wide, long woven shawl worn by women in New Mexico and Mexico

rico - rich, opulent, wealthy

río - river

saldado - soldier

señor - Sir, mister. Also used in the sense of "gentleman."

señora - madam, lady. Also used in the sense of "gentle woman."

señorita - young lady, Miss

sí - yes

Taos - the pueblo of Taos three miles northeast of today's town of Taos.

tejano - Texan

tierra - earth, land

tu - your

www.ingramcontent.com/pod-product-compliance
Lightning Source LLC
Chambersburg PA
CBHW052026220726
48293CB00015B/326